UNDER THE SHADOW OF THE ALMIGHTY

Book One

HIDDEN IN PLAIN SIGHT

SHARON D. MOORE

newseason
BOUNDARY BREAKING BOOKS

Hidden in Plain Sight
© 2016 by Sharon D. Moore

ISBN: 978-0-69276868-6

NewSeason Books
PO Box 1403
Havertown, PA 19083
www.newseasonbooks.com
newseasonbooks@gmail.com

AUTHOR'S NOTE

I t all started with a dream. As melodramatic as it sounds, this book started with a dream that stalked my sleep nightly the late summer / early fall of 2001. My dreams have often been very vivid (see: the one I had that was completely animated), but this one was different.

I began having this particular dream, every night, and sometimes multiple times a night. I felt like Bill Murray's character in the 90's film, *Groundhog Day*. I would dream the exact same story, situation, dialogue, names, and the exact same personalities. Every. Single. Time. There were two exceptions, but even these occurred infrequently. For example, sometimes I would imagine a recurring scene, but from a different character's perspective. Sometimes though, my subconscious would focus an inordinate amount of time on one scene in order for me to, I guess, absorb each of its idiosyncrasies. The dialogue would never change, but I had a new privilege, experiencing another side of the story complete with the complex emotions therein.

Cue the Twilight Zone theme music.

I was partly obsessed with the story and even looked forward to going to sleep at night just to experience it. On the other hand, I was a little more than freaked out and often wanted the crazy dream to stop. It didn't. In fact, it persisted until I gave in. The dream had a purpose bigger than just occupying my brain at night.

I tried to rationalize each nightly occurrence but did not have much luck. I thought perhaps my dreams were some sort of prophetic look into the lives of people close to me. After giving every pastor and church I knew the side-eye for a couple of months, I set aside that theory. This was something else.

After about a year of having the same dream, the frequency began to decrease. I went from having my sleep interrupted multiple times a night to once every other night or so. Many nights I did not dream at all. This persistent tale that initially freaked me out, began slowly disappearing. Not wanting to forget it, I started transcribing what I saw.

It wasn't until I began typing that it hit me how much I had absorbed. These people, this *thing* had lived in my head and spirit so long I could recount the story without deviation. I knew everything about each character down to their favorite foods and shoe sizes. I attempted to record everything I saw, heard, and felt from each character. Some things I can't say I actually 'lived' in the dream but they were things I perceived, intimated, and/or were simply intuitive.

It took me several months of marathon typing, but when I stopped I had over two million words. How I managed to dream all of that in one night, I cannot explain. Eventually I realized that my ongoing dream was a series of books. Once I came to this conclusion, it stopped. Maybe that was the point? Nearly thirteen years later, the dream has not returned.

I must admit I struggled for years with the even small amounts of profanity and racially charged language in this book. I would write it in only to take it back out fearing what people would think of me. In the end, I have chosen to remain true to the dream. When I chose to be true to the characters and their stories, I found peace. The language used reflects the raw honesty of each character and those moments are true to their speech patterns and how they interacted with me in slumber. I believe I was given this story to tell and therefore must tell it honestly.

This is the first part in these characters' story. This is the first part of the book series. This is the first part of my dream.

- Sharon D. Moore

Under the Shadow of the Almighty: 1) See Psalms 91:1 He that dwells in the secret place/shelter of the Most High God will abide in/under the shadow of Almighty. 2) Living in the background, under the shelter or control of a high profile person or persons (see: persons of influence/celebrities).

PART ONE

TRUTH

1

I *don't know how many more years of this I have left in me.*

As the gleaming, royal blue, Challenger 604 jet—complete with large, antique gold crests emblazoned on its sides—ascended into the late afternoon sky, Bishop James Collins sank deep into his custom leather chair and closed his weary eyes. Whoever said preachers didn't do anything but get up and talk for an hour twice a week, didn't have a clue about full-time ministry. It was some serious round-the-clock work!

The Bishop planned to take advantage of the short flight and get a well-deserved nap. Over the previous two years, he'd cut back his traveling and this was one of those days he remembered why.

See, the average person has the luxury of being critical of preachers like him because they don't realize just how draining the preparation and preaching part of ministry happens to be. Not to mention the prayer lines that usually follows a service and the stress of maintaining the business side of a church. There were nights when he laid hands on literally thousands of people, only to realize once arriving back at his hotel that there was yet another fire to put out at home—all before he could even think of going to sleep. Sure, the burden was on God to speak through him, but James was still just a vessel made of flesh; flesh that got older and more weary by the second.

Initially James limited his travel because frankly, he missed his home church. He felt disconnected when he was away too often and though it was a weakness, he liked to be as hands on as possible even with a more than capable staff to handle things. His congregation was filled with thousands of sons and daughters—spiritual children—who for the most part he didn't even know in passing, let alone personally. Sure, he would recognize the consistent familiar faces over the years, but he really didn't know them the way a father should. He wanted to interact more, spend out-of-church casual time with them, and minister to each of them on a personal level. Unfortunately, this was far from practical. James often tried to concoct ways to increase his hands-on exposure with his church members, but between scheduling and security issues, it was virtually impossible. He was just one man. Yet he often felt so distant from them. It was a burden he carried in his heart.

People were prone to forget that he was a pastor first and not just a conference keynote speaker. There were months it honestly felt as if everyone outside of Abiding Grace Christian Church wanted a piece of him. Even after turning down hundreds of invitations a year, there were still just as many that he granted, and the hustle and bustle of travel was getting to him. No matter how many stars the hotel had, nothing came close to his own bed with his own mattress, his own pillow and better yet, his wife, Victoria.

Every joint and muscle ached and he couldn't wait to get home and soak in a hot, Epsom salt bath. But before he could do that, the first thing he had to do after landing is sit in on some interview his wife was giving. If she hadn't asked him to do it some time ago he would have begged off of it but she was everything to him—his jewel—and he couldn't bring himself to disappoint no matter how tired he was. Plus, James didn't want to give the media any cause to suspect there could be trouble brewing in the Collins home. They often took small things, like a temporarily absent spouse, and ran with them as if it were a crime to be out of town or working.

James drifted off into much needed slumber.

"Bishop?"

James opened a bleary, sleep-deprived eye and stared sharply at the dark skinned, handsome young man stooped down in front of him. He hoped his look conveyed 'leave me alone' but the young man remained unmoved.

"What boy?"

"I just wanted to know if you needed anything…"

"Yes… some sleep!" James grumbled.

He tried to have patience with his adjutant but sometimes the boy could work his last good nerve. He wanted to slip back into sleep mode but the interruption irked him to the point that he just *had* to address it. With an exaggerated sigh, he said, "Son…"

"Yes, Bishop?"

"What's my name?"

"Bishop James Elliott Collins Sr., Sir."

James groaned inwardly at the stiff military-type delivery of the reply. He resisted the childish temptation to mock the young man by repeating it the same way that it was delivered. Still he had to get the boy straight.

"No… what do you call me?"

"Sir?"

That was all it took to rouse him completely. James sat up straight in his chair sending his pillow tumbling to the floor. He looked at his assistant who'd seated himself diagonally across the narrow aisle. The young man was tall, at 6'2 standing only an inch shorter than James, and from his closely cropped hair down to his shined shoes, possessed a military bearing that decried formality. His large brown eyes were framed in long luxurious eyelashes that, depending on his expression, made him appear younger than his twenty-three years. James sighed. The boy wanted to please him so much. His own little Elisha wanting to carry Elijah's mantel but not quite able to fit it yet because he was always trying too hard.

He doesn't get it.

Lee, his right-hand-man in training, was the consummate servant who was always on duty twenty-four seven. In public, when it really counted, he was the perfect adjutant: consistently on point, never missing a beat, and faithfully anticipating James' needs, carrying them out with speed and excellence. He was flawlessly able to 'flow' no matter the venue or the hour. However, in private, he still had a few things to learn.

Lee took himself and his role in ministry *way* too seriously—to the point of being strangely unsettling to those around him. He hadn't learned how to relax, how to enjoy life, how to separate home from the office or how to simply *be*. That was very dangerous and easily caused ministry burnout in people. James saw it happen time and time again over the years and tried to explain it so the young man wouldn't fall prey to it. Unfortunately, he might as well have been talking to himself because the boy either failed to understand him or didn't believe him.

"Son?"

"Yes, Bishop?"

"What is *your* name?"

"Sir?"

"Boy, you mean to tell me that you don't know your name either?!"

James was doing all he could not to appear exasperated but it wasn't working. How could any one person be so intelligent yet still so dense?

"My name is James Elliott Collins, Jr., Sir."

"Oh…so you *do* know your name!" James laughed in recognition of the ridiculous nature of their conversation. "So who am I?"

"Bishop Collins." The young man replied with a furrowed brow and anxious eyes.

"Lee…" He warned with more than a little agitation in his voice. "Okay… let's try this one more time. Who am I?"

"My father?"

"You don't know? Are you sure? Is there something I need to know? Do I need to call your momma and have an uncomfortable conversation?"

Lee laughed at himself now. He felt really silly. The Bishop had asked him a simple question and he failed to reply properly because he thought his mentor was about to expound on some deep spiritual revelation like when Jesus asked Peter, "Whom do men say that I am?" Instead, the answer his father was looking for was obvious.

"You're my Dad!"

"Exactly and I will always be your dad long after I am no longer your pastor or your Bishop or whatever else they come up with to call me. Remember that and relax for God's sake! You're giving me the willies!"

James shivered for emphasis. He still wasn't satisfied that his son truly understood what he was trying to convey so he took a deep breath and extended his forefinger which was a sure sign to his son that his father was preparing to launch into another lecture on life again. Lee tried to cut him off at the pass to avoid hearing it.

"Yes sir," he quickly replied hoping doing so would shut his father up. He looked away to insure the conclusion of their conversation.

Jesus!

The boy was so formal. James didn't know where he got that mess from. It sure wasn't his side of the family. James looked at his son intently from across the aisle as Lee avoided his gaze by looking out of the window. He knew that look. His son's eyes appeared heavy, almost closed, with his long upper eyelashes coming just short of touching his cheeks and the middle of his top lip sucked in. That was the *I have disappointed Daddy* look he perfected as a toddler. James knew he was probably trying to think of a way to make it right. He was too old to draw his father pictures in order to say he was sorry anymore and, in truth, James didn't want anything from him except to see him set free of whatever kept him so wound up. He decided to let him off the hook a little.

"Lee…"

"S…" Lee smiled, catching himself before he was reprimanded again. "Yes, Dad?"

"Do you know why I call you Lee?"

Lee, determined to have the right answer this time, answered quickly. "Because I have your name and calling me Lee was a way to tell us apart if someone was talking to us when we were both at home." He was so confident in his answer this time that he drew the words out in an almost singsong fashion.

"Ok… so then what does your mother call you?"

Lee looked out the window again and pouted slightly as he mumbled, "Jamie."

James grinned. He knew his son hated that name but his mother started calling him that almost right away and it had been hard for her to stop even after Lee got older and no longer liked it.

"So why do you think I call you Lee again?"

Lee kept looking out the window at the white clouds that encircled the small aircraft and the patches of freckled land beneath them. He was ready for this interrogation to be over with. He wished he'd never disturbed his father even if it did seem like a good idea at the time. He hadn't thought it through. Sometimes he could screw up royally without even trying. He should have known what would happen if he bothered his father when he was sleeping and now he was going to have to suffer through it.

He wanted to reply with, "Which story this time?" but instead said, "I honestly don't know dad. I guess I never thought much about it since Chris and Caleb call me Lee too. It's not that big of a deal."

"They picked that up from me." James replied with a considerable amount of pride. "And it *is* that big of a deal."

With the jet having leveled out and the *remain seated* sign extinguished, James unbuckled his seatbelt and slipped through the aisle to sit beside his oldest son. That was one of the perks of having your own jet—every seat was yours and you could sit wherever you liked, whenever you liked.

"Lee, do you even remember when I started calling you that?"

Lee shook his head no and met his father's intense gaze as he waited with polite curiosity for the answer. Bishop Collins sat back and began talking with a faraway look in his eyes as if he were seeing everything playing out in front of him as he spoke.

"I didn't think you would. You were still kinda small." He grinned. "Before you were born, we picked out all kinds of names for you. Most of them were biblical. You know how that goes. You were almost named after all the major and minor prophets and half of the apostles!" He laughed as he remembered him and his wife's innocent, albeit ignorant, and overzealous mindsets back then.

"You know we were all deep and spooky full of the Word but lacking a grain of common sense." James continued. "Then here you

8

come. Your mother took one look at you and called you James. I was totally against it because I didn't want a junior. I didn't want my son to feel like he had to be a carbon copy of me. I wanted my son to be his own man, an independent thinker." James paused as he vividly remembered the first time he saw his son's tiny wrinkled face. "But then I looked at you and was like WOW! I couldn't deny that you were the spitting image of me."

Lee smiled broadly revealing large, perfectly straight, white teeth just like his father's and James was almost certain that he sat up a little straighter.

"Your grandparents were at the hospital too and when they saw you, they had the same reaction. Everyone was gung ho about calling you Lil' James and eventually after a little convincing from your Grandpa Edsel, I got on board too."

Lee sat forward expectantly and listened to a part of his history that he'd never heard before.

"By the time you were two, you were my shadow. My God, you even walked like me! Everything I did, you did." James started laughing as he fondly remembered his son's clumsy attempts to copy him.

"You wanted to wear your Sunday suit every day because I wore a suit to work every day. You've seen the pictures. We didn't do that to you, man! You did it to yourself! You even wanted a part in your hair like I used to have. You would cry if we didn't give you one, too!"

James eyed his son and couldn't help chuckling again. Some things hadn't changed. Although his son's Brooks Brothers attire was a far cry from his own tailored, high fashion, signature suits, the resemblance was still undeniable. They had the same complexion, the same defined cheekbones, and the same almond shaped eyes. Their height and slight build were very similar and so was their shoe size. Everything down to their smile was identical. The only difference was that Lee had his mother's grade of hair and for that James was grateful. His son's large silky curl pattern didn't require the constant grooming that his did. If James ever missed a haircut, he'd instantly look like he had starter dreadlocks. There was a little of Victoria in Lee's face as well but James' fingerprint was all over him and that made them both proud.

"Anyway, people kept telling me that it was perfectly normal for you to want to be like me but the last thing I wanted was a Xerox copy of myself. That was the one thing that constantly ate at me. I think I called you everything during those first years: Junior, Lil' James, Elliott, JC… and then one day Lee just came out and I liked it because it was something I'd never been called. Somehow I felt it made you different. It separated me from you and gave you your own identity. Do you understand what I'm saying to you?"

Lee understood. He sat back in his seat and began looking out his window again. He saw everything and nothing. It was the same conversation they'd had many times before. Each time his father came at him a different way but the ending was always the same. He sat in silence for a while and when he finally turned back, his father was leaning forward and watching him, hopeful. He hated when his father did that. It never failed to make him jump.

"Dad, this *is* who I am!" Lee searched for the right words to say but he couldn't seem to put them together in a way that not only expressed how he felt, but once and for all convinced his father of their legitimacy. Sensing his building frustration, James sat back in his seat and patiently waited while his son attempted to make his point.

"Yes, I love and respect you, but I'm not trying to be you. Your example is one of the reasons I want to go into ministry. I'm trying to learn all I can from you but I really am being me—just me! This is who I am. This is who I've always been. I don't know how else you want me to be other than me. I'm being the best me I know how."

His voice trailed off as he realized he didn't have any more words to drive his point home and didn't want to risk being any more redundant. There was no need to provoke his father into another lecture on his communication skills or the lack thereof.

James looked into his son's deep brown eyes pleading for understanding. He reached over and gave his first born a strong, meaningful hug that temporarily buried Lee's face into his father's shoulder. It was his way of letting Lee know that he loved him regardless. Just as quickly, James pulled away from his boy so that he could look into his naïve face again.

"Oooookay. I'll drop it."

With that, James sat back into the chair again. He found a comfortable resting position and closed his eyes. He returned to trying to relax his mind and reclaim his sleep. For a while, everything was silent except for the hum of the aircraft and the low voices of his traveling staff who sat in the front of the cabin.

James didn't want to push his oldest son any further—at least not anymore that day. But the boy *was* beginning to make him nervous. He had hoped he would have seen more progress in him by now. He'd already publicly declared Lee the heir of his ministry but God forbid something should happen to him or Victoria anytime soon. Lee just wasn't ready to take over. Not even remotely close to being ready. How could his son be entrusted with the reigns of Abiding Grace Christian Church if he couldn't even trust himself to relax and live? James had considered sending Lee to aid a pastor in one of the churches that was birthed from and now came under the umbrella of AGCC but he ultimately knew that wouldn't help the situation. He knew that Lee would probably be given preferential treatment just because of who his father was and that was the *last* thing that boy needed.

What Lee *did* need was to be toughened up a little. He needed to be placed straight into the fire so that his own character and methodology could emerge to maturity. He wanted Lee to find his own path, his own specific anointing, and to stop following him step for step, word for word. James was at a loss about what to do and had been for some time yet every time he came face to face with the matter, it gnawed at him as if it were the first time he'd ever thought about it.

When Lee and Alecia got married in January, James just knew that his firstborn would mature into more of a solid, independent man. That seemed to be wishful thinking. In a sense, Lee married the female version of himself. Apparently the power of the marriage bed hadn't affected either one of them. They were both more humanoid than human.

James really didn't have anything to complain about. He was grateful for everything, including his robotic son. He had a good life, an excellent wife, and wonderful children. All three of his children were honor roll students all through school and all were virgins—well, at least Lee was up until January.

James couldn't help smiling at the thought of his prudish perfect son in an intimate setting. Now *that* was funny! James had tried to tease Lee about his marriage bed before the wedding but Lee looked so shocked and horrified that James left him alone. He was just trying to make sure the boy knew what to do. Thinking about this, James couldn't resist needling his son one more time.

"Hey."

"Sir?"

"When am I going to be a grandfather?"

James could feel his son blushing and he loved it. He opened his eyes a fraction just in time to see the telltale rosy flush creeping up Lee's neck and hear him nervously shuffling his feet. He elbowed him in the arm to drive his point home.

"Y'all are working on it, right?"

"Daaad," Lee whined.

He was so easily embarrassed sometimes and James took a sick pleasure in harassing him. All he wanted to do was loosen his son up. The thought of those two robots reproducing was hilarious. What would they have?! A microchip? He'd already vowed to do all he could to make sure his first grandchild wouldn't be… well… like his or her stiff parents.

"Huh?" James asked innocently. "We've only been married two months! You were the one that counseled us that we didn't need kids right away!"

"Oh yeah. I did, didn't I? Well…y'all hurry up and make something happen while I can still be a cool grampie!"

With that James rose dramatically, slid over to the sofa across the aisle from his son, and stretched out on it to finish his nap. Lee groaned, laughed, and pulled out a book to read.

"Hey."

"Sir?"

"Wake me just before we land so I can freshen up for your mother's   thing."

"Yes Bishop."

James' eyebrow went up and he sharply opened one eye only to catch his son struggling to withhold the smile trying to form on his full lips as he pretended to be interested in the book in front of him.

Well at least he has a sense of humor, James thought as he relaxed and finally drifted off to sleep, his dreams filled with things past and present.

2

T *hat was so fucked up.*

Jason sped away from his Aunt Theresa's Washington Lane house in his brand new, navy blue, 2002 BMW 745i. His mind was full of jumbled thoughts. He ran stoplights and wove in and out of traffic at breakneck speed. He didn't care if he got pulled over by the police or not. He didn't care about anything except getting as far away from her house as possible. His mother's older sister had just laid a lifetime of information on him and now his whole life—everything he ever believed—was turned upside down.

***

As the clean scent of Jason's Cool Water cologne slowly faded in his wake, Theresa White Bonner stared out through the Battenberg lace curtains covering her bay window. Just moments before, her giant of a nephew slammed out of the house and marched down her front steps, his coat flapping angrily around him. His body was tense and coiled like he was ready to strike anyone or anything in his way.

"Oh, dear Lord! I have truly messed up this time," Theresa White Bonner whispered.

She sighed with resignation. She had hoped for better, but some things never changed. He was a twenty eight-year-old man who acted more like he was two or eight. Anger was an honest emotion, but he'd never learned to control how he expressed it.

Jason had always been a stomper when he lost his temper. Unfortunately for him, all he'd ever accomplished with it was a lot of noise. It was a miracle he hadn't gone through the floor of his mother's apartment with the ruckus he made pitching fits and yelling at the top of his lungs as a child. Nevertheless, he was far from being a child now; he was an angry man with a volatile temper. This made Theresa wonder what exactly had possessed her to do what she'd just done.

It had to be done.

Theresa made peace with herself. She'd done what should have been done years earlier. It was the right thing for everyone concerned. Yet, the sound of Jason's fancy car squealing away from her row house, disturbed the peace of her otherwise quiet East Oak Lane neighborhood and made her stomach ache with fresh worry. She didn't know what he was going to do, but knowing him, it was going to be something big, something excessive, and something *she* might end up regretting for a very long time.

No matter what it was, Theresa's only nephew was always stood out. Of her sister Bridget's children, he was different—not just in appearance, but in demeanor too. His tall, athletic frame, rich brown skin, jet black hair, large eyes, full lips and strong jaw made him a high contrast to the fair, brown haired, narrow-featured, and small-boned White family. His physicality was an outward testament to how much he would forever refuse to conform to what the family had resigned to in life. In fact, Theresa couldn't remember a time when Jason was ever satisfied with anything.

Nothing was ever enough for him.

More than once, Theresa called him a *high-minded and ungrateful somebody.* From day one, it seemed like he walked around with a chip on his shoulder, like the world owed him something and he was demanding payment immediately. How did he adopt such a sense of entitlement? For someone who appeared so self-assured and controlled, Theresa knew Jason was bitterly angry. That anger sat simmering like hot embers, just below the surface, for years. And in this particularly moment, Theresa had just blown a fresh wind on those very embers with no way to extinguish them.

But burning fires were also cleansing, right? The White family needed a good cleanse after all of the mess they had put each other through.

Mess that could've been avoided years ago if someone had shown an ounce of self-control.

Theresa's therapist once said her family life had been tragic. *Tragic?!* She knew this was nothing but a polite way of saying dysfunctional. As insulting as the word's implications felt, Theresa knew it was true. After all, she lived it. The White family drama had the makings of a fantastic Lifetime Channel/Kleenex movie.

Unfortunately, Jason's birth initiated a very ugly time in the family. *No one could really blame a baby for being born, could they?* Jason always sensed the palpable undercurrent of resentment and shame around him and it often drove him to behave as if had an axe to grind. He channeled his energy into a drive toward perfection. He deeply desired to be the best, have the best, wear the best, and win—by any means necessary. At first, Theresa was proud of his persistence. *Who doesn't want a determined child who could excel?* Her husband Thomas, however, saw something more disturbing in Jason's behavior years prior.

If only I'd been there.

Theresa blamed herself for not being around more when he was a toddler. She thought that maybe he could have been molded into a more peaceful soul. Instead, she spent too much time trying to prove a moral point to her sister. If anything, she probably made the whole situation worse by manipulating her baby sister into a poverty-ridden disaster.

As Jason's fiery exit reverberated through the house, Theresa knew beyond a doubt that her well-intentioned effort to finally make up for her sister's plight might have actually made things worse. *Again.*

Theresa trembled as a chill ran down her spine. She was not going to second-guess herself anymore that evening. She shook herself back to the present moment, wiped away a tear from her freckled face, and slowly eased out of her chair.

Could've, should've, would've can't shape your future; it only holds you in your past.

Isn't that what Bishop Collins said on TV this morning? It was time for her to move forward. It was time for their family to move forward. Sure, they'd been stuck in neutral for almost thirty years, but it was never too late for change.

Since her mother died, Theresa had become the matriarch of her small band of misfits and she was determined that things were going to be different under her helm. It was time for the joy and security she'd known as a child to permeate the entire White family. It was time to live in peace for once and die without leaving a pool of secrets for everyone who was left behind to wade through.

***

Theresa looked up to see her husband standing in the archway that separated the living and dining rooms, watching her. Thomas Bonner was in his mid-fifties, but didn't look a day over forty. With a long lean frame and mesmerizing gray eyes, he was just as fine as when she'd first seen him sitting on his stoop taking apart a broken transistor radio.

God I love that man!

He was the one thing that had always been right in her life. Without him, the last few decades might have ended up very different for her. She'd been blessed with a good man early and had never regretted her decision to marry him for a minute.

Thomas walked over to Theresa and gathered her up into his arms. He smelled of that trademark woodsy cologne that made Theresa feel warm inside when he was near. His nieces swore it stunk to high heaven and was decades out of style, but Theresa loved it; it smelled like love.

He gently kissed her forehead as if it was something easily broken.

"You okay?"

Theresa mustered a weak smile more out of habit than sincerity.

"Yeah," she assured him.

She said this even as a sour taste invaded her mouth and her stomach burned hot courtesy of a new ulcer. There was no need to worry Thomas or beat a dead horse into the ground any further.

"Liar," he said with a snicker.

He knows me.

They both had a good stress-relieving chuckle. They'd been together too long for either to hide their true emotions. She knew better than to try, but she also knew that Thomas would carry her burden silently for weeks - long after she was over it. He lived to make sure her world remained perfect. After a deep cleansing breath, she regained composure, leaned back, and looked her husband of twenty-nine years squarely in the eyes. She *had* to ask him one more time.

"Baby, do you think I did the right thing? I mean, *really*..."

"Girl, didn't you just ask me that last night? And yesterday... and the day before that... and..."

"OK. I know but... did I? He's so angry and all I was trying to do was help. He was so distraught at the funeral and I thought this would... I don't know. I thought it would give him hope, but it feels like I just kicked a hornet's nest. Tell me the truth, Thomas."

"Terri, I can't answer that because I don't know. What I *do* know is I love you and I support you regardless, okay? There is no perfect solution to this. No matter what you did or didn't say, someone would have suffered the consequences. You can never go wrong with the truth so just let it play out. Let that boy go off and cool down. He'll see it for what it is and be just fine."

Satisfied with answer, she kissed him on his full lips and placed her head on his chest. The comfort of being in Thomas' arms was all that mattered. As usual, he knew how to make everything right with the world.

***

Jason was still coping with his mother's death and thought, *now this?* He didn't know what to do with what he'd just heard. *Why couldn't Theresa have waited to tell him this?* She had the worse timing of anyone he knew. Why couldn't they have had this conversation two months ago when he could have actually talked to his mother and gotten some answers? When he could have confronted her or let off some steam by yelling at her and telling her what he thought of the whole thing? Now he was scared to be mad. People always said not to speak ill of the dead and he would never speak ill of his mother anyway, but what in the hell had she been thinking? What was the point?

He should have known something was amiss when his Aunt Theresa called him out of the blue early that morning before he left for work. He loved her. She had always been good to him and without her, he would have never graduated summa cum laude from high school, earning a free ride to Temple University. That alone was worthy of eternal admiration, but still, they didn't have a drop-everything-and-see-about-each-other type of relationship.

In recent years, it was always some sort of family occasion or bad news that brought them together. It had to be that way or else he would end up with a headache from all of her Theresa-ness. He could only take her Brady Bunch, Sunday Morning attitude but for so long. His mother's older sister and only sibling acted as if she thought her way was the only way and that she was better than the rest of their family—heck, the rest of the world for that matter. For the most part, Jason and his sisters learned to ignore her because it was a lot easier than arguing with her.

For years Jason wondered why he, his mother, and sisters hadn't moved in with his Aunt Theresa and Uncle Thomas after his grandmother died and things got really ugly for them. Apparently his mother, Bridget, would have rather been homeless for six months than live under her sister Theresa's crazy rules. Jason could tell by the way his Aunt Theresa looked at his mother, prior to her death, that she thought she was better than her sister. He could even remember hearing them argue when he was little. Now he knew why.

God, I wish I didn't!

His feelings were all over the place. He was furious with Theresa, but he couldn't ignore all she had been to him over the years. She was the one person who'd always gone the extra mile for him when he was growing up and not just with his education. When, his sisters', Faye and Donna, fathers came around, those stingy, inconsiderate men only provided for their respective seeds. They never took Jason anywhere or bought him a single thing. At Christmas, his sisters racked up like bandits with the latest toys and clothes. He only received what his mother was able to afford and what Uncle Thomas and Aunt Theresa bought him, which was usually the budget basics like underwear, shoes and other things for school. He would never forget that. He didn't always like what he received, but at least they tried.

His aunt was also the one who had encouraged him to be better. She frequently challenged him by asking a simple question: "Do you want to live in Richard Allen for the rest of your life?" Theresa Bonner had never lived a day of her life in the projects and never understood how her little sister, Bridget, could do it so willingly. Aunt Theresa cheered the loudest at Jason's high school and college graduations and he knew she was genuinely proud. And she still sowed those seeds into his family with his baby sister, Donna, who would have to live with Theresa and Thomas now that his mother was gone. Their home would give her hope.

Jason's sister, the middle child, Faye was a lost cause. The projects were all she knew and all she wanted to know. She was engrained in that environment. Jason neither liked nor wanted his nephews raised in the so-called "ghetto heaven" of the Fairhill Apartments, but it wasn't his decision and he was tired of arguing with Faye over how she parented her kids. But all wasn't lost for their family. Donna would make up for everything Faye wasn't and didn't want to be. He was sure Aunt Theresa would see to it.

Jason felt off-balance. His mind meandered from the past to the present and all points in between. He did not like feeling less than centered. He needed something to ground him and glancing at his cell, he had a good idea of *who* would do the trick.

Some might consider Jason to be a commitment-phobe but he preferred to think of himself as a man who chose not to be tied down. He appreciated the variety life had to offer and it currently consisted of five young ladies he rotated regularly. They didn't know about each other and he knew about as much as he wanted to know about any of them. The only one he even remotely cared about was Denise Edwards.

His Nieci. She held the number one position in his life but was currently out of town at some sort of conference related to her work as a psychotherapist. Doctor Denise would probably come back and try out some new psychobabble technique on him that he didn't understand. She was determined to "fix" him, and he was equally determined not to be fixed! But...she was sweet. She was almost wife material. Almost. Part of him wished she were in town so he could go to her and tell her everything he was feeling, but another part of him was glad she was unavailable.

The person who held the number two spot had recently been relieved of duty and needed to be replaced. Jason remembered how he felt as he stood with Donna and Faye beside their mother's casket receiving condolences from mourners at the viewing prior to her funeral. As Jason hugged one of his mother's church friends he saw someone move toward him from his peripheral vision. Before his mind had time to process, he felt someone wrap her arms snuggly around him. He looked up into the face of Nadine. She grinned like she was pleased with herself. She was grinning—at his mother's funeral. At his mother's funeral? Before he could react, she looked to his other side.

"Oh! Are those your sisters? Are you going to introduce me?"

He almost yelled "Hell No!" but even he knew better than to curse in church. Instead he reached his left hand across his body and tried to discreetly extricate his other arm from her smothering grip.

"No, I'm not and you *can* let go of me." He hissed.

"But..."

"But nothing. Let's go!"

With that, he practically dragged her back up the carpeted aisle and into the vestibule. He then steered her into an open door that led to a supply closet filled with boxes of paper, hymnals, and dusty fake flower arrangements. Once inside, he spun on her while snatching off his sunglasses revealing bloodshot and swollen eyes. She was beautiful and could easily pass for Naomi Campbell's twin sister but he didn't see any of that in that moment. He saw red.

"What are you doing here?! Just what are you trying to pull?!"

She appeared offended.

"I came to be here for you! I thought you would need my support. You're welcome."

"Did I tell you about this? Were you invited? Did you even *know* my mother? I don't appreciate you disrespecting my family by showing up. You need to leave."

She stared at him blankly.

"I said, leave! Get out! Go! Now! Don't make me do it for you." Jason waved behind himself at the door.

In a split second, her face changed from hurt to something much colder and conniving. Nadine lifted her head, tossed her hair and swept past him without giving him a second look. Jason noted the change in her demeanor, but he didn't care how mad she was.

"How did you find out about my mom anyway?" Jason asked. He needed to know who had run their mouth.

She gifted him with a brief, backward glance and smirked. "I know people."

"Who?"

Nadine turned once more, looked him up and down as if he were nothing, and strolled out the open doorway. Jason almost ran after Nadine, intent on shaking the information out of her, but he caught himself. He didn't rough up women even when he felt they deserved it. Instead, he took a few calming breaths and remembered where he was.

The situation with Nadine bothered him for a lot of reasons. She was sneaky and he could not have any of that. She'd just successfully freed up space in his life, but he didn't have the time to make sure she knew it. She was more than a little decent in bed but so were many other women.

Jason considered his options then hit number four on the speed dial. The phone rang once and a digital recording informed him that the number was temporarily disconnected. He cursed under his breath.

Her loss.

ReRe was fourth in his current female rotation. She was his wild woman. His ghetto chick. She was his round-the-way bad girl who was perfect for the sheets, but not someone to be seen with in the streets. Not that he cared, but he could never seem to remember what the

"Re" in ReRe stood for. Renee? Rita? Something with an R. He never had to use it and she never seemed to notice or care.

Stopped at a traffic light, Jason surveyed the address book in his phone. He considered his next option and then hit number five on his speed dial. After a couple of rings, he was met with a silky smooth voice. Marisol currently held the number five position and was even lower maintenance than ReRe because he could go months without calling her, then just show up and wham! He was in there!

With a sigh, Jason thought about the woman he had, literally and figuratively, on the line. He'd added her to his harem effortlessly because she was one of those Latino chicks who had a thing for the brothers. Marisol was not hard on the eyes at all. She was a walking goddess with a coke bottle shape, creamy skin, big hazel brown eyes that crackled when she talked, and long, flowing, dark brown hair. She definitely had what he and his best friend Tyrone called "arm status," which meant that they could take her with them anywhere and see nothing but envy and longing in the eyes of every man in the room. But there *was* one problem: she was a breeder. Jason always made sure he was wrapped up well before he lay down with her. He had no intention of leaving anything behind that would crawl into his wallet and stay there for the next eighteen years.

At twenty-six, Marisol already had four kids and when she answered her phone he could tell from the noise in the background that the little parasites were still up. That was a *big* no-no. For the briefest second, he considered stopping at a store to get some good old Nyquil to knock their bad butts out. Just as quickly Jason had a flashback of his last encounter with them and decided he didn't want to go through the hassle. After a few polite words, he pretended to hit a dead spot and hung up on her. She was simple and would buy that. He might try her again some other night when things were different.

Jason turned at the next traffic light, pointed his BMW toward Center City, and hit Angelina's assigned number on his speed dial. His number three and last resort. She was his mixed chick with an identity crisis. He never knew whether he would be dealing with Angie, the *sistah*, or Angelina, the Italian babe. Both of them knew how to hold it down so, again, he really didn't care. It actually kept everything interesting. She was petite at five feet tall, but had a rough and nasty mouth on her that made a lot of men walk away. But Jason was confident it was because they didn't know how to handle her. He liked her tough facade because as sassy as she was, she was equally as passionate. That's why she held down the number three spot. He made a point to connect with her at *least* once a month.

The phone rang several times, but Jason didn't get an answer at her house. He wasn't leaving a message. She had a steady boyfriend and he didn't want to disturb that relationship just to feed his need on a single night. Angelina was always his safest bet because she didn't try to get attached. She liked the excitement of cheating and, like he did, believed variety was the spice of life. Nevertheless, Jason was truly disappointed that she was unavailable. He made the first available U-turn that he could so that he could go home to Chestnut Hill. He had no choice but to call it a night. He wasn't in the mood to recruit any new talent into his bed.

A streetlight illuminated one of the clear cases on the seat next to him as he drove. His aunt had given him VHS tapes of his biological father's sermons. Jason wanted to watch the tapes but equally wanted to hurl them out the window.

"So, this motherfucker is supposed to be my father," he said to himself.

It didn't even sound right. All his life Jason believed his father was a minor hero in the Navy who died in a military-related accident. How was he supposed to adjust to a completely different script after twenty-something years? His mother fed him the same story over and over from the time he could talk. She added more information as he became older, but the crux of the story was always the same.

According to Bridget, his father was a young sailor named Earl who was stationed at the Navy Shipyard in Philadelphia not far from Roosevelt Park where she and her friends spent many hours hanging out in the summer. Young and starry-eyed, his mother had a dalliance with Earl before he shipped out. He promised to come back to marry her, but died before it could happen. Bridget said she'd never met

Earl's family or known very much about him, but that was okay. He had a dad once upon a time.

There had been times in Jason's life when he'd watched families on television, complete with fathers and two sets of grandparents, enjoying themselves and wondered about his other grandparents. He also wondered if he had another set of aunts and uncles out there who could provide for him like his Aunt Theresa and Uncle Thomas did. Deep down Jason had held hope that one day his other family would show up with toys and surprises, but it never happened. It was all a lie.

3

According to his aunt Theresa, Jason's father was not Earl, was not dead, and he'd never been in the Navy. Jason sat staring dumbly at her trying to make sense out of what she was saying as she told him. Time seemed to stand still for a few moments like in the Matrix movies. He could slowly feel anger building up inside. His aunt had over twenty-eight years to find a better way to tell him all this, but didn't. Instead, she threw the information out there like darts. Each dagger dug deeper as she shared the full history behind his conception and the slow, systematic, destruction of his extended family.

The story began during the summer of Bridget White's high school graduation. She'd met a young man from North Carolina visiting Philly on his summer vacation at a house party one night. Although Theresa had never met her sister's new boyfriend, she remembered how smitten Bridget was with him. Theresa warned her little sister about taking irresponsible risks and behaving less than ladylike, but Bridget ignored her. Sometime around the beginning of August, the young man returned to North Carolina and not long after, Bridget discovered she was pregnant. Theresa dropped her head at this point in telling Jason the story and began to cry. Her tears had no effect on him. He was too stunned and anxious to console her.

Theresa recounted the day Bridget was forced to tell the family about her condition. The mom-to-be had been washing dishes while Theresa dried when their mother came in the kitchen and stood near the sink staring. She had been watching Bridget a lot in recent days. Even Theresa sensed a blow-up on the horizon, but had no idea why.

"Everything alright?"

Both sisters looked up and chorused, "Yes, Ma'am."

"You sure, Bridget?"

Florence White stood stock still as she stared at her youngest daughter. Her serious expression wiped the smile off of Bridget's young face.

"Ma'am?"

"Is there something we need to talk about?"

Before Bridget could reply, her mother strode over and spun her daughter around to face her. She stared first at the girl's neck, then at her face, and lastly at her abdomen. Bridget blanched. Theresa moved out of their way and proceeded to wipe the splattered remnants of dinner off the stovetop. She didn't know what her sister had done, but she didn't want to get caught in the crossfire.

"What have you done to yourself?" their mother whispered angrily as she turned red and tears filling her eyes.

Bridget stammered, "I…I…" She then burst into tears. "I'm sorry Mommy!"

Theresa looked between the two of then confused. Her mother yelled out for their father.

"Leroy! Get in here, please!"

A sense of dread filled Theresa's stomach and turned her undigested dinner into a weight. This had to be bad. There weren't many discipline-related matters her mother deferred to their father on. He got to handle the big things, which could only mean one thing. Theresa stared at her sister with horror and a tiny measure of jealousy. She did not want to believe Bridget could be pregnant. Theresa was the oldest and the one who was engaged, not Bridget. Her little sister needed to wait her turn.

Leroy came in the room looking satiated from his evening meal but irritated that he'd been taken away from his television program. Before he could ask his wife what she wanted, Florence yanked Bridget away from the sink sending her skidding across the brown speckled vinyl floor toward her father. Florence could barely get her words out.

"Look at her. Look at your child! Look what she's done to herself!"

Leroy's eyes scanned his daughter not seeing anything to get worked up over but one look at Bridget's small yet rounded belly confirmed everything for Theresa. She began fighting back her own tears.

"Look at her!" Florence shrieked. "Can't you see she is carrying a baby? Your daughter is expecting!"

Leroy's fair complexion had always run closer to red than brown. This plus his curly, auburn hair and sprinkling of freckles caused his friends to dub him Redman. That night, Redman glowed crimson. The veins in his neck and forehead throbbed. At 5'6" he was just a few inches taller than his wife and daughters but Theresa thought he seemed to grow about ten inches taller in that moment.

Leroy reached out and grabbed Bridget firmly by the shoulders.

"Are you expecting?"

Blubbering Bridget nodded and managed a "Yes, Sir."

"We raised you better than this! Didn't we? *Didn't we*?"

Again she nodded.

"Who is he? Who's his family?" Leroy bellowed ready to search the young man out and do him harm.

Bridget stood crying and trembling. "You don't know him. He's not here. He's gone."

"What do you mean he's gone? You don't know who he is? Did someone hurt you?" Leroy yelled in his daughter's face.

Theresa groaned. "I bet it was that boy from down south."

The girls' parents turned toward Theresa causing her to quickly backpedal lest she get in trouble too.

"I don't know him. I don't even remember his name! She just talked about him all the time, that's all."

"How could you do this to us?" Florence wailed, her attention back on Bridget. "What are you going to do with yourself? You can't go to college like this."

"Yes I can! I can still go to school!" Bridget insisted, her heart breaking at the thought of losing out on what she'd worked so hard for.

"Not with my money, you're not!" Leroy said.

"Yes, daddy! Please! My classes start in a couple of weeks," Bridget begged. "I can stay here and still go to school. That's what I was going to do anyway. I can still do it!"

"Oh no you're not! You are not staying here. You think you are old enough to lay down and make a baby then you are old enough to get out on your own."

Florence and Theresa gasped. Bridget cried harder.

"Daddy!" she screamed trying to grab onto him, but he pushed her away. She came toward him again and he slapped her. She turned and ran up the stairs toward her bedroom wailing. Leroy followed behind her yelling.

"You need to get your clothes and get out of my house! Don't take anything else! You are lucky I am letting you have that much!"

Theresa stood dumbstruck as her mother rushed from the room and up the stairs. Florence called to her husband and begged him to see reason. Within minutes, Theresa heard the first whizzing snap of a belt followed by Bridget's anguished scream and her mother's cries of, "That's enough Leroy! That's enough!"

Theresa entered the hall and looked up in time to see Bridget running from her father and him in hot pursuit, belt swinging in his hands. He hit her not caring how hard or where the physical blows landed much less the emotional ones.

Bridget was cast out into the street. And with nowhere else to go, she temporarily moved in with an older female friend. Theresa eventually located her sister after a few days and took her items from time to time. Unfortunately, they ended up arguing each time. Bridget was determined not to go crawling back to her parents. She could live without ever speaking to them again. In the interest of restoring their family and Bridget's original life plan, Theresa tried to talk her little sister into having an abortion. She refused. She wanted her baby. Theresa believed it was largely because Bridget was so in love with the father. Sure enough, she wrote to the young man from North Carolina multiple times to tell him about her condition and ask him to come back or send for her. He never replied. His letters were never returned, so the sisters assumed he had received them, but didn't want to be bothered.

Jason nodded slowly as he listened to the story unfold. Hearing it confirmed a deeply hidden suspicion he'd had all of his life. Even his girl, Denise, mentioned a time or two that Jason seemed to have anxiety about rejection, which could be the reason why he chose to be so arrogant. Jason knew he was super sensitive so Denise's words rang true though he'd never admit it. This was probably why. No one had to come right out and say they didn't want you for you to feel unwanted. You don't even have to know them, see them, or talk to them to sense it. The soul knows even when the mind chooses not to believe it or entertain it.

Jason's aunt continued on. She told him about how his mother discovered she was pregnant with twins and fell apart. She was so distraught that she almost gave in and crawled back home to her parents. Almost. Leroy White didn't allow Theresa to even mention Bridget's name in the house. She was dead to him. Bridget eventually became happy about having two babies, but she was scared. Theresa wanted to do more for her baby sister. She tearfully admitted she wasn't a consistent source of help for Bridget like she should have been. And Bridget, once again, took matters into her own hands.

Through her classmate's mother, Bridget managed to get a small one-bedroom apartment in the Richard Allen projects and that was where she stayed until Jason's twin, JaLisa, died. In the meantime, Bridget's parents argued continuously over the fate of their youngest daughter. Her mother wanted Bridget back home with her grandbabies, but her husband didn't want anything to do with her or them. He was prideful, embarrassed, and angry. With all the tension in their home, Leroy White finally left for work one day and never came back.

Almost immediately after their father's disappearance, Florence became ill. Theresa blamed Bridget. She believed her sister was selfish for throwing away her education and ruining their family just to have some boy's babies. More than that, when Leroy vanished, he wasn't there to walk Theresa down the aisle for her wedding a few months later. Everyone in their family was so bent out of shape about Bridget's situation that a dark shadow was cast over Theresa's wedding plans. There were two big gaps in Theresa's already sparse bridal party and she resented Bridget for years after that.

Listening to his aunt pummel him with this story, Jason couldn't help feeling like she *still* held a grudge. Sure, his mother made some mistakes, but at least she never held herself over people like she was better than them. His mother was a young, scared, pregnant girl with twins. She was beaten and thrown out of the house by the people she expected to love and take care of her. And all his aunt could think about was her wedding? His mother never had one nor had she ever had a man to call her own—at least not for very long.

When Theresa began to cry recalling all the pain again, Jason watched her with a detached curiosity laced with disdain. She scooted to the end of her chair in an attempt to get closer to him. She asked for forgiveness. Another person might have pitied her. She had carried all this for a long time. Jason should have at least accepted her apology. But his anger won out instead. He took mental notes and created an ironclad case against his aunt, a woman he once admired, but who now appeared pathetic.

"Back then I didn't know Jesus for myself like I do now. I didn't understand that taking a human life was wrong. I am so sorry for trying to get Bridget to get rid of you. I don't know what I would have done without you in my life. I am so proud of you and love you like you were my own. I thank God she didn't take my advice. I am sorry."

Theresa looked at her nephew almost expecting absolution. Jason stared at her, silently cursing her and everything she believed in. He may have hated her right then, but he knew better than to disrespect her in her own house. He could offer no words of forgiveness or comfort. His thoughts, however, did their own vengeful and angry dance, as he looked out of the lace-covered window.

After an awkward silence, punctuated only by his aunt's sniffles and sobs, she finally continued her story and regained his interest. Perhaps there was a punch line to this twenty-nine-year-old joke.

"When you twins were born," she recalled, "I was the only member of the family to visit the hospital to see you."

In truth, Theresa didn't stay for any length of time during her visits and there were precious few times she saw Bridget and her babies before they moved back into the family home on Ellsworth Street with their mother.

JaLisa's death at fourteen months shook everyone and caused Bridget to finally make amends with her mother. It was a shaky truce, but not long after their initial tearful conversation, Bridget took Jason to live there. Bridget was never the same after JaLisa's death. She gave up on everything, especially herself.

Bridget began a series of short-term relationships and bounced from man to man faster than Theresa could blink. She ended up with two more children—each with a different man. Before Bridget could snap out of her downward spiral, her and Theresa's mother died. Although the family house was willed to Theresa, she gave it to Bridget. She and her husband, Thomas, had already purchased a home of their own. Within a few short months, however, it was clear Bridget was unable to keep up with the demands of homeownership. She'd let yet another less than reputable man convince her to re-mortgage the house, leaving her without a dime. She eventually lost the house less than three years after moving in.

Jason bristled as his aunt shared details he was never privy to because he was so young at the time. His aunt couldn't hide her frustration.

"All she had to do was tell us when she couldn't fix something or pay the taxes. She didn't say anything. She didn't do anything but run up more debt. She just let that house fall apart. Even if she had come clean and told us about the loan, we would have tried to help. But no, she didn't say anything until the bank took it."

Theresa shook her head in disgust.

"I don't know if you remember that house or not. It was a really nice piece of property in Overbrook. It could have been where you grew up. If she couldn't handle it, we could have used it as rental property or sold it to give you and your sisters a strong start into your adult lives, but your mother took all of that away. I hate we lost it."

The loss of the home was part of the reason why Theresa and Thomas didn't invite Bridget and the children to stay with them afterward. Bridget was too proud and headstrong to ever ask and Theresa didn't want Bridget's transient lifestyle moving through *her* house.

I thought you said you were sorry, Jason thought as he stared at her self-satisfied expression. *This is exactly why you could never have kids of your own. Karma is a bitch and so are you.*

***

As Jason drove home, he realized that all this new "truth" – or at least the truth as Aunt Theresa believed it to be—made it easy to shoot holes through his mother's lies. If his mother never heard from Earl again, how did she find out he was dead? Many times she said she couldn't remember his last name, but if she knew it and knew he was dead, why didn't she try to find his family? Surely the military would have helped her if they knew a soldier had fathered a child with a teenager. So much of what Bridget White told her son rang blatantly false. Jason's rage boiled over at the thought of his innocence at the time. He wanted to believe. He needed to.

Without pictures, Jason relied on his childish imagination to concoct what his father may have looked like. He often studied strangers on the bus wondering if his father looked like one of them, spoke with a similar voice, or had a similar laugh. Jason's mother and his two sisters were much lighter than he was growing up and they all had similar features. Jason was markedly different from most everyone in his small family. Each sported the same barely beige clear skin, straight noses, thin lips, and naturally wavy hair. In fact, his sister Faye had successfully lied and passed herself off as Latino when she was in the fourth or fifth grade until Bridget found out about it and slapped her middle child silly for behaving as if she were ashamed of being black.

Jason caught a glimpse of himself in his rearview mirror and wondered if he really looked like the man who used to be the boy from North Carolina. He flipped over one of the videotapes and glanced at the photo on the cover through the punctuated darkness of his car. As much as he hated to admit it, there were some obvious similarities—his dark skin especially. He tossed the tape to the side with disgust and gripped the steering wheel with both hands.

Un-fucking-believable! Out of all the men on the planet, my father has to be him?

If it had been anyone else, he may not have cared. Any dude that impregnated his mother then walked away without a backward glance wasn't worthy of a second thought. But this one? Who he was added another dimension to the deception. Through the television and radio, he had been in their house every day. He was treated by his mother (and everyone else) like he walked on water. Yet, she never said a word. Never batted an eye. Never looked the least bit guilty or ashamed. Instead, Bridget White sung his praises. How could she do that knowing what he'd done to her? And if she didn't mean it, why perform? There had to be more to this story. Jason never considered his mother weak, but if everything he'd learned from his aunt was true, maybe she was, and this did not sit well with him at all.

The news ate at Jason like a cancer. His mind replayed incident after incident from the past. He knew each scene would have been drastically different if his father...*his* father had been involved. He wasn't angry his parents never married. They were young and dumb, and it obviously wasn't a serious relationship. Jason certainly wouldn't marry any of the women he rotated if one of them got pregnant, so he couldn't be a hypocrite and expect the same. But this man never did *anything* for him. Not a single, solitary thing. Would it have killed him to send him a card every year or so? A picture? A letter explaining why he wasn't around? Wasn't that what people were supposed to do when their illegitimate children grew up without the wayward parent in their lives?

Jason's temples throbbed and sweat began to bead on his nose and in the vertical groove above his upper lip. *How could a person be so incredibly selfish?*

* * *

One particular Friday night—a Friday like many before and afterward—Bridget White entered her small, second floor apartment slowly. Her face was drawn with fatigue. At the sound of the key in the door, a young Jason hopped out of bed gingerly and peeked out into the hallway just in time to see her come in.

"Thank you, Ms. Edna. I'm sorry I'm late. They made us stay and do inventory tonight."

Bridget smiled weakly at the older woman who watched Jason, Faye and Donna, Friday through Monday nights when she worked her third job into the wee hours of the morning.

"I'm not doing anything I wouldn't be doing in my own place. Don't you worry. I know how hard it is raising kids by yourself. But BeBe?"

Bridget looked up at her expectantly.

"You can't keep working yourself to the bone every single day on those jobs. You're going to send yourself to an early grave. You get help from their father don't you? Give up one of those jobs and enjoy yourself. Life's too short to do nothing but work."

Bridget smiled tightly.

"Thank you, Ms. Edna. I'll get it together one of these days."

She showed the older woman out and made sure she saw her into her apartment downstairs. Afterward, Bridget collapsed into her favorite chair, an important rescue from the foreclosure. It was a yellow plaid, Queen Anne style chair with a skirt at the bottom. The best part was the rocking mechanism hidden under the skirt—perfect for keeping the kids busy, if only momentarily. Jason and his sisters sat in it and rocked every chance they got. Within minutes, Bridget was asleep. And like so many nights before and after, young Jason crept forward to stare at his mother's face, count the dusting of freckles on her nose and cheeks, and gently kiss her. There was a time he would have crawled into her lap and joined her, but he'd grown too big.

Bridget never stopped working hard and Ms. Edna had been right after all. He was there. Bridget had literally worked herself into an early grave. Jason felt responsible for this. She received a small monthly child support check from each of his sister's fathers, but she had to do everything for him solo. The irony was that she somehow always had money for the man he learned was his father, sending in tithes and offerings when she could. It was mindboggling. He was certain his mother would have enjoyed her life and him and his sisters would have been able to enjoy her more if his father was around. He was even more certain that his sister, JaLisa, would still be alive.

Tears welled up in Jason's deep brown eyes. A few found their way onto his long lashes as they dove onto his cheeks. The tears only made him angrier. He'd lost control and that was unacceptable. He tried to suck it up and bite back the grief.

***

JaLisa was Jason's Achilles heel. Just the sound of her name hurt his heart. JaLisa was his womb-mate. His first playmate. He was forever connected to her. At fourteen months old, her life was snatched from her after being bitten by, of all things, a rabid rat. Their apartment in the projects was infested with them. Many of the rodents grew to the size of small cats. Jason vividly remembered their stench and how they ate through the ceiling tiles in their apartment. The rats weren't intimidated by traps, poison, or any other forms of pest control. The only thing their building superintendent was able do was shoot them on sight and put up wire where they'd been so that they couldn't chew through *that* spot again.

As a young child, Jason laid awake many nights listening to the rodents scratching in the walls and chewing their way through panels. He tried to monitor their locations throughout the night afraid that they were going to get him next if he wasn't vigilant. Even now, as an adult, any phantom sound in his bedroom at night could have him up for hours with the light on. This was one of the many reasons he was still single. How could anyone explain that sort of trauma? He wasn't about to set himself up to be judged or ridiculed.

His Aunt Theresa told him that his mother had done all she knew to do to protect her children from the rats, but JaLisa was bitten anyway. As a young, inexperienced mother she didn't immediately know what happened to her baby when JaLisa suddenly became violently ill. She didn't know what to do about it until it was too late. Who could she have called? Her parents? That bridge had burned.

Although he hadn't been able to conjure up a true mental image of her in decades, Jason missed JaLisa on a level he'd never missed anyone before. Instead of seeing her face, she was a represented by a shadow, a smell, a feeling. His mother had never gotten around to taking infant photos, so he had no photograph to jar his memory. JaLisa existed on a birth certificate, a death certificate, and in an empty place in his heart. But in this moment, with nowhere to go and no warmth of a woman's curves to assuage his pain, he was clear about one thing. If anyone were to blame for his sister's death, it would be the man on the videotapes. In his mind, this man killed his twin sister by sheer neglect. The irony of it all was that Jason's biological father was a preacher. But men in robes hiding behind pulpits were just that—men. Jason didn't trust them and didn't put anything past any of them.

Under the veil of night, Jason allowed his tears to flow. He missed his mother so much that he felt physically ill. He was ashamed of his anger toward her. Maybe if he'd been a better son she would've told him more. She often chastised him about his temper. Maybe she feared if he knew about his father, he would have attacked him. Jason knew this could be a possibility. His anger for *that man* was deep. Jason wanted to hold him upside down off the Walt Whitman Bridge until he answered all of his questions. Then, he'd drop him. Drop him the way old preacher man dropped his mother.

4

Mrs. Lucretia Pope Stewart was the First Lady of Abundant
Holiness Metropolitan Missionary Baptist Fellowship
Church in Raleigh, North Carolina. It all sounded very
impressive but, in truth, her journey was far from it. At forty-five, her
life was a series of regrets; a series of painfully depressing experiences,
each heavily shrouded in deceit. After all of these years, she was tired
and ready for it all to end.

In 1979, Lucretia met Evangelist Quincy Jefferson Stewart when
he came to her hometown of Washington, North Carolina for a tent
meeting. Folks would dress in their summer best and head to Lil'
Washington's revival. They'd sit downwind under a huge, faded yellow,
plastic tent erected in an old cow pasture owned by a prominent black
farmer. They came to hear from whatever out of town preacher they
could convince to drive down to the North Carolina coast.

Quincy was a young man then, just a few years her senior, but he
could preach the Bible like nobody she'd ever heard before. And he
was a sharp dresser on top of that. Even his name sounded like
money. She never forgot the first time she saw him preach. She was
seated in an aisle seat midway in the tent. He was so tall and lean, yet
had strong wide shoulders and a loud and commanding voice. It gave
her chills and she was immediately taken with him.

"...and so then Moses stood in the gate of the camp, and said,
'who is on the Lord's side? Let him come unto me'. And all the sons of
Levi gathered themselves together unto him.[1] They didn't look around
to see who was going to go first. They knew who they wanted to run

38

with! You gotta know who you runnin' with! You can't stop and think about it or wait for your friends to decide. You gotta step up!"

He leaned back and strutted around the pulpit like he owned it. He preached until sweat ran down his dark skin and soaked his shirt. And even when his voice was hoarse, he kept preaching. Every once in a while someone would hand him a cool drink while the old people in attendance encouraged him with shouts of "That's all right son. Take yo' time" or "Tell the truth and shame the devil! Yassah!"

It was during one of those times that the impressionable twenty-two-year-old Lucretia was certain he looked right at her. She could barely breathe each time their eyes met. He represented all she thought she wanted and deserved. But twenty-four years later, she knew it was nothing but a well-orchestrated show. Back then though, their feelings seemed to be mutual.

Every night after Quincy preached, Lucretia sat perched on the front row. During each sermon, they stole looks at each other. Hers were curiously innocent and hopeful. His were more knowing, more calculated. He preached just to her. The other unmarried women flocked around the handsome, single evangelist, but Lucretia kept her cool. Her mother taught her better than to carry on like that. Inside though, her heart raced. Nevertheless, she was determined to never let him see her sweat.

Quincy had eyes that could go from fierce and penetrating to smoky and sultry without missing a beat. He possessed pronounced, chiseled cheekbones, a strong, lantern jaw and the prettiest teeth she'd ever seen. When Quincy smiled it lit up the place, making her want to melt. To this day, he kept his mustache and beard closely trimmed and neat. When she shook his hand that first night, she was amazed at its softness. *Feels just like a baby's cheek.* No black man in Lil' Washington at that time had hands like his unless he was what folks called 'questionable.' And yet somehow Lucretia knew Evangelist Quincy Jefferson Stewart was entirely too manly to even consider that life.

After the revival, Lucretia learned through the grapevine that Quincy had asked around about her, so she was only mildly surprised when he called her home a few days after the tent meeting had ended.

At first she wasn't sure they'd both felt the same spark, but she should have known better. Lucretia was secretly scorned by many of the women in the community. Her clear, high yellow skin and exotic features that some insisted were Chinese or maybe Cherokee, easily passed the paper bag test. By any criteria, but especially by the colorism of the day, she was stunning.

She learned early on to use her wide, light-colored eyes to mesmerize men. Her light brown hair bordered on a dark blond so the fact that she had what people in her community called "white folks' hair" didn't help her case any with her darker classmates who were born with tight, kinky curls requiring hours of work. She was born with what her grandmother called wide, childbearing hips and the kind of full breasts that many men looked for back then—a sign of a passionate and fertile woman. Although Lucretia was hard pressed to find a long-lasting, female friend, the men always hung around, panting like thirsty puppies in the summer's heat.

The day Quincy finally called, Lucretia's mother had barely hung up the phone before she broadcasted the news to half of Lil 'Washington, Pantego, and every town along the North Carolina coast. Dodie Pope was always good at that. Any information someone wanted to disseminate quickly could be transmitted to the world lickety-split by telling her.

Lucretia's mother bragged to every ear she could connect with, "That young evangelist done called my daughter Cretia and is plannin' to come down to see 'bout her! Can you imagine that?" If her mother could have swelled up any bigger with pride she would have levitated.

So many people had high expectations for Lucretia and coddled her. Most hoped to be in with her so they could benefit when she hit it big. Few were as big a fan or a more anticipatory benefactor than her mother. From the beginning, Dodie never hesitated to boast about her baby to whoever sat still long enough to hear it.

"She sounded just like that Aretha Franklin!" Dodie Pope boasted of her then sixteen-year-old daughter Lucretia after she won the Miss Waterfront pageant.

"She sounded better to me!" Dodie's best friend Hattie chimed in. She need to go to Motown or Hollywood somewhere and get a record going. She's gonna be like Gladys Knight singing with men folk behind her doing all that steppin' and such." Hattie attempted a few steps to Dodie's amusement. "Just you watch and see!"

"Oh I know it." Dodie said bursting with pride. "But you know she don't need to limit herself. Look at that Pam Grier. My baby can do that. She can be in the pictures and model like that Beverly Johnson. Can't you just see her face on Ebony? That'll sho' be something." Dodie looked wistful.

"Mmmm hmmm…" Hattie agreed. "Speaking of the Johnsons, she might get her a rich man like that Eunice Walker Johnson. That'll be somethin' for sure!"

All of Lucretia's looks and charm worked in her favor until she graduated from high school. Lucretia was not the best student. She also had a flair for the dramatic, which garnered lots of special attention. So even when her grades didn't allow her the privilege of an active part in the chorus, band, cheerleading, or even the drama troupe, Lucretia still practiced at home and performed at church. She was going to be a big star one day and didn't believe she needed school to do so.

Although she was not a fan of manual labor, Lucretia was content to work in the seafood market her father and uncle owned. She grew up around fish all her life and was convinced that most of their male customers shopped there just to get a look at her. She felt her presence in the family store was good for business especially when the men bought more than they planned as they fawned over her. Her wink followed by a "Bye now. You come back and see me, you hear?" never failed to make even the oldest man blush.

Lucretia hated the smell of the seafood, standing on her feet all day, and having her father yell at her for moving too slow. She only tolerated it because she just knew someone would discover her and take her away from the fish and small town living. The world would see her shine. The young evangelist showing up and taking interest in her was perfect timing. He could be her ticket up and out.

Less than a year after they met, Quincy Jefferson Stewart and Lucretia Pope were married. All of the important people in Lucretia's small community attended. Even the white mayor made an appearance to witness Walter and Dodie Pope's baby girl walk into her destiny. It was the biggest black function Lil' Washington had ever seen at the time and as the center of attention, Lucretia was in her element.

Quincy's family, though, was conspicuously absent from the affair. When asked about them, Quincy told everyone about the heartbreaking illnesses that kept his family sick and shut-in. A quick sermon about how God had raised him up to heal his family of their infirmities satisfied everyone's curiosity. It was years before Lucretia learned the truth about *that* particular lie. If only she were smart enough to have looked a little closer and actually listened to what he said back then. If only she'd had the presence of mind to ask more questions and demand straight answers void of church-speak and clichés.

The newly married Stewarts moved into a small apartment in the black section of Raleigh and Quincy immediately began grooming his wife. It was as if she were Eliza Doolittle to his Professor Henry Higgins.

"You wear this here skirt with this blouse. That's how them white women is wearing it nowadays," he said, explaining his choices. "And put some stockings on your legs!"

He would steer her down the street with his hand firmly placed on her back directing her where to go. Lucretia never forgot the first time he hit her. Quincy had been teaching her how to speak properly and how to greet people like a pastor's wife.

He said, "Good morning, Sister Stewart! How are you?"

Lucretia's response should have been a nod of the head followed by a pious, "Blessed, thank you." But she was tired and feeling a bit silly so she said her line as if she were in a minstrel show. She never saw the slap coming, but it sent her to the floor of their apartment with her head spinning and face stinging.

"You wanna play? This funny? I am doin' this because you are not goin' to embarrass me! Now get up here and do it right!"

She did as he commanded and the ringing in her left her ear lasted for weeks.

Quincy taught Lucretia proper city manners and how to have "airs." Those were a few of the things she needed to know in order to be a famous evangelist's wife—or so she thought back then. Within no time, she knew how to: walk with dignity, like she was concerned and listening to someone when she really wasn't, gracefully wave her cloth handkerchief encouragingly as Quincy preached, and even how to do the Holy Spirit two-step, shoutin' dance for when she wanted to catch the Holy Ghost in church.

Quincy barely made any money going around evangelizing in those days and since he didn't have a home church to sponsor him, there was very little in the way of income coming into the household. Lucretia didn't mind though. She was smitten with her husband and convinced he would be on TV one day like Oral Roberts or Billy Graham. It was amazing how time changed her perspective so dramatically.

One of the things she quickly learned was that Quincy was one smooth talker. He could talk the hair off a dog and cajole a fish straight out of water. His gift of gab got them clothes to wear that they otherwise couldn't afford. It put food on the table when they had no money, and provided an impressive Lincoln Continental to drive when they couldn't afford a single car payment. The car had been used and was a much older model than what Quincy wanted, but it definitely was a certified preacher's car and they looked sharp riding around in it. At first, Lucretia was worried someone would come to their home and demand their things back, but when no one did, she learned to relax and accept the blessings that came.

Sometimes the fruit of Quincy's mouth made Lucretia uncomfortable, especially when he talked to other women. She felt he overtly flirted with them, but Quincy insisted he was just being nice. They argued about it frequently in the beginning, but he always won her over by using his words or his hands against her. When they disagreed, he'd call her names: country, crazy, backward, stupid, and silly. Then he would point out her humble beginnings and remind her that he'd made her into something more refined. She could not refute any of it so she shut up. That was how she coped all these years. If she said nothing, then he would also say nothing and better still, he would do nothing.

Lucretia also got good at seeing past things. She learned to ignore Quincy giving their unlisted phone number to attractive women or overtly flirting with them at the churches they'd visit. She pretended not to see Quincy ogling their breasts and rear-ends, and she pretended not to notice a lot of other humiliating things that made her cry in private. Instead, Lucretia tried to be the best wife possible. She cooked Quincy the best meals she knew how to make. Sometimes he acted like he enjoyed them, sometimes not. It only really bothered her when Quincy gushed over the meals prepared for them by women at the churches they visited. It was contrived and slimy, but the women never failed to fall for his charms. Those women could not hold a candle to what Lucretia prepared for him at home and she knew that he knew it. As embarrassing as Quincy's behavior was, Lucretia held her head up high, went home, and tried even harder. She loved her husband and did all she could to give him a good home.

Although it often left her ashamed and embarrassed, she even tried to make him happy during their marital intimate time. Lucretia had no idea where a sanctified preacher like Quincy learned all of the strange and awkward things he taught her but she sucked up feeling like a cheap prostitute and performed her wifely duty. She fully believed that the day Quincy became a famous worldwide preacher, she would be right there by his side to share in the glory and the spoils. The hard times were just their testimony for later. It never occurred to her that the spot by Quincy's side would ever become crowded.

Quincy's invitations to speak at churches began to decline quickly mid-way during their first year of marriage and money became tighter than ever. He refused to let Lucretia work. No wife of Quincy's was going to work outside of the home. Her job was to stay home, keep house, and raise their children even though they had no little ones yet. That was another sore spot. Lucretia tried desperately, but after a year, she still had not become pregnant. Immediately, Quincy declared something was wrong with her and made her go to a gynecologist. Lucretia assumed Quincy was right about her body, after all he was right about everything else. Ultimately the doctor told her she was fine and to relax; a baby would come when they least expected it.

Lucretia had no idea where Quincy went during the day and even decades later she still didn't know. Whenever she asked him about his day, he became angry and told her that he was, "Out doin' the good Lord's work and bringin' in the money so we can eat." Lucretia didn't want to make him angry, so she eventually stopped asking.

One day Quincy arrived home a little earlier than normal.

"We fixin' to have our own church. I heard from the Lord on it today! We gonna call it Stewart's Baptist Grove."

Quincy kept her up half the night with his vision for it, drawing pictures, and dreaming big. Lucretia was excited. She was going to be a proper first lady. Seven months and a miscarriage later, they found themselves no closer to starting their church or having a family. They were poorer than ever. Quincy's surly personality intensified as he yelled at Lucretia for every little thing real or imagined. She knew he was frustrated. She was too. She took the verbal and physical abuse in silence believing he didn't truly mean any of it. His disappointment was doing the talking, not his heart.

On the day of the first miscarriage, Quincy left the house early that morning to handle ministry business. Lucretia had not felt well all morning and hours later began having painful cramps. With no way to contact Quincy, she opted to lie in bed with a hot water bottle pressed to her stomach, but the pain only increased. When she began to bleed, she knocked on her neighbors' doors until she found someone home. No sooner then when the neighbor hurriedly agreed to take her to the doctor, Quincy returned home and took her instead.

When the emergency room doctor explained what happened, Quincy's face turned grim and Lucretia cried. They did not even make it to the car before he began yelling.

"What kind of woman are you that you can't even carry a baby right? Is you that stupid?"

Lucretia cried even harder.

"I'm sorry. I didn't mean to."

In the car he turned toward her, spit flying out of his mouth as he berated her.

"You did it on purpose, didn't you? You can't stand for me to have nothin' so you killed my baby, didn't you? *Didn't you?*"

Lucretia was so horrified that she couldn't talk. Her mouth hung open and her throat went tight and dry. The tears poured down her reddened face. She shook her head no.

"What you say? Answer me woman!"

Lucretia couldn't get her throat to work so she shook her head even faster as she stared wide-eyed at her husband. Quincy grabbed a fist full of Lucretia's hair and slammed her face into the dashboard. Her scream filled the car. Quincy looked around, but no one looked in their direction. He cranked the engine and put the car in reverse. Lucretia held her forehead with both hands as she moaned and cried.

"I ain't through with you either," Quincy menaced. "I'll finish dealing with you when we get home."

And he did.

Quincy's next foray into ministry involved starting a bible study in their apartment. He tried what another local black pastor did to begin his ministry. That pastor had gone on to create a mega ministry that boasted nearly a thousand members—unheard of in their town in the 1980's. Quincy's attempt was short-lived though. No one ever attended the bible study. Lucretia finally began to understand that Quincy wasn't as famous in Raleigh as he was back in her hometown of Lil' Washington. Still, she foolishly held out hope that with her love, hard work, and devotion he would – *they would* - become something big sooner rather than later. They just had to keep pressing.

As time went on, Quincy's anger hardened. Lucretia suffered another miscarriage and just when she thought she couldn't take anymore of her husband's ranting and acting out, he came home one day with good news. Abundant Holiness Baptist Church needed a new pastor and Quincy was going to interview for the job.

The weeks that followed were filled with Quincy preparing a trial sermon and practicing his best preacher moves. Lucretia watched her husband strut, shout, hem, and haw for hours until he felt confident he was ready. He carefully picked out Lucretia's outfit and made sure she had everything in place for the big day. Quincy reminded her that no matter how well he preached, if she wasn't perfect, she would ruin everything for him. That was the last thing she wanted to happen so she determined to try her hardest for him. For them.

5

The morning of the interview, Quincy and Lucretia Stewart woke early and went over every detail of his trial sermon with a fine-tooth comb. In the middle of their respective preparations, Quincy went to his wife in haste.

"We need to do somethin' about your name. It don't sound right."

"What?" Lucretia replied. She liked her name. She was named after her godmother who died a few years before she met Quincy.

"We changing your name." Quincy enunciated with a tinge of threat in his tone. "Lucretia sound like you an old woman. And we definitely ain't gonna have folk calling you Cretia. That sound even more backwater than Lucretia. We need to find you a good name."

Lucretia was dumbfounded, but Quincy continued.

"You ever heard tell of any important pastors with wives that got a name like yours?"

She shook her head no.

"That's right! So we gonna fix that today. We gonna give you a good soundin' name."

Lucretia didn't protest because she was convinced Quincy knew what he was talking about. He always had. So on the day of his trial sermon at Abundant Holiness Baptist Church, Quincy's wife, Lucretia Pope Stewart, became Lucy Stewart. She was relieved that, on the surface, things finally seemed to get better for them, but behind closed doors, they only got worse—at least for her.

Later that morning when he spoke, Quincy preached his best sermon ever. He revisited the message that he had preached the very first time she ever laid eyes on him. There was something even more captivating about him this time.

Quincy stood at the podium with his arms wide.

"Who is on the Lord's side? Which of you would choose the Lord over earthly things? Which one of you would choose the Lord over your friends and family? Which one of you would turn your back on the Lord for a calf made of gold like the Israelites did?" He scanned the crowd staring at each person as if they were the ones who would choose the golden calf.

"You gotta know who you runnin' with! You can't stop and think about it or wait for your friends to decide. You gotta step up! As the song says, 'Stand up, stand up for Jesus, ye soldiers of the cross. Lift high his holy banner we shall not suffer loss.' You can't lose with Jesus!"

Quincy had the entire church on their feet cheering. Lucy was so proud. She tried to remember everything Quincy taught her about being a proper first lady then tried to do it all—twice.

At the end of the day, the church members seemed impressed. The women gathered around the charismatic Evangelist Quincy Jefferson Stewart and the old stodgy male church board gathered around Lucy. She tried not to notice Quincy's fan club and instead used her best English and her best first lady mannerisms. A month later, Quincy was hired as the new pastor of Abundant Holiness Baptist Church. A few months after their arrival, Lucy suffered her third miscarriage. But this time, Quincy didn't seem to notice or care. She was almost five months into her pregnancy when the unthinkable happened. The ladies of the church came by the Stewarts' modest apartment to support her, offer advice, and a shoulder to cry on. They, not Quincy, helped her through her loss. But at least he didn't beat her, yell at her, or call her names. In fact, he didn't do much of anything. This made Lucy feel worse than if he'd yelled his head off and slapped her until her ears rang. She began to believe he'd given up on her. He'd given up on them.

Once he became pastor at Abundant Holiness Baptist Church, Quincy spent all his time there. It was his first church and he was determined to become the best pastor the ministry ever had. Thinking back, Lucy was never sure how sincere Quincy actually was about the gospel back then. Maybe he really *had* tried and when he failed, he took another road. Only God knew the precise start of Quincy's change of course, but when he started pastoring Abundant, he took Lucy along to members' homes for dinner, to their hospital beds when they were sick, and he even invited several prominent members over to their new home. Thanks to their new financial stability, Quincy and Lucy were finally able to purchase their first home on Quartz Court in South Raleigh. It wasn't much of a house, but it was the first major thing Quincy ever owned and he made a big deal out of it.

The church grew at a steady clip and in 1985, after four miscarriages, Lucy gave birth to Michael Wesley Stewart. The church made a fuss over their first lady and for once, Quincy seemed proud of her. That was until he arrived home one day to both Lucy and Michael crying.

"What's wrong with you? Can't you get that baby quiet?"

"He's hungry but..."

"But what? Feed him!" Quincy barked staring at her bare engorged breast.

"I'm trying!" Lucy wailed. "The milk won't come out. He's not getting enough, so he hungry."

Quincy glared at her and shook his head. For a minute she feared he would slap her. Although he still yelled and called her names, he hadn't hit her since they found out she was pregnant with Michael. She had hoped their son's birth would signal an end to the beatings, but she feared maybe she was wrong.

"First you can't get pregnant. Then you kill my babies one after another and now that you finally give me one, you can't even feed it? What's wrong with you? Why can't you ever do anything right? My God...I don't know *why* He gave me less than half a woman!"

Internally Lucy recoiled. The insult stung as if she'd been slapped. But she busied herself with quieting her son. She did all she knew to do to get her milk to flow.

In public, Quincy treated Lucy like the best thing since sliced bread. He demanded she sit up in the pulpit behind him so that everyone could see his beautiful wife in the clothes that he chose and purchased for her. And he made sure everyone knew that it was all his doing. Lucy always wore a sharp suit, a fancy hat, matching shoes and sometimes, even gloves. Her job was to sit behind him, look pretty, and demonstratively support every word he spoke as he preached. She did her job well. Quincy had enlisted the elderly motherboard of the church to care for Michael during Sunday services and they spoiled the First Son rotten.

The whole church doted on baby Michael, but Lucy wasn't the least bit deceived. She knew what was behind everyone being so hands on with her baby. Before he asked the church mothers to keep Michael, Quincy told Lucy more than once that she was a sorry excuse for a mother. He threatened to let the older church mothers keep his son so that she wouldn't embarrass him at church with her maternal ineptitude. And, in a way, that's exactly what he did. Lucy's memory was excellent. She never forgot a single, hurtful, word Quincy said to her. Each hateful word and every painful incident slowly turned her devotion into a resigned hatred.

After Michael was born, Lucy's intimate time with Quincy became alarmingly infrequent. Initially she didn't really mind since that was all Quincy wanted when they first got married, but she soon began to miss it. One day, Lucy found herself in an unusually good mood. She sang along with the radio as she cleaned the house and Michael happily played in his playpen. As she belted out *The Glamorous Life* with Sheila E, Quincy came into the house and slammed the door behind him. She looked up smiling, but one look at his face wiped the smile from hers. Quincy stalked over to the radio and snapped it off.

"What's wrong, Quincy?" Lucy asked, fearing something terrible had happened at the church.

He advanced on her like a tiger stalking its wounded prey.

"What's wrong?! What's wrong?! My wife don't know how to be no decent first lady, that's what's wrong! What you doin' listening to that worldly mess in my house? You releasing all kinda spirits all over my son! What if somebody from the church stopped by here?"

Lucy was stunned. Michael began to whimper.

"You ain't supposed to be listenin' to no secular music, stupid!"

Quincy swung and Lucy didn't move fast enough. The back of his hand connected with her head sending her careening over to the nearest wall. And just like that, the hitting began again. Michael wailed.

"Hush up all that fuss, boy!"

Lucy pushed off the wall and hurled herself toward Michael, afraid Quincy would hurt him next.

"Quincy! No!" Lucy shrieked, as Quincy reached down into the playpen and picked up their toddler.

He stiff-armed her away. "Shut up!"

In a somewhat kinder voice, he spoke to Michael who wailed as he perched on his father's broad arm.

"Your momma been bad so Daddy had to give her a whuppin'. That's what happens when you bad. You get your butt tore up. Now stop all that crying, hear?"

Quincy gave his son a soda cracker. A calmer Michael munched contently. Lucy was humiliated but relieved that her son remained unharmed. For the next couple of years, she recalled this incident every time her young son slapped her in the face to express his displeasure. It took her much of his toddler years to break him of that terrible habit.

By the time Michael turned two, Quincy stopped touching his wife and began staying away from home more, even overnight. He no longer took Lucy along with him when he preached away from their home church. Quincy made her stay with the baby instead. As Michael grew, the violent instances continued. Lucy never knew what would trigger Quincy and she always feared for Michael's safety. But he never attacked their son. Even when Michael was old enough to know what was going on between his parents and tried to intervene, Quincy would not strike him. Michael would come running once he heard his mother's screams or the sound of her crying. Often he would put himself in harm's way, covering his mother's body with his own or getting between them when his father went on a tirade. Quincy would have to go through Michael to get to Lucy. He would often threaten Michael who never once backed down even as angry tears ran down his young face. Most of the time, Quincy would simply stop and leave them both alone.

Quincy continued to stay away from home and Lucy often went days without hearing from or seeing him. Lucy wasn't as dumb as Quincy thought she was. She knew her husband's weaknesses. They never discussed it but somehow it became an understanding between the two of them. Quincy did whatever he wanted to do and Lucy pretended to graciously allow it without so much as a raised eyebrow or a question on her lips.

Abundant Holiness Baptist Church continued to grow and the Stewarts reaped the benefits. Their congregation showered them with gifts for some form of anniversary or another. Mainly because Quincy manipulated them into doing it. His "suggestions" were always carried out quickly and often repackaged as a surprise gift. Over the years, Lucy grew tired of pretending to be surprised and moved by the generosity of the extravagant, coerced tributes when she'd known about them all along.

One night after another pastor's anniversary service, Quincy was in a particularly good mood and Lucy decided to make a brazen move. She had never initiated their intimacy before but that night she decided to try it to see what would happen. Maybe they would end up with another baby. Lucy showered and oiled her body with sweet smelling almond oil. She fixed her hair the way Quincy liked it and put on a skimpy teddy that Quincy had given her early in their marriage. It barely fit but what hung out was what he liked anyway. Stepping into their bedroom, she paused. Quincy glanced over at her then went back to watching television. Lucy wasn't sure what to do next. *Please look at me. I did all of this for you. At least tell me you like it.* After all these years, she was out of practice when it came to flirting. Part of her wanted to run away and hide, but she pressed on. Her body was ready for him and she was willing to do whatever he wanted that night. She risked her pride and as her heart pounded in her chest, approached the bed with her mind on the baby girl she so desperately wanted. Quincy continued to stare at the television, so she spoke.

"Hey."

Quincy mumbled something she couldn't hear. Lucy climbed onto their queen-size bed and crawled toward him placing her hand on his chest, her face inches from his.

"You tired?"

Quincy glanced at her, took in her body with a single dismissive glance, then rolled his eyes and crooked his head to see around her to the television.

"No. What you got on all that for?"

Lucy ran her hand slowly over her husband's chest.

"I thought we'd have some married time tonight."

Quincy snorted. "Woman, go to bed. I don't want no married time with you tonight."

Lucy was stung, but she persisted. "I thought we might try for another baby. I thought..."

"There you go tryin' to think again!" Quincy mumbled coldly, removing her hand from his chest and dropping it on the bed between them. "What you need to do is go to bed and leave me be!"

Devastated, she rose, changed into her normal sleepwear and returned to bed with her back to him. He never saw her tears.

The next morning, she was awakened to Quincy noisily opening and closing dresser drawers as he removed his clothes. She sat up bewildered.

"What you doin'? Where you goin'?"

"I can't stay in here with you no more. You quenchin' the spirit of God and I can't have that. I need to be able to hear from God to get my sermons ready for Sunday, so I gotta sleep where I can have some peace. I'mma stay in there." Quincy nodded out into the hallway and presumably their guestroom.

Lucy felt her world tilt. She was hurt and disappointed, but at the same time relieved. She was unsure of what this all meant for her future, but knew better than to ask. The look on her husband's face let her know that any questions would be answered with the back of his hand.

Their sleeping arrangement remained that way ever since. Everything in Lucy screamed for her to leave Quincy, but she had nowhere to go. Also if she left him, she would have to leave her precious Michael because Quincy would sooner kill her than let her take his son away from him. She couldn't go back home to Lil' Washington because her family bragged endlessly about them and their church. If she went back there, she would be a failure. Somehow it would be all her fault. Her stupid mistake. Her family's embarrassment would kill her mother.

Lucy was born to be a star and at least in Raleigh, her star was shining a little. Even if she left Quincy, what would she do for money? The only job skill she possessed came from the few years she worked in her father's fish market and there was no way she could go back to doing *that*. She was stuck. And she hated herself for allowing it. Maybe even more than she despised the man who caused it. Lucy needed a sounding board to sort the thoughts clashing in her mind. But as badly as she wanted to spill her frustrations to someone, she kept her peace. Quincy had made it clear that what happened in their house, stayed in their house. God only knew what he would do to her if he found out she was running her mouth to anyone about anything dealing with him.

Lucy was completely in awe of her husband when they first met. She fell madly in love with him or at least everything he represented. Then she came to fear him, his moods, his temper, and the way he constantly attacked her with his words and hands. After over two decades, all she had was deep loathing and pity for the man she foolishly married. Lucy suffered in silence, but she stayed. Sometimes she wondered which suffering would have been worse, dealing with her husband or leaving him when she could have had a chance to make it on her own.

The following years after they came to Abundant and Michael was born, brought a lot of changes into their lives. They added onto the church building. Quincy began to broadcast his sermons on a local radio station, and he became a bishop. The appointment to bishop was the biggest joke of all. Since their marriage was one that now functioned in name only, Lucy was able to look at her husband with a far more critical eye. What she found there was just plain sad. The only two things that consistently motivated him were money and keeping up appearances.

As the older deacons, trustees, and elders of their church began to die off or leave the ministry, Quincy replaced each of them with a roster of Who's Who in the black community, local government, and business. Lucy wasn't even sure some of the men he appointed could spell 'God' let alone act like a certified Christian. And she doubted if Quincy even cared. The presence of an elite class at Abundant Holiness Baptist Church attracted people, mainly social climbers, which was probably what Quincy wanted anyway. In no time, Abundant Holiness Baptist Church became the place to be and be seen on Sunday mornings.

It was during a particular popularity spurt that, to the embarrassment of Lucy, Quincy changed the name of their church several times. Each time he heard of a church with a name he liked, he would tack on the new word or phrase. Lucy thought it was absolutely ridiculous, but no one asked her and since Quincy copied everything else he did, she resigned that he might as well copy that too. By 1997, the church's official name was Abundant Holiness Christian Metropolitan Missionary Fellowship Baptist Church. Quincy took pride in letting everyone know that he re-named the church, never realizing how ignorant it sounded.

Over the years, Lucy often wondered why God only seemed to speak to Quincy when he was out of town or alone. After a few years of curious contemplation, she figured it out. Quincy may have pegged Lucy as stupid, but she was no one's fool. Her husband didn't have an original bone in his body. He copied other pastor's sermons—sometimes word for word—then preached them at Abundant Holiness Christian Metropolitan Missionary Fellowship Baptist Church as if God had told Quincy and *only* Quincy that particular message. He never once gave his original source any credit.

Quincy would buy the VHS and cassette tapes of other ministers then slink off to his room and listen to them for hours. Sometimes Lucy heard him in there imitating the way certain preachers said things and it was all she could do to keep from rolling on the floor laughing. He would rewind the tape and go over the word or phrase several times until he had it down and could claim it as his own.

Such a sad lil' man. He has no idea how stupid he sounds.

Quincy wasn't a complete idiot though. He never copied any local pastors. After all, his imitation might have gotten back to those pastors (or others) and make Quincy look bad. Instead, he mimicked out-of-town pastors he assumed his congregation had never heard. Most of the members and visitors to Abundant Holiness Christian Metropolitan Missionary Fellowship Baptist Church didn't even bring a Bible to church, so she doubted they watched Christian television shows or read a Christian instruction book. Quincy had nothing to worry about. Much of the congregation showed up on Sunday for the thrill of spectating, showing off their latest *whatever*, and enjoying the lively music.

Behind the scenes, the church was on shaky ground and it never ceased to both anger and amaze Lucy how the nonsense continued as long as it did. The money that came into Abundant went two places: Quincy's wallet and the music ministry. He never put more than just enough into the church account to keep the utilities on, even if doing so meant the church lived just by the skin of its teeth.

One Thursday evening, Quincy came home in a foul mood. When he arrived at the church earlier that day, the electricity had been turned off for nonpayment. There wasn't enough in the church account to cover the delinquent bill, so Quincy had to write a personal check to cover it. He was not happy.

"These negroes need to learn how to give. They stingy. They sittin' up in there breathin' our good air in the summer and warmin' up with our heat in the winter, but don't give nothin' to keep it goin'. I'mma fix that. You watch and see. I'mma set them straight on Sunday. Watch me, Lucy. You watch me. I'mma have them throwing money on the altar like they do over in them big time churches. Just you watch and see."

And he did. Lucy cringed inwardly as her husband preached that Sunday. Quincy was known to regularly call for special offerings (usually to bless himself) and would pressure the church members to give beyond what his wife had felt was reasonable or normal. It wasn't the people's fault the church had no money. It was Quincy's. But he didn't see that.

"This mornin's Word from the Lord comes from Acts five. It's a little story about a man and his wife who stole from God. They stole from the church. Brother Clarence, read!"

As Brother Clarence read the assigned scripture, Quincy strode around the pulpit grunting. He did this to emphasize certain words the congregation heard.

"So let me get this here right. There was a man named Ananias married to Sapphira[2]. They had good jobs. They came to church every Sunday. They sang in the choir and ushered and all that, but when the offering plate came by..."

Quincy posed with one eyebrow raised. This drew a strong reaction from the crowd as they encouraged him to continue.

"You see they had things they wanted to do with their money. They didn't care if the church had lights or not. They didn't care if the water bill got paid. All they wanted was their stuff, so they decided before they even got to church that they wasn't gonna tithe and they was gonna be cheap in their offering. But the Holy Spirit told on them! He hemmed them up. God don't play. The Holy Spirit whispered to Peter something like this: 'Hey man. You see these two? They stealin' from the church. Ask them if you don't believe me. But if they lie, get ready, cause I'mma take them out!' Sure enough Peter asked, they lied, and just like that—dead."

Quincy moved to the edge of the pulpit and stared out at his congregation.

"Now if I went row by row and asked some of you the same thing, what you think would happen? How many of y'all gonna drop dead up in here today?" Quincy paused dramatically. "Let me tell you somethin' you ain't even know. Just this week I had to dig into my own pocket to pay the church light bill. I paid for it. Me! I ain't call none of y'all to pay the bill. I'm the pastor and I paid the bill. But that should've never happened!"

Quincy hung his head trying to affect humility. The church ate it up, as sounds of shock and support resonated throughout the building.

"Our God is a God of second chances. That's what His grace is for. It's so you can get things right. So today is gonna be amnesty Sunday. If you ain't been giving like you should, today is the day to settle up and get right. The altar is open to receive your gifts. Ushers come forth."

In a flurry of activity, people began practically running to the altar with cash and checks. Some stepped up into the pulpit to place money in Quincy's hand. Lucy wanted to vomit watching her husband squeeze this type of money out of them. Sometimes she wished he would just cut to the chase, pick everyone up by their ankles, turn them upside down, and shake them down. It would save them all time, effort, and the awkwardness of multiple offering collections nearly every service.

Quincy didn't mind or even care if people gave their last dime. Instead, he rationalized their lack by regaling them with the Bible story of the widow's mite[3]. Lucy often wondered how some members made it financially from week to week. Quincy belittled her biblical knowledge, but she *could* read and the way she always understood the story of the window's mite was the lady quietly gave God all she had and then went about her business. Jesus never called a giving line to shame people into giving the way Quincy did. Apparently God laid it on that poor lady's heart and she gave her all not expecting to be recognized for it by anyone let alone to be remembered for eternity in the Bible. All Lucy could assume was either their members never read the story or they didn't understand it.

Quincy notoriously held Sunday service hostage for thirty or forty minutes until the ten or twenty "obedient" souls came up and gave the hundred dollars each that he'd declared *God* told him they would give that day. Lucy couldn't stand to watch it week after week. Couldn't they tell the difference between God speaking to their hearts and

Quincy speaking to their wallets? She never wanted to look at the giving parade but she knew if she dropped her head or showed any disapproval, there would be hell to pay when she got home. So Lucy sat stone-faced and pretended to believe in her husband.

In recent years, as television ministries became more prevalent, Quincy quickly ran out of material to steal. At first, Lucy was glad. She silently hoped Quincy would finally be exposed for the lying, conniving, snake he was. Maybe then he would go back to being more like the man she thought she'd married. But in spite of her best hopes, Quincy found a way out of this dilemma. To supplement his shallow store of sermons, he hosted major church conferences five or six times a year. He featured every major preacher the Christian world had to offer and the appeal of the speakers packed their church building and increased the church's income like never before. Soon, Quincy was forced to rent the Civic Center in Raleigh and as the masses filled it, he walked around like a stuffed peacock. For months, attendance rates and the "numbers" were all he talked about.

The swell in notoriety made it easy for Quincy to steal some of the best musicians and vocalists from churches all over the Triangle area with promises of recording contracts and television time. Most of these promises never bore fruit, but by the time the musicians realized it, Quincy had already sucked them into his web of control. Abundant had an unrivaled orchestra, a praise team, and several choirs better than those heard on the best Gospel radio stations. Hearing the choirs sing was one of the few joys Lucy had in attending her husband's church.

6

Jason pulled up to his condo building just as his mobile phone played Jagged Edge's latest hit, *Where The Party At?* He hesitated and let the call go to voicemail. The phone stopped for a moment, but then sang out again. Annoyed, he looked at his best friend Tyrone's flashing number on the display. Any desire to talk, had long gone, so Jason continued to ignore it.

Gathering the videotapes from the passenger side, Jason went into his house, slamming the door behind him. As he turned on the lights, he froze momentarily, cursed, and sent the tapes whizzing through the air and crashing onto the back of an oversized, black, leather chair. He felt like he was losing his mind! For a moment, even the inside of his home didn't look the same.

Jason often said, *what doesn't kill you only makes you stronger.* He had beaten all the odds and survived his childhood, despite his home environment and the predictions of his grade school teachers. In fact, he didn't just survive—he thrived. He was strong. Hardened. Independent. Successful. No one and no thing could break him. Especially not some preacher man.

Fueled by the burning heat of purpose, he stripped himself of his work attire, threw on a pair of Nike shorts, and jumped on his Bowflex. Working out always cleared Jason's head after a hard day. He trusted the familiar routines to help bring him back to himself. He went at it hard, chasing the man he had been when he woke up that morning, and doing so many reps he lost count. He only stopped when his arms and legs shook uncontrollably. His body was renewed, but his mind still wasn't a hundred percent. He couldn't deny the pain was still there and it was real.

Jason crawled off of the machine in an exhausted stupor, stumbled to the bathroom, jumped into the shower, and let the water run. He was too spent to even take off his shorts or go through the motions of washing himself properly. The water felt good and disguised the tears that wandered down his face again. There was too much hurt, too much disappointment boiling inside of him. He missed his mother, but also felt their bond was forever tainted.

Jason rehearsed over and over in his mind the earlier conversation he had with his aunt. He examined each detail and tried to make sense where there was none. His Aunt Theresa asked him to stop by because she wanted to check in with him. She claimed to sense his feelings of loneliness after Bridget's funeral. It had taken everything in Jason not to roll his eyes and curse whenever she said something like that. His aunt seemed to always feel something in her *spirit*. When he arrived she immediately launched into an apology.

"Baby boy, I am so sorry…"

Jason frowned. "For what Aunt Terri? You haven't done…"

"But I have. I mean…" She sighed, clasping her hands together. "I feel responsible for what you are going through right now."

Jason shook his head. "Mommy died of an aneurysm. There is nothing any of us could do. How could you be responsible?"

He almost added, "It's not about you," but held his tongue. They were all hurting and everyone processed pain differently.

She shook her head. "It's more than that. There is a lot you don't know that you should and I—*we* should have told you a long time ago. I am so sorry. I just want to make it right."

So much for doing that, Jason mused as he dried himself off.

If anything, his aunt had added more to his pain and he couldn't help but resent her for it. The normally succinct, former school teacher took forever to get to her point. The only thing that kept Jason from showing his impatience was his curiosity.

"I would never speak ill of Bridget to her children or even try to sully her memory because I love her. She will forever be my baby sister. I love her as much as you and your sisters do. I just…I don't know how to say this. There are some things you need to know and it will not show your mother in her best light. I'm sorry. I wouldn't tell you if you really didn't need to know."

Jason sat quietly, but was intrigued. He wanted to hear what was behind her dramatic build up. He was going to give his aunt the benefit of the doubt. However, if she was going to sling more dirt on his mother, he was more than ready to sling some back. Hours after her rambling, he'd almost wished he'd left before she said another word.

Hearing the sordid story after so much time offered a measure of relief. It had finally satisfied the countless questions Jason had about the period of his life when his family was homeless. The didn't have a home for nearly a year. Bridget eventually got a tiny apartment in the Richard Allen projects where she stayed until the year before—2001—when the city destroyed the blighted complex in favor of new and improved housing. Rather than allowing Jason to upgrade her living situation, she followed Faye into another public housing complex where she remained until she unexpectedly died of a brain aneurysm.

Once he graduated from college and began working, Jason tried repeatedly to get his mother to move out of her depressing neighborhood, but she refused to leave. With the new information from his aunt, Jason realized that she probably felt like she deserved to be there after foolishly losing her parents' home. Nevertheless, Jason still wished he'd known about it all years ago so he could have made it right for her before she died.

His chest felt tight. Thinking of his mother's death didn't seem right, but Jason couldn't deny its reality. He'd seen her lifeless body lying in that coffin looking like she was getting ready to step out the door for church at any minute. The whole thing was surreal. This had been the longest two weeks of his life.

If only she were honest with him. Maybe he would have been able to buy his grandparents' former house back for her or something. Anything to return her dignity. Jason put his hand to his chest. His heart hurt. He would gladly give up everything he had in a second if he could somehow set this whole mess in order. But it was impossible and he knew it.

Now she was, as his aunt loved to say, in God's hands.

In God's hands, huh.

When Theresa told Jason the rest of the story, it was supposed to be more redeeming, but it only made him grind his teeth more. He felt a complexity of emotions.

In the early part of 1990, Bridget finally gave in to Theresa's constant lecturing and began going to church with her. What started out as a way to pacify her older sister, soon became voluntary. After her first visit, Bridget became a Christian. Jason remembered the time period well. He and his sister, Faye, hated having to go to church and their mother's new attitude on life. Donna was too young to care one way or another. They tested their mother's newfound salvation by attempting to get out of going to church as much as possible. Unfortunately for them, her resolve was greater and they went anyway.

According to Theresa, it was during that time that Bridget forgave Jason's father. She stopped wondering obsessively about what happened to him and was finally able to move on emotionally. Bridget loved watching her televised church services early in the morning before she went to her first job. One day, five years after her conversion, she turned on the television and there he stood. Jason's father seemed to be looking right at her through the screen. She knew it was him. He looked exactly the same, just older.

Jason curled his lips remembering his mother sitting up straight and reading her bible along with the television like she was a student in class. He always felt there was something degrading about it. If his mother could be so dedicated to learning all about Jesus, then why didn't she go to school to learn something that would pay the bills and better herself? Apparently, she wanted some magical quick fix because she bought whatever the preacher on the television was selling.

"She was shocked to see him on television all those years later, but she tuned in to see what he said. She couldn't help but be proud of him. He had turned out so well and she wanted to support him. She told me she mailed money anonymously to support his television show and church. She didn't want to cause trouble. She wanted to help him," Theresa said.

In 1999, when the televangelist came to Philadelphia for a three-day crusade, Bridget secretly planned to go. She had to see him in person. Her seat wasn't close to the stage, but it was close enough for her to see the man she had loved for so many years. She never approached him. It was only after she left the crusade that she told Theresa she had found Jason's father after all of these years. If she had known beforehand, Theresa assured her nephew that she would have stopped Bridget from going to the crusade before she made a fool out of herself. Bridget made it a point to pray for him and speak well of him up until the day she died.

"I couldn't believe it! I watch that ministry almost everyday and I had never put two and two together. I never knew his name when he was seeing your mother, so how could I know?"

Just like her sister, Theresa didn't hate Jason's father. In fact, she believed everything that occurred was God's plan for all of them—the good, the bad, and the confusing.

"After all, Romans 8:28 states that all things work together…" Theresa recounted, but Jason tuned out his aunt's holy diatribe. When he started listening again, he heard her say, "…there could be a very good explanation. Maybe this situation is what God used to make his men's ministry so strong and why he can address relationship issues with such authority!"

Jason was bewildered. To him, his aunt had completely lost her mind. She was always using God's name and the Bible to say stupid stuff, but she'd outdone herself this time. But in truth, he didn't really know who to be angry with. He felt cheated, lied to, and completely disrespected. He finally understood why his grandmother always got so mad at him when he asked questions about his grandfather. She probably died still blaming the birth of her only grandson for her husband ultimately leaving her. That hurt. Jason never got the opportunity to apologize to her for wrecking her life even if it had been out of his control. Maybe just hearing the words would have given his grandmother peace.

Theresa had given Jason the handful of videotapes that haphazardly lay in his chair.

"Here," she'd said handing him a stack of videotapes. "I thought you might want to see him and see what a great man of God he became. Watching might help you understand everything a little better."

Theresa had hoped Jason would watch the tapes and develop a sort of respect for his father. Maybe he'd finally give his life to the Lord. This was a regular prayer of hers for years. Maybe he'd be the first stroke on a new canvas for her habitually dysfunctional family.

Jason's thoughts raced. *I don't care anything about that nigga or whatever he's become. Man-of-God? Please!*

To Jason, this "man of God" treated his mother like a two-dolla-holla and left her with two babies at eighteen-years-old. This "man of God" successfully ruined three generations of lives in one fell swoop all because he didn't give a damn.

Now he's supposed to be the shit? Oh really?

Sure, his father wasn't the first man to turn tail and run when a pregnancy was involved. Jason knew the type and had no respect for them. His mother never got the chance to go to school and get a degree because of this man. Yet to hear his aunt talk, the preacher man hadn't done too badly for himself.

Jason could still hear his aunt's words, the ones that set him completely off, reverberating in his head. "Jason, we all make mistakes. The Bible tells us that we all have sinned and come short of the glory of…"

Jason had rudely cut her off. Quoting scripture didn't help his mother when she was pregnant and scared to death. Quoting scripture didn't help them when they practically lived on the street going from shelter to shelter and relying on the fickle help from Bridget's immature friends. Quoting scripture was just Theresa's attempt to bury her guilt with useless words.

Jason sat in his dark condo, engrossed in his memories. After several hours, Jason got up and fixed a glass of strong, Chivas Regal. The videos, resting nearby, caught his eye on the way back to his favorite chair. He picked a tape up, slipped it into the old VCR he still held onto from his college days, and watched.

7

Bishop James Collins and his wife Victoria started their ministerial career by accident. After they both graduated from college, James felt compelled to abandon his previous aspirations in politics and pursue ministry instead. Initially, he surprised even himself with the decision, but he chose to obey the voice of God without hesitation. James and Victoria were never elders or deacons. They never held any major office in the church they attended while in college. But they were faithful. For the most part, they sat in services and quietly soaked up every sermon like sponges. They applied what they learned to their lives. They also enrolled in a two-year bible school held at their church, rarely missing a class. At the time, they didn't know what the benefits of their discipline would reap.

A year after deciding to go into ministry, James and Victoria started a bible study in the clubhouse of their apartment complex. Within weeks it was a standing room only event and, surprisingly, the Collins' were the only black people in the room. It wasn't intentional. They simply taught what they learned about God and His word and whoever came, came. News spread throughout their apartment complex. People brought family members, employers, co-workers, friends, and strangers they met on the street. Not long afterward, one of the attendees offered the after hours use of his modest breakfast-and-lunch-only restaurant and the bible study moved to that location. Three months later, the bible study, too large for the restaurant, had to move again. They met everywhere—including the local park during the spring and summer months.

It wasn't long before people came to James and Victoria with their personal issues and they found themselves informally involved in the hands-on pastoring of some of the attendees who did not have a local church. To their surprise, they discovered that their bible study was the only "church" most of those people attended.

In 1980, one month after the Collins' graduating from bible school, Abiding Grace Christian Church was born. They started out of the proverbial gate with three hundred and thirty people. Twenty-two years and three buildings later, the church had grown phenomenally.

James didn't feel worthy or equipped to lead the people, much less the pastors who frequently came to him and called him their spiritual father. As a man, he couldn't necessarily relate to their problems, trials, challenges, disappointments, or struggles. The issues he had as a young man were so far removed from his present experience that they were nothing but distant memories. So James truly relied on God-inspired wisdom to counsel people.

The growth of the Abiding Grace Christian Church was a shock to James. They never send out flyers or announcements during the early years. He did not speak at a bunch of other churches to advertise his own. He didn't even have a radio or television show back then. Word of mouth alone brought people by the hundreds, which was profound. James never forgot that. His own spiritual father, Bishop Wallace, often joked about the Collins' life and their apparent Midas touch. Though James knew he was just being teased, it embarrassed him. He had no idea why God favored him this way. He knew better than anyone else that he had not been perfect, and there were far more deserving individuals. To compensate, he made a point of dispersing his good fortune as much as he could. Unfortunately, his generosity only added to his fame. He could not seem to escape it.

Because of what God had done in his life, James believed beyond a shadow of a doubt that if he preached the unadulterated word of God, was honest and fair with people, they would come, and they would not come alone. Unfortunately, not all the pastors he mentored grasped this premise. They often operated under their own power, will, or agenda. How could anyone claim to be led of God if they never consulted Him? Some of the more brazenly, eager young pastors even tried to duplicate everything about Abiding Grace Christian Church down to the carpet color and the style of faucets in the restrooms. This was a major sore spot with James. Sure, imitation was the sincerest form of flattery and of course, there was no reason to reinvent the wheel, but James had a feeling God wasn't consulted when those decisions were made. They simply coveted the work done at Abiding Grace and did all they could to replicate it for themselves.

It wasn't rocket science. God would speak. James and Victoria would do. It was just that simple. Victoria liked to refer to them as the "Forrest Gumps" of the Christian community. They were too green to know any better, so God was able to use them freely to do his will. He gave them clear, specific instructions, and they followed them to the letter—never deviating. Still, a part of James missed the smaller groups he began with. He missed knowing everyone by name. He missed talking to people one on one, and visiting their homes. He missed hearing their problems and celebrating their victories. Now that his ministry staff was so large, all of those things were handled long before they could ever reach him.

The closest James came to fellowshipping with a large segment of his members was in the recognition of familiar faces who frequented the first few rows of his services. Or, in conversing with those he met in the new members reception. It seemed the larger the ministry grew, the more inconsistent the parishioners seemed when it came to serving the ministry. Back when the church was small, James never had to deal with some of the personnel issues he now had. From what he heard though, many pastors dealt with the same thing.

This generation was different from his, for sure. It seemed harder for the younger people to receive the sermons God gave him and to at least try to put them into practice with any consistency. James was frequently misquoted or misunderstood. This was one of the reasons why him and his team developed the new members class. He only wanted people at Abiding Grace who truly wanted to be there. With Easter not too far away, James knew he had an opportunity to reach people who did not regularly attend church. The evangelist in him looked forward to that.

8

Other than money and women, Bishop Quincy Jefferson Stewart's major weakness was Bishop James Collins. Quincy hated the man despite the fact that copied so much from him. Sure, he'd always add his own twisted spin, but the core Collins was there in most of the things he attempted in ministry. In the early eighties, Bishop Collins planted his Abiding Grace Christian Church and it grew tremendously. Lucy knew it angered Quincy that Abiding Grace was a positive and extremely productive ministry. Collins was a prolific minister of the word of God and his reputation was in stark contrast to the undercurrent of fraud that often clouded the Stewart name around the rumor circuit.

By the late nineties, Bishop Collins' church had over ten thousand members and was the largest in North Carolina. Bishop Collins was everywhere—on the radio, television, and the covers of both secular and religious magazines. His church set the pace for other churches worldwide. The people of Abiding Grace Christian Church were committed to the community and earned the loyalty and respect of many. Politicians and the media called on Bishop Collins for his opinion on both moral and political matters. Several new churches branched off from Abiding Grace Christian Church under Bishop Collins' leadership and these ministries did equally well.

It was in early 1998, when James Collins was ordained a bishop in a huge celebration that, unbeknownst to Collins, detracted from one of Quincy's big name conferences. Not to be outdone, Quincy had a ministry friend ordain him a bishop. But no new churches were ever birthed out of Abundant Holiness and no decent pastors ever wanted to link up with Quincy. He couldn't compete with Collins, not even on the man's worst day.

To assuage his bruised ego, Quincy talked about Bishop James Collins horribly from the pulpit. He told extravagant and easily disproved lies week after week in order to ensure his members would never leave. Lucy was well aware of her husband's fear. He was afraid his congregation would defect.

In 1999, Abundant's secretary retired and Quincy needed to hire someone new. The church body wanted to vote on the replacement and several members jostled for the position, but Quincy insisted he had to hand pick the new secretary because only he knew what was required. A few months later, Quincy introduced Miss Stacy Lewis to the congregation. She hadn't been a regular visitor or even a member, but Lucy knew better than to voice her disapproval. It wasn't worth the battle or the beating.

At the time of her hiring, Stacy was a thirty-one-year-old single woman who previously worked as a secretary for a large company in Research Triangle Park. In stating her credentials, Quincy gushed that Stacy came highly recommended. One look at her and Lucy pretty much knew what those recommendations were. Stacy was curvy, wearing her clothes a little too short and a little too snug for Lucy's liking. A woman had to take extra pains not to look seductive and everything Stacy wore made her look like she was about to solicit herself on a seedy street corner. The members of the church were split on Stacy's arrival. The older crowd shared Lucy's concerns while the younger members warmed up to her instantly.

Lucy had to grudgingly admit, if only to herself, that in spite of her appearance, Stacy did bring order to the church office. She introduced computers and helpful programs to the ministry and suddenly everything became easier for all those serving in it. Many things the church outsourced to local businesses could now be handled easily in-house.

Stacy was a whiz at everything in the office and an asset to everyone, especially Quincy. He couldn't praise her enough. She even volunteered to type Quincy's sermons because she said it would make it easier for him to follow on Sundays. It was a move that allowed her to tamper with the content—something Lucy thought was the she-devil's motive all along.

At first, Quincy didn't notice the subtle changes in his sermons. The more the liberties Stacy took with her "corrections" went unnoticed, the more comfortable she felt making more changes. When the church responded more enthusiastically than normal one Sunday, Quincy rechecked his notes to find out what had affected his congregation so he could repeat it. That's when he finally caught on. Whether it was his infatuation with her or his genuine appreciation, Quincy enlisted Stacy to write his sermons for him from then on. Quincy thought no one knew his secret, but Lucy knew and it turned her stomach to see the congregation cut up when he preached the gospel according to Stacy. She envied the young woman because Quincy never accepted one suggestion or criticism from her during their entire marriage, yet he soaked up everything Stacy said.

With the church doing better than ever, Quincy built an impressive, new house in an exclusive Northwest Raleigh subdivision. With formal and casual areas, a huge chef's kitchen, and a guestroom on the main level with a maid's quarters in the basement, it was a home designed for elegant entertaining. Michael had the third floor to himself and it was complete with a den filled with a big screen television and every electronic toy suitable for a modern, affluent, teenaged boy. Quincy and Lucy occupied twin master suites on opposing sides of the second floor. Their doors faced one another, a position that summed up their marriage perfectly.

Even before they moved from their starter home into their estate, Lucy suspected something more than church business went on between Quincy and Stacy. Lucy wasn't surprised. It was just a matter of time. Stacy was Quincy's only companion when he traveled. There was no real need for his secretary to attend a conference with him, especially when he wasn't scheduled to preach. Actually, a male armor bearer would have been more appropriate. But being appropriate never crossed Quincy's mind. The two spent an inordinate amount of time alone, behind closed doors, and though it didn't look decent or proper, no one working in the church office dared to say anything. They all acted as if everything was normal. And, for them, it was.

When the doorbell rang at six each Wednesday evening, Lucy girded herself for battle and crossed the expansive foyer to the large, mahogany front door. She knew who it was even without the woman's shape announcing her through the beveled glass insets. The tramp showed up at the same time every week. Lucy never understood why the shameless hussy had to come to her home to give Quincy the papers. She could have easily handed them over to him at church earlier in the day.

She opened the door and stared coolly at the young woman.

"Good evening."

"Good evening, First Lady. Is the Bishop in?" Stacy asked with the fakest smile Lucy had ever seen.

Lucy looked her up and down. She wore a beige suit that fit like a glove. The skirt stopped high on her toned thighs and her long legs poured into a high-heeled pair of brown boots. The cream-colored lace camisole under the suit jacket left little to the imagination. Lucy struggled not to smirk as, in her mind, she hoped the hussy caught her death of cold dressed like she was.

"He is, but I think he's busy. Is that his message for Sunday?" Lucy asked extending her arm to take the manila envelope crooked in Stacy's arm. "I'll get it to him."

"Thank you, First Lady, but I need to go over a few things with him and find out if he has any questions. Is he available?"

Lucy paused. She didn't want Stacy in her house. It was bad enough she had to see her at church, but because Quincy invited Stacy over, there was nothing Lucy could do but let her in. She knew any pushback to his request would resurrect his fist.

At that moment, Quincy called out from somewhere in the house. "Who's that at the door? Is that Stacy with my papers?"

Lucy gritted her teeth noting Stacy's smug smile. The young woman had the audacity to call out, "Yes Bishop," as Lucy stepped aside.

Out of sight of the other, they each rolled their eyes. Disgusted, Lucy grabbed her coat, purse, and keys as she headed for her car.

At seven on Wednesday nights, Abundant conducted a weekly bible study that met in the Sunday school wing of the church. Quincy never attended the study and the majority of the church's members didn't show up either. It was the one day when the remaining older members would gather to pray, read scripture, testify, reminisce, and then go home. Lucy loved to attend. Initially, she went because she felt strongly that at least someone in the Bishop's family should be present to support the service. But she soon discovered how much of a comfort the service was to her spirit.

Walking down the hallway plastered with children's drawings and Bible story posters, Lucy could hear the gathering of folks worshipping. Their strong voices singing, hands clapping, and feet stomping in time easily filled the sparse room. This was another world, far from the lights and glitz of the regular church service. In this no-frills space, they celebrated with one breath, a common faith, a common hope, and a yearning for Jesus.

A familiar raspy voice belted out, "Down through the years, God been good to me. Weee-eelll down through the years, God been good to meeeee. Down through the years, God been good to me. God really been good to me!"

After a few verses of that song, a mother of the church stood up on shaky legs and declared, "First giving honor to God who is the head of my life, I'd like to say I'm glad to be here in the house of the Lord one more time. I coulda been dead, sleeping in my grave, but God stayed His mighty hand so I could be here today to give Him glory. My God is good—all the time. He's a bridge over troubled waters. He's a mother to the motherless and a father to the father-less. He's a doctor in a sickroom and a lawyer in the courtroom! He's the lily of the valley, a bright and morning star. The rose of Sharon and author of our salvation. He's a mighty good God, yes He is. Y'all pray much for me as I pray for you."

Those words were like a starter gun going off. Testimonies of God's goodness sprang up all over the room. Requests for prayer and words of encouragement came next and were followed by more singing. Afterward, the group completed a brief study of scripture. All of it fed the empty places in Lucy and she was usually one of the last people to leave. It was her place of safety and for an hour and a half once a week she felt hope, an escape from the life she pretended to live.

9

O n yet another Wednesday evening, Lucy left the house early for bible study and passed Stacy as she pulled into the driveway. They didn't bother waving at one another. No one was watching, so there was no need to perform. Lucy rolled her eyes and pulled onto the main street secretly wishing the little witch had been walking so she could run her over.

In spite of running into Stacy on her way to the church, bible study was especially sweet that night and Lucy left with a warm glow in her spirit. She hadn't felt that way since she was back home in Lil' Washington over twenty-four years ago. Back then, she felt the presence of God at church nearly every time she went. It was personal and made her feel that yes, Jesus loved her and she mattered to Him. It made her feel as if the scriptures were written to and for her—they weren't just empty words in a book for Quincy to twist and destroy. There was nothing else like it. Lucy learned to reverently fear God in that small, country church and how to love Him with all of her heart. Having been around Quincy for so long, she had begun to believe that this sweet part of her Christian experience was long gone. But Wednesday nights reminded her that, despite it all, the Holy Spirit was still with her.

In closing their time together, one of the older members sang "Pass Me Not Oh Gentle Savior." It remained in Lucy's heart and she sang it all the way home. The house was quiet except for the occasional rumble of Michael's rap music. She didn't mind the subtle noise. At least he was at home for once and at a decent hour no less. Lucy took her medicine and went to bed feeling a measure of peace that she would try with all her might to hold on to until the next Wednesday night.

Sometime after one in the morning, Lucy woke with a start and sat up in her bed.

"Hello? Who's there?" Her voiced quivered as her heart and mind raced.

Lucy imagined burglars or someone with a grudge against Quincy breaking into their home. She waited, struggling against the medicated drowsiness that tried to overtake her. She would do whatever she needed to do to protect herself and Michael. It wasn't long before she heard a thud followed by a pitiful mewling sound again. Lucy grabbed her green fleece robe and pulled it around her shoulders. She eased her feet into her slippers and crept up to her bedroom door. She cautiously pulled the door open and listened carefully. She thought she heard somebody moaning like they were in pain. Her mind flashed to Michael. Was he hurt? Immediately, she flew into momma mode and began moving toward the stairs to Michael's third floor room to check on him.

"He probably done hurt himself doing all that crazy dancin' he do," she thought, imagining the vulgar gyrations she caught Michael doing on more than one occasion. He could have anything from a broken leg to a broken neck the way she witnessed him going at it listening to that hip hop music.

Before she made it to the first step she heard the sounds again. It was *not* the sound of someone in agony and she turned furious! She snatched a house shoe from off one foot and started marching up the stairs to beat a hole in her hardheaded, disrespectful, actin-just-like-his-sorry-daddy boy. If Michael had some little fast girl in her house, she was going to light a fire under both of their behinds!

Just as she reached the top stair with her fingers poised over the doorknob, she stopped again. It occurred to her that the sound that broke her sleep wasn't coming from the third floor because she had steadily moved away from it instead of closer to it. When realization set in, she felt sick.

As she spun back toward the direction the sounds came from, she heard muffled giggling and Quincy's deep baritone voice followed by more noises that let her know exactly what was going on. Her hand flew to her mouth both from shock and a sudden queasiness. Lucy remained frozen with one foot on the step below her and the other hovering in the air. She didn't want to listen, but she was unable to move. The noises seemed to engulf the house.

Everything in her wanted to march into Quincy's bedroom and take a stick or some scalding water to both of them. Quincy would slap her down for sure if she did. Lucy paced the hallway between their bedrooms like a hall monitor for a few moments. Her mind was ablaze with indignation. After a few moments, she walked stiffly back to her room and tried to block out the noises that now seemed louder than they were before.

How could he? In my house! With me nothin' but five feet away!

If she heard them in there acting like two wild dogs in heat, then Michael probably had too! What did Quincy think he was doing?

Her head began to pound out a relentless rhythm with every beat of her heart. Another migraine. Just what she needed. Lucy never suffered with them until after Michael was born and Quincy moved out of their shared bedroom. She reached for her prescription medicine. She took a pill and tried to lie back down. She couldn't sleep. The noises continued. Lucy got out of her bed and noisily went downstairs to get something to drink thinking that would make them stop. It didn't. She paced the lower floor debating what to do.

Finally, the house grew quiet. A dejected Lucy slowly returned to her room awash a myriad of dark and desperate emotions. It took some time, but Lucy finally fell back asleep. She tossed and turned though as she fought a battle in her head spawned by the woman in Quincy's bed. In the morning, Lucy woke up later than usual, still exhausted and very much depressed.

With no strength or reason to get up, Lucy laid listless in her bed for the first part of the day. She had finally given up on becoming a renowned celebrity or at least the wife of one. The days of kidding herself by chasing the elusive were over. She had wasted decades of her life and it seemed like she was only marking time until she was tossed into a grave somewhere where Quincy could no longer hurt her. The only joy in her life was her son, Michael, but it seemed like he was becoming more like his trifling father every day. She felt useless. Quincy was right. She was stupid. She was fat. She was old and ugly. Only a fool would intentionally stay in this humiliating situation as long as she had. Lucy hated that she didn't do more with her life earlier. At least then she would have had an escape route. Everything was Quincy's. She was just one of many possessions in his trophy case.

Lucy finally rolled out of bed in the early afternoon. She caught her reflection in the gold, ornate, dressing table mirror and became more despondent. An old hag stared back at her. No wonder Quincy preferred that fresh young thing to her. She hurled herself at the mirror. She screamed at the top of her lungs and pounded against the glass until her wrists ached. In one fell swoop, she swept everything off the expansive white dressing table that met the mirror's top. Lucy didn't feel any better. If anything she felt even more trapped. She stumbled over a novel she'd been reading and hurled it at the mirror.

Lucy's head began to pound again. She had worked herself into another bad migraine. She slowly walked to her en-suite in search of her medicine. At least the meds would ease the intense pressure that had built behind her temples and the back of her neck. Once in the bathroom, she carefully lifted her bottle of prescription anti-depressants—she'd begun taking them "as needed" over the last few years. She stared at it for a moment before she popped the lid, turned the bottle over, and completely emptied the contents into her hand.

Now that'll fix somethin' for sure!

While carefully holding the tiny mound of anti-depressants in her left hand, she carefully opened her bottle of migraine medicine with her right hand and allowed all of those pills to also fall into her left hand with the others. Several bounced off the mountain of pills, making skittering noises on the white tile. She opened her mouth wide and shoved everything in. Her mouth was crowded, but she managed to work every single pill down her throat. She had to work hard to keep the medication down, but she was determined. Lucy had no use for her life. She wasn't worth it. If Stacy wanted Quincy so bad, she was welcome to him.

Lucy calmly walked into her bedroom and sat atop her floral Laura Ashley comforter. The details of her white, four-poster bed, her yellow cotton gown, and the tiny pink embroidered roses on the bedding caught her eye. She wondered if anyone would send pink roses to her funeral. A quick smile crossed her lips when she thought of how embarrassed Quincy would be when the news of his wife's death got out. His wife found dead of an overdose?! He may drop dead of pure shame right beside her. What would people say if they found out everything he tried to hide all these years?

As Lucy sat imagining Quincy's humiliating downfall, her thoughts turned to Michael. She cried bitter, angry tears. Even he was leaving her. He would be going to college in a few months. If she stayed, she would lose her only ally in the house. She couldn't face a life with Quincy without Michael as a buffer. There would be no one to love her. The realization of such a bleak future made her cry even harder.

Pulling herself together, Lucy stumbled to her desk and scrawled a note to her son. She told him how much she loved him and how sorry she was to leave him. She apologized for the life she had given him. She told him to be an honorable man and love Jesus with all of his heart. As she read her words, a light penetrated her thoughts and she realized the finality of her actions.

Have you lost your mind? What are you thinking? Do you really want to leave that boy with Quincy? You don't want to die!

Lucy jumped up, pulled on a pair of pants under her pajamas, yanked her hair back with a scrunchie, grabbed her purse as she ran down the stairs and jumped into her Mercedes. She had to get to the hospital before it was too late to fix her mistake.

Lucy headed out of their impressive, gated subdivision and up New Falls of the Neuse Road. She did not care how fast she went or if the police tried to stop her. Her clothes were mismatched, she didn't have on a bra and she was without makeup. As she crossed the overpass at I540, she began to feel a little lightheaded. She blinked hard and let a window down hoping the fresh air would bring her more focus. Within minutes, as she drove down the very busy road, she felt pressure in the center of her chest and a queasy sensation took over her stomach. It was hard for her to breathe. She drove faster. Traffic lights became optional. Haloes of light developed around the edges of her eyes, nearly blinding her. She only had two or three miles to go and then she would be OK.

The impact was forceful. The last thing Lucy remembered was her muffled cry: "God help me."

10

Oh my God! My head! Sweet Jesus!

With every beat of her heart, explosions of pain rocketed around her skull.

Oooh my head. It hurts so bad!

Her stomach heaved and bile raced up her throat.

Oh Lord! I gotta… I gotta…

She tried to keep from soiling her pants, but she couldn't as everything faded to black. A sea of putrid smelling vomit jolted Lucy into consciousness as it spilled out of her mouth and down her face. Or at least what was left of her face. It seemed heavy and numb like when her foot fell asleep sometimes. Someone or something was lifting her up and she panicked.

A garbled voice mumbled and she almost laughed because it reminded her of the teacher's voice in the Charlie Brown cartoons. She tried to concentrate and thought she made out the word "choking." Then the single garbled voice swelled into a choir. What were they saying? She felt pressure and thought maybe someone was touching her.

Who's got me?

Lucy's heart raced. She tried to open her eyes, but they felt as if someone had sat on each of her lids. She felt so cold, so bare, and sore. She assumed that wherever she was, she wasn't in heaven because she would have a new body in heaven and angels don't throw up, right? But then that meant either she was in Hell or she'd gone blind. Both options sounded equally bad to her.

Lucy heard deep, ghostly moans coming from somewhere near her. They were faint at first, but seemed to get louder as her head throbbed with each sound.

What is that?

She heard someone call her name from afar, but she didn't recognize the voice and still couldn't open her eyes to see. She felt people touch her and before she could protest, it all stopped. She was floating. She gave in and drifted off into a thick sleep.

Lucy had no idea how much time had passed, but the voices were gone and everything was quiet. Her mind raced with anxiety and she tried to calm down by taking deep breaths. The pain returned and the attempts to focus were useless.

Think good thoughts… think good thoughts… think… think…

She tried to concentrate but couldn't seem to keep her mind trained on any one thing for more than a second. She tried thinking of something simple.

Something simple. What did I have for breakfast this mornin'? This mornin'… This mornin'…Oh my God!

Everything came back in a flood. She blacked out under the weight of it all.

11

Quincy felt on top of the world. The previous night with Stacy was incredible. He'd spent the day at North Ridge Country Club networking and enjoyed a playfully competitive game with some local, wealthy businessmen. His heart was filled with something close to nirvana. Who said he would never amount to anything?

Hmph! It don't matter what they say. Let Quincy tell it, the people who doubted him couldn't shine his shoes now. He was living. For him, life was about money, power, and influence. He couldn't say he had finally arrived, but he was feeling mighty close.

Then his day went straight to hell.

He almost didn't answer his phone. Part of him wished he hadn't. His normally mellow son sounded terrified. Lucy's dumb, no-drivin' self had wrapped her Mercedes around a light pole and was in the hospital. His first thought was that she had better not have destroyed the car. His second thought was that she always picked the worst possible moments to do something stupid. It was as if she knew when he would be most inconvenienced. He was sure she'd done it just to spite him.

When Quincy arrived at the hospital, Michael was waiting for him. Lucy was unconscious and the medical staff feverishly worked on her. A permission form was shoved his way and insurance paperwork still needed to be completed. Michael sat wide-eyed waiting for word from the doctors while Quincy handled the business.

When he finished the paperwork he was motioned in to see Lucy. He paused at the entrance of the emergency ward to prepare himself for the worst but when he got to her bed, his momentary fear turned to anger.

Look at her! He thought. *Where she call herself goin' lookin' like that? How dare she embarrass me and Abundant Holiness comin' out the house lookin' like Miss Celie?*

He wanted to just slap her! This was another example of Lucy not thinking things through. He couldn't wait to hear her backwards explanation.

The doctors explained that they needed to run additional tests because witnesses had reported Lucy appeared to be passed out before crossing over three lanes of traffic, jumping the curb, and hitting a utility pole. Luckily everyone else traveling on the road was uninjured. The paramedics also noted that she seemed under the influence. They asked Quincy if he knew of any prescription medications she was currently taking and if she abused alcohol or illegal drugs.

That woman and her durn pills! She's always takin' pills for somethin'! Always havin' a headache! Everything makin' her sad and givin' her a durn migraine.

Quincy calmly told the doctor about her recurring migraines and bouts with depression. He placed the blame for those conditions on her previous miscarriages citing that they had left her a little "weak in the head." That said, he wasn't about to have everyone in Raleigh thinking his wife was unstable. The doctor seemed to believe him and thanked Quincy for the information. He then told Quincy they would keep Lucy for overnight monitoring until she regained consciousness. They wanted to make sure there were no further injuries. Quincy agreed and eventually they moved Lucy into a private room.

Quincy and Michael sat in Lucy's room for a few hours watching her sleep while various members of the hospital staff came in and out. The father and son barely spoke two words to one another. Michael was concerned about his mother's health and Quincy was concerned about the car and whether or not anyone they knew saw Lucy looking so shabby. He also fumed about his plans for the day being altered because of Lucy and her foolishness.

Lucy had a large purplish knot on her forehead, a busted lip, and a huge green and yellow bruise running down the side of her neck. Every so often she grunted a little, which caused both father and son to sit at attention. But then she'd fall silent again, returning to her rest. Finally, a doctor came in and broke the monotonous silence of the room. He introduced himself and asked to speak to Quincy privately. Quincy didn't understand most of what the young Indian doctor said, but he nodded just the same and pretended otherwise.

The part Quincy *had* understood was that the tests detected abnormally high levels of anti-depressants and Sera-something inhibitors in Lucy's system. The doctor wanted to know specifically what medications Lucy was prescribed and the dosages. He had no idea. He didn't even know the name of her regular doctor—the one who had given her all those pills to begin with. Before he could think of an answer that wouldn't make him look bad, Michael yelled at the top of his lungs for help. The doctor rushed back into the room with Quincy behind him just in time to see Lucy throwing up in her sleep. Michael tried to help, but was too repulsed to be of any real use. He moved back and forth, toward and away from his mother like he was doing the cha-cha.

The doctor brusquely asked them to leave the room as a nurse rushed in. Back in the hallway, Michael continued pacing while trying to steal glances into his mother's room. Quincy felt himself growing increasingly ill. The sight of Lucy vomiting turned his stomach. The smell of it had taken root in his nostrils. It was too much for him, so he quietly left while Michael paced in the other direction. So much was going on and he assumed no one would notice his departure. Quincy figured he looked green around the gills too, and there was no need to have two people throwing up.

Back home, Quincy went straight to his wife's bedroom. He'd decided that if anyone asked him why he left the hospital so suddenly, he would say that he rushed home to get her medical information. He found Lucy's bedroom to be an absolute mess and had to hopscotch over items on the pale pink carpet just to make it to her bathroom. Her pill bottles were still open and a handful of pills dotted the marble floor.

What she call herself doin' in here? She was never usually this nasty but there was no tellin' with crazy folk. One day they be fine, and the next they climbin' walls and eatin' dirt.

Quincy went down on his hands and knees and gathered up all of the pills he could find and tossed them into the two open prescription bottles. He wasn't sure what went where and he didn't care. He would let the doctors figure it out.

Quincy looked around Lucy's bedroom and tried to think of what she might need during her hospital stay. He wasn't good at these things so he called Stacy. She was at his side within 20 minutes. He didn't know what he would do without her. She helped Quincy pack a few things for his wife. When she spotted the note Lucy had begun to write, she quickly handed it to Quincy with a somber look on her face.

"Baby, you might want to take a look at this."

Frowning, Quincy took it from her. His face morphed into an angry mask that she had never seen before.

"That stupid cow! She did this on purpose! I thought maybe she had just dropped her pills, but I should have known better! She is forever doin' somethin' to get attention. I give her all of this," Quincy said waving his arms around the room, "but she can never be happy. She always gotta do somethin' crazy. I don't know how I ever expected that backwards fish-sellin' girl to be a first lady. This is my fault. I should have left her right where I found her."

Stacy sat silently on Lucy's bed, listening as Quincy ranted about the lunatic he married. The longer he went on, the easier it was for her mind to wander. The last person she wanted to talk about when they were alone was Lucy. But the fool had obviously tried to kill herself and Stacy tried to give Quincy a few minutes to process it all. No one said she had to actually listen though.

Stacy wondered if it was a coincidence that the day after she spent the night in their house for the first time, Crazy Lucy decided to kill herself. It wasn't like she and Quincy were quiet about it. Quincy tried hard so she always exaggerated her responses to make him feel good.

Not that he was a terrible lover, just insecure. She'd thought she heard someone moving around the house last night and couldn't help wondering if it had been the batty First Lady eavesdropping.

Serves her right!

She honestly felt sorry for Quincy. Being married to a pitiful woman like Lucy must have been hard on him. Quincy began flinging Lucy's things at her overnight bag, as he complained. Stacy had heard enough. Knowing what he liked, she began to lean back on her elbows, arching her back so her full breasts looked their best under his lustful gaze.

Come to mama, Bishop. I'll make it all better.

She understood even more now why he needed her. No man—especially not a successful man—needed the kind of grief that tired old woman brought to his life. Quincy had too much to do and his so-called wife held him back. Stacy sincerely wished the old bat had died. Then Quincy wouldn't have to suffer anymore and could move on to better things unencumbered by Lucy's mediocrity.

Her eyes followed him and her heart went out to him as he vented. He was such a distinguished looking man especially now that his beard had so much grey in it. He kept his body up which was something Stacy truly appreciated. He needed her and she wanted him. Before she was finished with him, he would rival even T.D Jakes and *she* would be his Serita not his current Looney Tunes wife.

"I bet she did this to embarrass me. She is always trying to embarrass me and make me look bad in front of people. Doesn't she know we got church members who work in that there hospital. She don't care. She don't never care about anyone but herself. Best thing she could have done was take all them pills and lie down somewhere and go to sleep. But what she do? She drive down the street tearing up my car and making a scene! You know the city gonna make us pay for that pole too. Just wasting my money at every turn!"

Quincy had worked himself into a lather. Spit flew from his mouth until it looked like it was foaming. Stacy knew she needed to do something to calm him down and make him feel better. Since he didn't take the bait and join her on the bed, she got up and wrapped her arms around him. She tightly pressed her body flush against him, filling every nook, cranny, and groove. She used her body to absorb the negativity. It succeeded in calming him down quickly because he stopped mid-sentence like he forgot what he was saying. Maximizing the moment, Stacy lifted her head and kissed him deeply with a searing intensity. The Bishop's mind recalled vividly their passionate night just hours before. Her naked body under his, over his. All the things she did to him. Quincy didn't want to lose what they were clearly working up to, but he knew he had to leave.

"Whoa now, girl. Watch yourself. You about to start somethin' I can't finish right this second." He licked his lips, as his eyes remained transfixed on her mouth.

"Let me run this here mess up the street. You stay here and get ready for Big Daddy. I'll be back as soon as I can and then we can finish this the right way." He grabbed a handful of her round bottom and kissed her long and hard. Then he snatched up Lucy's luggage and raced down the steps toward the garage.

Once Stacy heard the distinctive whirr of the garage doors rolling up and was sure Quincy had indeed left the house, she wandered through Lucy's large walk-in closet trying on some of the many hats and suits she had quietly admired. She modeled a few items in front of a filigree floor length mirror imagining her life as the Bishop's wife. The clothes were definitely big on Stacy's size-eight-frame, but the vision was clear. Even without alterations, she looked a thousand times better than Lucy Stewart ever had.

Stacy's eyes narrowed as she thought about all the hard work she put into both Quincy and the church.

That fruit loop has never stepped her big face in the church office to so much as hand her husband a piece of paper as long as I've been there. What kind of First Lady is that? In Stacy's mind, Abundant Holiness Christian Metropolitan Missionary Fellowship Baptist Church deserved better. Quincy deserved better. Even young Michael, with his fine self, deserved better. Stacy knew exactly what her destiny was and no one was going to keep her from walking into it especially not some old washed-up crazy woman! As Stacy surveyed the contents of Lucy's jewelry box, she began picking out the pieces she would wear and the pieces she would sell or donate as soon as the woman was gone for good.

At the hospital, Michael remained planted at his mother's bedside. His father had run away like a child during the heat of the crisis, but he wasn't going to leave his mother. He rubbed her arm, then reached out and smoothed her hair. He wanted to make everything better for her, but he didn't know how. He prayed the best prayer he could manage and hoped God would do what he asked. Michael was fully aware that some of the things he'd done in his recent past were supposed to be wrong, but his father said every growing boy did them. They were normal and helped a boy become a man. Still, when it came down to someone to believe, Michael knew his mother was far more credible than his father. He saw how his father acted with other women, especially Miss Stacy. He had watched his father lie to and otherwise manipulate people for years to get whatever he wanted. Now here in this hospital room, his mother's words about his lifestyle choices haunted him. Maybe God would help his mother, even if the request came from him. She deserved it. He didn't.

Michael dozed until his mother's groaning startled him awake. He reached over, rubbed her hand, and to his relief she slowly opened the golden brown eyes that mirrored his own. Without ever taking his eyes off of hers, he pushed the call button for the nurse. When they answered, he anxiously told them his mother was awake. He didn't know if his handholding and hand-rubbing did any good, but it was all he could think to do. His mother's eyes seemed out of focus and that scared him. It was like she was there but wasn't switched on. Her vacant stare made Michael wonder if the accident had blinded her. He began frantically calling her but she acted like she didn't hear him—at least at first. A nurse gently touched him on his shoulder then moved into the space between Michael and his mother. She bent over Lucy looking her in the eye and began loudly calling her name.

"Mrs. Stewart? Mrs. Stewart? Mrs. Stewart, can you hear me? I'm your nurse, Elaine. I am going to take care of you this evening, is that alright?"

Hearing her name, Lucy tried to answer but she couldn't get her words together. Her tongue felt like it was sewn down to the inside of her mouth. Her chest ached and it hurt to breathe. She struggled to focus her eyes on something. Anything.

Where am I?

Lucy tried to ask the person she heard if she were in a hospital, but the silence afterward made it obvious her garbled sounds couldn't be interpreted. She tried again but made an effort to speak slower.

"Momma! Momma, it's me! I'm here. Can you see me?"

Michael's voice caught her ears and she peered in that direction. All she could make out were blobs of brown, white, and a series of bright colors that all bled into one another. Everything in her line of sight swirled together and she squinted in order to focus.

Eventually her efforts paid off and she was able to see Michael's face. He looked much older than his seventeen years, as worry and grief filled his big scared eyes. He was such a handsome young man. She could never figure out why he still insisted on wearing his hair in those ridiculous cornrows. With a nice neat haircut, he would look so refined. But no, he liked to wear crisp white undershirts, baggy pants, sports jerseys and anything else that swallowed up his slim body.

Michael spoke to her again, but there seemed to be a delay between the words leaving his mouth and their sound reaching her ears. She had no idea what he was talking about but it didn't matter. Lucy smiled and that simple act appeared to soothe him.

Just then, Quincy blew into the room like a force of nature. He carried a matching leather garment bag and a small travel suitcase. Quincy could feel Michael's catlike eyes judging him. His son was defensive when it came to his mother. The last thing Quincy thought he would ever raise was a mama's boy, but he got one anyway.

Quincy shoved Lucy's overnight bag haphazardly into a narrow closet and glanced critically at her. She looked pale and drugged. Dark circles framed her swollen eyes and sweat had plastered stray hairs to the sides of her face. The sight of her like that made him sick. Lying there, she had become a waste of twenty-four years of his hard work. He should have left her in that backwater town where he found her.

Handing the nurse the bottles of Lucy's medication, Quincy turned on his charm and excused himself. He went on about having someplace urgent to be and named Michael as their immediate contact person. He'd spent all of two minutes in the room.

Michael was pissed. He knew exactly where his father was going. He wasn't stupid. He'd heard Stacy in his father's room the night before. No matter what was going on between his parents, Michael thought having Miss Stacy in the house was some fucked up shit. Now his sorry excuse for a father was putting Stacy and his johnson before his family, again.

Michael had been raised to respect his elders, but he could not respect Stacy. Everyone knew she was a whore. He didn't know why his father thought he was so special. Word around the church was a few of the men there had sexed her down before the Bishop finally got a chance to sample her. Michael had also tried to seduce her. Part dare and part test, she did not disappoint. He backed off before anything happened because he would never go in behind his father. That'd be gross. But he did wonder if she ever told the Bishop about *that?* His father was so selfishly stupid, it probably wouldn't matter. He honestly couldn't stand the sight of the man some days and couldn't wait to leave for college in Greensboro.

As Michael settled in to spend the night with his mother, he figured his father was probably already half way home. For a moment, he wished his father would have had the accident instead of his mother. He wondered why bad things never happened to trifling ass people, only to the good ones. Michael watched his mom drift in and out of sleep. He briefly looked up at the partially closed closet door. There was no need to check the stuff his dad dropped off. He knew there wasn't a thing for him in there. Whether he had a change of boxers or not, he was staying with his mom.

The next morning, Lucy was awake and alert long before Michael. She watched as her boy baby slept twisted like a pretzel in the hard, unforgiving chair. She desperately wanted to hold him like she had when he was a sleepy toddler, but her body hurt too badly and the machines she was connected to prevented anything but modest movement anyway. Lucy lay back and reviewed as much as she could about the previous twenty-four hours. She had questions, but she wasn't sure who could answer them. The morning nurse came in and Lucy startled the young woman by saying, "Good morning!"

"Well good morning! Welcome back. You had yourself a good long rest didn't you," the nurse said with a smile, as she checked the fluids in Lucy's IV bags.

"What hospital am I in?"

"Duke Raleigh Hospital. My name is Leslie and I am one of your nurses this morning. How do you feel?"

Lucy nodded. She was glad she made it there.

"Sore. And my head hurts. But I'm okay. How did I get here? I don't remember."

The nurse moved around so Lucy could see her face. She looked concerned.

"EMS brought you in yesterday afternoon. You don't remember? You had yourself a car accident. Do you remember driving?"

Lucy shook her head.

"I remember getting in my car but not no accident." She turned her head toward her sleeping son. "Michael! Michael!"

Her underused voice was strained, but it was enough to wake him. He hopped up scratching and stretching. When he realized that his mother was awake, he practically leapt to her side and began rubbing her hand again. Lucy launched into a series of questions about the accident, which completely surprised him. He hadn't expected her to come back to herself so fast! Maybe God *did* hear him after all!

Michael filled in a few of the blanks and Lucy tried to stifle a laugh when she heard her Mercedes was totaled. She never wanted the car to begin with. Quincy bought it for her after Bishop James Collins bought his wife, Victoria, the exact same car for her birthday. Lucy was sure Quincy hit the roof when he learned she demolished the car. Somehow, that alone satisfied Lucy and made the pain worthwhile. He always showed off like he was so much; like *they* were so much more than they actually were. The Bible verse about how pride comes before the fall skipped through her mind and it left a smirk on her face.

94

Sometime after 8:30, a steady stream of people, doctors mostly, came in and out of the room. This went on for several hours and Lucy was tired. Many asked the same questions the previous person had asked:

"Have you ever tried to hurt herself before?"

"How long have you been taking these medications?"

"How many did you take the day before?"

"Who prescribed them to you?"

"Why did you think they were prescribed?"

"How often are you depressed?"

"Are you depressed today?"

"Were you depressed yesterday?"

"Do you want to hurt yourself?"

"On a scale of one to ten, ten being the best you have ever felt, how do you feel emotionally today?"

"How about yesterday?"

With each round of questions, Michael got angrier. There was no need for them to keep asking the same thing over and over again. Couldn't they just compare notes? Finally, when he couldn't take any more, he jumped up with his fists clenched.

"Get out! Every last one of you! Get out of here and leave my mother alone! She's answered your questions a hundred times already! How can she get better if you keep bothering her?"

Angry tears formed in his eyes.

"Michael! Calm down baby. That's enough. They are just doin' their job."

"No, they're not. If they were doing their jobs, they'd be trying to make you better not talk you to death. They need to leave and stay gone."

Michael was beside himself. Where was his father? It was almost noon and that sorry piece of shit had yet to call or come by. He didn't even send his wife a flower or see if his son had eaten or needed to go home.

Michael didn't like people treating his mother like she was crazy. He knew she wasn't. It was his father that made her say things. Do things. Then his father would stand back and tell people lies to make her look worse. The people at the hospital didn't know this about his parents and there was no way for Michael to show them. The medical personnel had already dismissed his requests to leave his mother alone and Michael knew they wouldn't believe him if he told them how his father treated his mother.

Just after one that afternoon, Quincy strolled into Lucy's hospital room wearing a bold turquoise-colored suit with huge yellow windowpane checks, playing the role of the concerned husband. Michael turned to see his father's grand entrance and immediately flew into a rage. He could feel his face grow hot. He clenched and unclenched his fists as he stood near his mother's bedside. Quincy eyed his boy like he was a bug he was about to squash. Michael wished he would try it. Nothing would make his day more than to beat the rested and satisfied look off the old man's face. He turned his back to Quincy, refusing to acknowledge his father's presence or play his role in the Bishop Stewart show. The room crackled with their tension. Before a nasty confrontation could ensue, Lucy's doctor came in the room to update them. He informed them that although there was no sign of substantial injury, he wanted to keep Lucy for at least one more night for additional observation.

Michael was relieved his mother was on the mend, but Quincy wouldn't hear of her staying another night in the hospital.

"Now doc, I know you a reasonable man. This place is not good for my wife. I bet y'all have folk in and out all day long and she needs her rest. This here bed is no match for the comfortable one I got her at home. I just can't see her staying here another night when she would be better off at home with her family. You know, I'm a pastor here in Raleigh and we have a pretty large congregation," Quincy said, as he rolled back on his heels adjusting his suit jacket. He looked more puffed up than the humble look he was going for.

"Some of them work here and I would hate for our family's privacy to be violated unnecessarily. I am sure you understand."

Quincy grinned and adopted his most authentic preacher pose. Michael stood in the doctor's line of sight shaking his head.

The doctor noted Michael's displeasure as well as Quincy's concerns.

"Your wife is on some pretty serious medication. In her current mental state, I am not sure…"

"Doc, I hear you, but I know this woman," Quincy said smiling confidently. "Sometimes she just forgets things. This was nothing more than an oversight. She didn't mean no harm, did you, honey?"

All eyes turned to Lucy who lay in the bed wide-eyed. She had no choice. She shook her head no.

"See there, doc. I told you. This was an unfortunate mistake. It ain't gonna ever happen again even if I have to give her the medicine myself. You know how women are."

He flashed his seasoned trademark smile and shrugged as if to say in husbandly camaraderie, "What can you do?" But the doctor didn't appear convinced. His patient had almost ten times the normal amount of meds in her system and was lucky to still be alive. There was something going on that he couldn't put his finger on. Nevertheless, her tests had come back clear and he didn't really have a medically necessary reason to keep her longer. Sensing a fight if he tried, he agreed to release her later that day with a strict list of conditions. The doctor left the Stewart family to continue his rounds with patients who were more receptive to his recommendations.

Satisfied that he gotten his way yet again, Quincy addressed Michael as if his son were still a small child.

"Why don't you go get yourself a soda or somethin'? I'd like to talk to your mama."

Michael stood unmoving for a minute. He didn't want to leave her with that man. *Your mama. He can't even call her his wife!* Michael stared his father down.

"I am not leaving you alone with her."

"You hear me, boy?"

Michael glared at him. *I got your boy right here.* Michael flexed his clenched fists and continued to stare his father down.

"Why do you want to talk to her now? Where were you last night when she needed you?"

The two men glared at each other. Michael had never been more ready to swing on his father. All the old man had to do was flinch.

"You listen here, boy. I go where I please, when I please. Don't forget yourself."

Lucy slowly lifted a weak hand indicating to her son she was fine. It was only then that Michael reluctantly obeyed. He took his sweet time leaving and he shot his father a prolonged nasty warning glare. Quincy rolled his eyes dismissively and turned toward Lucy. Approaching the bed, he smiled his fake preachers smile at her. It stopped having an effect on her years ago, but he evidently hadn't realized that.

"How you feelin'?" He asked.

"Okay." Lucy whispered, watching her son's slow retreat from the room.

"Good. Good."

Reaching out with his long thick fingers and stroking her hair he let his large hand travel down the side of her bruised face. Lucy didn't know what Quincy was up to, but something in his touch made her skin crawl. She drew back repulsed. The door to the hospital room closed and almost in concert with the *click,* Quincy swiftly and firmly grabbed Lucy's chin, squeezing just hard enough to make his point while not leaving a mark. He never left a mark. Lying there weak, Lucy was helpless.

"I know what you tried to do Lucy and I swear to God if you ever pull a stunt like this again, I'mma kill you myself. You hear? You hear me talkin' to you, stupid? You better nod or somethin' before I slap you back to…"

Quincy caught himself before he erupted into his usual rage and drew unwanted attention. He leaned forward and growled his words into her face. "I done warned you not to embarrass me. Do *not* try me. You hear me, woman?"

Lucy winced as the heat of his spearmint scented breath splashed across her face. She struggled to nod her head under his unwavering grip. Quincy's eyes were cold and his face twisted with so much hate, it stunned her.

How could I have ever seen him as good, or loving? Was he that good of an actor or was I that big a fool?

After squeezing a little harder, Quincy let go of her chin, straightened up, and prepared to leave. Walking toward the door he stopped suddenly and spoke to Lucy's shaken figure behind him without turning.

"I brought you somethin' to put on. It's in that bag in the closet. You will *not* leave here lookin' like you came in! You understand me?"

The implied threat was so clear to her that it caused her to tremble uncontrollably.

"I'll be back for you later. If not, I'll have Michael fetch you home. Okay?"

Lucy swallowed hard. She couldn't answer him. Her heart was lodged in her throat and her stomach felt like it had turned in on itself. Maybe death would have been better after all. She couldn't go back into that house again. Lucy prayed silently that she would somehow get sicker and be forced to stay in the hospital where she was safe. Maybe pulling one of the tubes out would work. But then the doctor would probably tell Quincy and things would be even worse. Quincy left the room and Lucy stared speechless at the closed door

In the hallway, Quincy donned his trademark smile once again and played his well-rehearsed role as the benevolent pastor. Michael rolled his eyes, brushed past his father without a word, and went back into his mother's room. Quincy pretended not to notice the blatant disrespect from his son. He left the ward but not without greeting the staff as he came upon them, thanking each of them for caring for his wife, and shaking hands as if all were well. Alone in the elevator, Quincy's true nature reemerged as his smile departed. He was sick of all Lucy's foolishness. He'd come too far to let that country heifer mess everything up.

The reason Quincy married Lucy was simple. At the time, she looked good enough to play the role of wife. He thought she would give him some pretty light-skinned babies and she was just dumb enough to do whatever he said. If he were smart, he would have let her go as soon as he noticed her defects. Maybe he could have gotten himself a real woman and gone places. Done things. He had goals. And in just the short time she was employed with the church, Stacy had introduced Quincy to a whole new world. He wasn't going to let his crazy wife hold him back one more day if he had his way.

All his life people told Quincy what he couldn't do. White people looked down on him because he was black. Black people looked down on him because his family was the poorest of even the poor. Folks acted as if being black and poor was *his* fault. He was born into his family's problems; he didn't create them.

Quincy's father was the eldest son of a sharecropper and worked on the farm instead of going to school most of the time. He couldn't read, write, or even speak well for that matter. Quincy's mother's background wasn't much better. Quincy worked hard in school, but with no support at home, he was a below average student even after his best effort. He soon discovered that the gift of gab and an excellent memory got him places no amount of education ever could.

When a young Quincy stumbled upon an excellent impersonation of his church's pastor, people suggested he become a preacher himself. As time went on, the seed of those suggestions took root. Quincy wasn't sure he had ever heard God "call" him to preach, but he'd definitely heard the people's call. Their encouragement was the first consistently positive thing he could remember and he milked it for all it was worth. He went to church every week just to watch and memorize. The attention and praise he received sparked his determination to become the number one colored preacher in North Carolina. Nothing or no one was going to keep him from making that happen.

Quincy unashamedly wished Lucy had died in her car accident. He thought about Stacy waiting for him in his bed and smiled. She knew her place and held it well. He may be fifty-years-old but he still had it. Things would be different soon enough though. One more incident and he was either going to have Lucy locked up in Dorothea Dix Mental Hospital or he was going to send her back to her country, broke-down, backwater family so they could deal with her. He didn't care what he had to do just as long as she was gone.

PART TWO

GOOD FRIDAY

12

ere we go.

As the airplane ascended, Jason White looked out of the window and a strange feeling came over him. The upward trajectory of the plane gave him a sense of distancing. For a few moments, he felt like he'd left his life and past behind him somehow. He closed the book he had been reading, leaned back, and rested his eyes. Everything in him said that he was doing the right thing. His answers—his peace of mind—were just an hour and fifteen minutes away. Jason could see the man's image floating in his mind and could hear that distinctive voice playing over and over in his head like a recording.

Jason found himself online visiting the website of his biological father's church. He read each page carefully. Looking. Learning. He wasn't sure what he would find but he would know it when he saw it. It was the only way he could find out all he could about the man in order to get his measure. So far, Jason had learned that the man was a bishop, which meant nothing to him. He'd noted that the man's wife was a fair-skinned black woman just like his mother. Jason's feelings vacillated from indifference to anger on that. He wondered why it wasn't his mother on the site.

He needed to know. It ate at him and stalked his dreams whenever he slept. His daily life had shifted into a quest to find the truth of his identity. He had already invested countless hours reviewing the videotapes his Aunt Theresa had given him. When watching the videos wasn't enough, Jason found himself reviewing the broadcast listings on the church's web site. He watched every broadcast he could find, sometimes listening to the same sermon multiple times.

And for someone who previously avoided anything religious, he soon could quote each sermon almost verbatim. The sermons were decent enough. Jason had to give him that much. He didn't even like church, but this man talked a good game. He could actually hold Jason's attention. The points his father made were ones that Jason couldn't argue.

Even a broken clock is right twice a day.

Jason opened one eye, glanced at the book in his lap, and studied the face of the man who got his mother pregnant. He inspected those features over and over again. His father had been right under his nose all along but he never knew it. Jason had been happily living his life in the dark and under a big fat lie. He barked a laugh. The whole situation was absurd. Jason knew better than anyone else that the best place to hide something was out in the open. He practiced that concept every day of his adult life as he juggled his harem.

Jason had begun perusing Christian bookstores where he was able to pick up a few books about the man he never knew. His newfound hunger for the truth about the man only grew with time. Whatever was driving Jason had him reading his father's books two or three times. He searched for anything to help piece the puzzle in his head together. He needed the piece that would explain how this man could leave his family.

Selfish motherfucker.

Jason wasn't exactly sure what he was going to do but he knew he had to do something. He had to see this man face to face. He quietly slipped out of town without telling anyone, not even his boy, Tyrone.

Immediately after dropping this toxic bomb on him, Jason's Aunt Theresa called him daily in an effort to get him to talk to her. He never returned her messages. He didn't have anything to say. In fact, he didn't accept many calls while on his mission. His favorite five wore his mobile number out and filled up his voicemails with suggestive messages. When he didn't respond to those messages, their pathetic pleas for attention soon filled his box. He ignored those too.

Jason smiled wryly to himself as he thought of all the stunts they pulled to get his attention. He could make them jump through fiery hoops anytime he felt like it. Jason shook his head slowly. He didn't have time for games; his mind was occupied with weightier matters.

The one time Jason tried to explain to Tyrone what he was going through after learning about his father, he realized that his best friend didn't get it. Tyrone actually had the nerve to accuse him of being weak!

Tyrone DeGraffenreid became Jason's best friend in the second grade. They were part of a small group of kids who played together at school and afterward. Over the years, the others in their group wandered away, but Tyrone and Jason hung tight. They were a brotherhood of misfits who understood each other—or so Jason had always believed.

The two friends competed academically and were always alternately number one and number two at every grade level. By their high school graduation, they'd each received academic scholarships to Temple University and the competition continued there. Sometimes the battle got out of control, but no matter how unpleasant things became between them, they managed to get over it and stay tight. Just like family.

Jason and Tyrone studied hard, but they played even harder. Neither had any problem getting the attention of women, young or old. Tyrone was a tall, light-skinned, muscular, black man with deep dimples, tattoos, and the quintessential bad boy attitude. Jason was his dark skinned counterpart minus the dimples and tats. He had big eyes and long, thick, eyelashes that dusted his cheeks when he looked down. His thick eyebrows grew naturally in a shape women paid to have theirs snatched into. Together they were dangerous and virtually irresistible.

Jason and Tyrone didn't just do well in school and with women; they also successfully crossed to the other side of the proverbial tracks. They seamlessly learned the ways of the upper echelon. Both wore the best clothes, drove the best cars, lived in the better neighborhoods, hung out at the hottest spots, and had the brains to make the money to support it all. They loved every minute of their adult lives and prided themselves on their ability to flow from the streets to the boardroom without missing a beat. They were young, black, successful Renaissance men and proud. As far as they were concerned, life was good and could only get better.

More than anything else, they shared their hearts with each other. Tyrone grounded Jason. They had seen each other through trying circumstances and were always there for one another. If Jason were going to take a bullet for someone, it would have been Tyrone. He'd always thought the feeling was mutual. When Jason told Tyrone about his father, he didn't know what reaction to expect but it certainly wasn't the one he got.

"Wow. So Ma Bee pulled a Lisa on you. Man! I would have never thought she'd do that but hey, nothing surprises me anymore!" Tyrone shook his head chuckling as he drank his protein shake.

The two men were seated in the café located in their health club and hadn't seen each other in a few weeks. Jason was a little stunned at Tyrone's response. He placed his empty glass down on the table.

"I'm going to need to you to explain because I *know* you know better."

"Don't get your panties in a wad, Son. You know exactly what I mean. Lisa lied to me about my father and your moms did the same thing to you. That's all." Tyrone shrugged with a smirk. "It's not that serious. It's what they do."

Jason scooted his chair back and prepared to rise. Tyrone cut his eyes at him not feeling the least bit intimidated.

"Man, sit your ass down!"

The loud exaggerated clearing of a throat caused both men to glance at the juice barista who nodded toward a large sign posted behind the bar that said, *No Profanity Allowed. Violators Will Be Fined.* Tyrone grabbed a five-dollar bill out of his wallet and threw it in the barista's direction without even watching its trajectory. He focused his eyes on Jason.

"Look. I know what you are going through. It's fu--" He glanced at the barista who watched him with a hard stare. "It's messed up. You remember how I felt when I found out PacMan was my father? At least yours is a preacher. Mine is a drug dealing pimp! You win the biological father sweepstakes. Let it go and live your life. So what if he didn't bother with you. You know how many niggas can say the same thing? You aren't special. Suck it up, Buttercup!" Tyrone said, laughing.

Jason didn't. He seethed. Tyrone's mother, Lisa, was a strung out crackhead who sold her body to feed her habit and not her son. As a child, Tyrone was passed around to most of his relatives so much it seemed like everyone got a chance to raise him for at least a day. When they were juniors in high school, Tyrone saw his birth certificate for the first time and discovered he was named after his father. Within a year he found out that his mother's pimp, PacMan, was actually his sperm donor.

Jason tried to keep his voice calm and steady.

"If memory serves me right, you ran up on PacMan."

"I didn't run up on him. I asked him what his government name was. He told me. I asked him if he was really my father. He said he didn't know, but could be because I looked a lot like his uncle. Boom. The end."

"I remember it a little differently, but whatever. You got answers. That's all I want."

"Leave it alone man. This isn't something you want to start up."

"What do you mean? I'm not starting anything."

"Don't poke the bear, man. I'm telling you. Leave it alone. He's nobody to you. Stop acting weak, man."

"Fuck you mean? Weak? I am *not* weak. I just need to wrap my head around this thing. I feel like everything in my life up until this point has been a lie. It's like I don't know anything anymore."

"And playing detective on this nigga is going to solve all that? I'm telling you man, leave him alone. You do not want to go poking around in that man's life after all this time. It is not going to turn out well. I'm telling you. Get out of your feelings and look at this thing clearly. Throw those books and shit away, and move on."

"I can't. Look at it from my side. What if it was you?"

"If I were in your shoes, I would let it alone. For all you know Aunt Terri got it all wrong. She was giving you hearsay and you know how that goes."

"Exactly! So now I am going to get it from the horse's mouth!"

"You're acting like a real bitch, man."

As the men's voices rose and their words tumbled over one another, the barista began to snap his bar towel at them. If Jason hadn't been so mad, he would have laughed at the old goat. All the man had to do was tell them to "keep it down" or "stop cursing." Tyrone and Jason stood, opened their wallets, tossed a few bills at him, gathered their things and left still debating the issue.

***

As the plane cruised toward Raleigh, Jason looked back down at his father's face on the book cover. In his heart, he knew the Bishop was his father. End of story. When they met, old dude had a lot to show and prove.

After their harsh words the previous month, Jason and Tyrone retreated into their private worlds. This was only the second time they'd ever put their brotherhood on hiatus in over twenty-two years and, admittedly, it hurt Jason. He didn't have time for haters though. If Tyrone wasn't going to support him, he could go straight to hell with everyone else—including his sperm donor.

Jason looked at his watch. He had twenty minutes before he would land in North Carolina. His heart pounded in his chest. He wondered if anyone back in Philadelphia even noticed he was gone. He made Friday a vacation day from work, dropped the videos in the mail to his aunt, and took a cab to the airport. It departure was nice, neat and clean. No good-byes, no drama, and no one trying to talk him out of doing what he knew he had to do.

He remembered the most recent television broadcast of his father's church services. They had been aggressively advertising a massive Easter service and promised a good time for all.

Perfect timing!

Jason knew he had to be there. There would be two resurrections talked about that day.

Yep, your son has risen from the dead too, Jason mused.

Growing up, his mother frequently admonished him that what was done in the dark would soon come out in the light. Jason was about to give his father a living lesson. With his job closed for the holiday, Jason had plenty of time to shine the proverbial klieg light all over the reverend and be back in Philadelphia just in time to celebrate his twenty-ninth birthday. Maybe, if she were lucky, he would finally get around to calling Denise to see how she was doing since she returned from the conference. But he had to get through this first.

The plane landed and as Jason came down the escalator in RDU, a large billboard came into view. His only barely caught himself before his jaw dropped. The man was everywhere! He stopped in front of the ad briefly and took it all in. Unbeknownst to Jason, a baggage handler came up behind him.

"Nice, isn't it?"

Jason turned and gave the man a blank stare. The guy looked about his age and was just standing there grinning like Howdy Doody. Even with Jason looking at him like he was stupid, Baggage Boy didn't move.

"Have you ever been there?" Jason asked. His words reeked of indifference. He really didn't care, but he felt obligated to say something.

"Been?!" Baggage Boy loudly exclaimed. "I'm a member! Been going since 1988. I grew up in that church."

Good for you, Jason thought.

Baggage Boy stood there beaming, but Jason didn't have an award for this fool. He pretended to look for someone, but Baggage Boy didn't take the hint. *Doesn't he have some work to do, a bag to carry, a floor to mop or something?* Jason gave up on polite pretense, turned, and began walking away.

"You live here or you visiting?"

Jason's steps were halted briefly. It was all he could do not to turn around and punch the guy. Baggage Boy wasn't going to go away, but he decided to keep walking.

"Visiting," Jason said over his shoulder as he picked up his pace.

"Come see us!" Baggage Boy shouted out behind him.

Jason wanted to flip the guy off, but instead threw up his hand in place of only his middle finger in reply. He quickly collected his bags and got out of the airport before Baggage Boy decided to follow him for more unwanted conversation.

13

Margo opened the long flat box that had just been delivered to her boutique, Margo's Closet. She let out a sigh of relief. *Finally!*

First Lady Victoria Collins had ordered the suit several weeks ago and it seemed the package had gone everywhere but to Margo's shop in Raleigh. It was the only one the designer had left so re-ordering it was out of the question. Mrs. Collins had been gracious, but Margo had been a wreck. It was a major boost for her to land the Collins' account and one mistake was one mistake too many. She picked up the phone and called the Collins residence. Much to her surprise Victoria answered the phone and was delighted to hear from her. She thanked Margo for the call and told her she would be right over to pick up the suit. Margo hung up with another sigh of relief. Everything was going to be all right. Her shop was still new, but once word had gotten out that *the* Victoria Collins shopped with her, she'd have the local elite, socialites, and wannabes pounding down her door.

Regan, Margo's cashier, straightened the displays. Rolling her eyes, she watched her boss run around like a maniac. Just the other day she had been talking about this very thing with her best friend Jennifer.

"You ought to see how she acts when they come in the store. She be bowing like they royalty or something."

"Why? That's dumb," Jennifer said.

"I know, right? You would think these women were Jesus, the way she acts. Don't let one of them call or come by the store. She starts showing off, yelling at me like I'm her slave. She's the one acting like a slave! One of these day's she's gonna mess around and say, 'Yessuh, Massa.' and 'No Massa.' Just you watch!"

Jennifer laughed. "Those people ain't special. They nobody. Margo needs to get a grip. That's why people walk all over her like they do. How many churches in Raleigh and she trippin' over them?"

"Exactly! She only acts crazy over a few of them women."

"You need to quit and get a job at the mall. She don't carry nothing in that store for you to wear. All she has are those old church lady clothes. You need a job somewhere with a good discount. So you can hook me up."

The two girls laughed.

"I know, but remember my sponsor hooks me up with a hundred large every time I pick up the phone. I already got five hundred dollars since Christmas. That ain't at the mall!"

"Oh I forgot about *that* hookup. No, you stay right where you are so you can loan me some money when I need it."

Regan swatted her friend playfully and they laughed. What was funny a few days ago wasn't nearly as funny now that she had to deal with her boss once more.

Regan waited until Margo went into the back storeroom. She walked over to the counter and removed a business card from her pocket. She dialed the number and was instantly connected.

"Hey. This is Regan at Margo's. Yeah. That Collins woman is coming in today to get her Easter outfit." She paused. "Uh huh. It's a suit she ordered. I don't know, but I gotta go. Okay. Thank you!"

Margo came back into the retail area huffing and puffing. She pulled out the vacuum cleaner and started barking orders at Regan. The cashier rolled her eyes and proceeded to clean even though nothing was really dirty.

"All of this for one woman to come in the store for five minutes," Regan mumbled out of earshot.

She was pissed but she kept her opinions to herself and kept working before Margo fussed about something else.

A short time later, Victoria Collins walked into Margo's Closet followed closely by Tina, the First Lady's personal attendant and bodyguard. They were both petite women but their presence packed a powerful punch. Victoria's sense of style was impeccable and the source of many a local fashion trend on Sunday mornings. No matter what she wore, she was flawless. And she spared no expense on her wardrobe.

Victoria gave the women in the store a warm smile.

Did that disrespectful little girl just look me up and down and roll her eyes?

Victoria was accustomed to being treated poorly by older women, but this salty child looked barely out of high school! She gave the girl a wide smile and silently prayed, *Father, forgive this baby. She doesn't realize what she's doing.*

Margo had Victoria's suit steamed and ready to go, but Victoria wanted to look around. She hadn't been there in almost a month and was anxious to see the new arrivals. Margo Best kept small quantities of high quality, couture items in her store. No woman, especially one of a certain stature, wanted to see her spitting image walking down the street. Victoria loved the store and would sooner shop there than any place she'd ever been. It didn't hurt that Margo had a knack for finding things that were exactly her style. While Tina canvassed the room, Victoria gathered a handful of hangers in her tiny, French manicured hands and went into a fitting room.

As she settled with her finds, Lucy Stewart pulled up in front of the boutique. She was relieved to finally be out of the house until she noticed the familiar opal black Mercedes CLK and groaned.

"Not today."

She'd already endured a stressful morning and didn't need or want any more added to it.

The April issue of Contemporary Christian Woman Magazine had arrived a few days earlier and Victoria Collins' Barbie-doll-like face was spread all over the cover. One glance at it sent Quincy into a fury and he had been on a warpath ever since. When he burst into Lucy's bedroom and ordered her to go to Margo's Closet to get something new to wear for Easter Sunday, she jumped at the opportunity to leave the house. He'd been on the phone loudly, harassing the poor staff of Contemporary Christian Woman Magazine and countless other publications about why they had not interviewed his wife instead. Quincy sounded so ignorant but, to him, the reprimands were necessary.

"The church is a mess, my husband is a crook and a skirt chaser, and I hate him!" Lucy smiled to herself as she imagined the look on the interviewer's face. Just envisioning Quincy reading her true thoughts about him, and watching his head explode, was so satisfying.

Still smiling, she checked her reflection in the mirror of her new Lexus LS 430. It was metallic gold with ivory leather trim and she absolutely loved it. Quincy had a fit when he saw it but she didn't much care anymore. Lucy figured he was just mad because he didn't buy it for her nor had she asked for his permission before making the purchase. It felt wonderfully liberating to take control and making a decision for once. She patted the hood as she walked by.

Lucy stepped into the boutique and smiled at the ladies behind the counter. The younger one smiled back broadly, but Margo looked like she was going to faint.

"You okay?" Lucy offered.

"Yes, yes. Thank you, First Lady Stewart. How are you today, First Lady Stewart? Is there anything I can do for you?"

Lucy couldn't help feeling a tad rushed. What was wrong with Margo today? Why was she talking so loudly and why did she keep saying her name like that? Normally, Margo was more relaxed and friendly. Was she scared because Victoria Collins was in the shop somewhere? Lucy's eyes quickly scanned the boutique, but didn't see Bishop Collins' wife anywhere. There was another well-dressed woman hovering near the fitting rooms. *Maybe that's her Mercedes,* she thought and relaxed a little. She'd seen so many black Mercedes' on the road over the last year that she was starting to think the dealerships were giving them away.

Lucy turned her head and her eyes fell onto a lovely suit hanging at the register. "Ooh...I *love* that!"

Margo could have died. Lucy Stewart had her cat-like eyes fixed on Victoria Collins' suit. The suit that was already weeks late. Margo had no clue how to finesse Lucy Stewart's attention away from it. It was a disaster in the making!

Lord! Just let the ground open up and swallow me now.

Margo mustered up a little courage, plastered a huge smile on her face, and said, "I'm sorry, that's the only one and it's been sold." Noting the fire in Lucy Stewart's eyes, Margo quickly added, "... but I *do* have many other nice things that just came in if you... uh..."

Margo rushed from behind the counter as she spoke and tried to casually guide Lucy toward the new items. Unfortunately, Lucy's eyes were transfixed on the suit. Regan couldn't help grinning. She wanted to call her friend Jennifer *so* badly, but Margo had a fit when Regan made personal calls on the shop phone.

"Well can't I at *least* try it on? After all, it's still here so it ain't sold *yet*, now is it?" The edge in Lucy's voice was undeniable. She was feeling empowered for some reason. She was ready for war.

Margo felt perspiration form on the bridge of her nose. This was bad. This was really, really bad! How could she tactfully tell this woman her butt was too big to get into *that* suit and the owner was in the dressing room probably listening to this conversation? Margo licked her lips as she attempted to find a discreet way to focus Mrs. Stewart's attention elsewhere.

"Uh...I don't think that's your size First Lady, but if you'd like, I can see what I do have for you?"

Margo busied herself flipping through a rack and glanced at Victoria Collins' assistant. The stoic woman never returned her gaze. The boutique owner didn't know what to look for on the racks, but she knew she couldn't look in Lucy Stewart's direction. Margo knew what was coming and braced herself. It happened every time Lucy showed up.

"Well, what size is it?"

"I believe it's a six," Margo stated with a nervous cough.

"I think I can get in it."

Margo dug further into the clothes rack like a dog burying a bone. That woman hadn't seen a six in years, but every time she was in Margo's Closet, she insisted she wore a smaller size than she actually did. Why women played these games and wasted her time, Margo would never know.

"Here's something you may like!" Margo pulled out a brightly colored ensemble. It was the only one she had and it would fit over all of Mrs. Stewart's curves. "These colors will compliment your complexion beautifully!"

Lucy never looked her way. She focused her eyes on Regan. "Can you hand that to me so I can try it on?"

Regan grinned like the Cheshire cat in Alice's Wonderland. She just knew that Lucy woman was going to pop every seam in the skirt and that was going to be funny.

How in the world does she think she's going to pour all of that in that itty-bitty suit?

Margo looked like she was about to jump out of her skin. And for Regan, that was funnier than anything else! The boutique owner cut her sales clerk a "you'd better not move" look and was about to address her patron again when the dressing room door opened.

Oh my God! This is better than some reality TV shows, Regan thought.

She wanted to yell "Leeeet's get ready to Rumbllllllle!" like the announcer at the beginning of boxing matches.

"I'll take these as well," Victoria said, while extending her garment-covered arm. Thankful for the diversion, Margo rushed over and practically snatched off the woman's slender limb to retrieve them.

Fetch girl, fetch! Regan tried her best not to laugh out loud.

Margo noticed her grinning and wanted to slap the smile off the silly girl's face so badly she could taste it.

Margo moved so fast, she looked like a human tornado. She got the suit down and put it with Mrs. Collins' other purchases. All the while she avoided the hair-raising, glowering gaze of the angry first lady who still stood almost directly in front of her. Lucy's glare was like a dagger-shooting weapon. Her eyes narrowed and her nostrils began to flare so large they'd turned red around the edges.

"Are you just going to just stand there posing or are you going to help Lady Stewart?" Margo hissed at Regan.

She didn't like having to behave that way in front of her clients, but the young girl had pushed her buttons. Margo knew full well that Regan could see she had her hands full! Why didn't the girl put herself to good use and help? Margo was going to have a strong conversation with her later to remind her of her duties as well as how to conduct herself in the shop.

"Can I help you find anything?" Regan offered with zero enthusiasm. Lucy Stewart ignored her and continued to stare at Margo as if the shop owner had suddenly grown horns. Regan wandered over to Victoria Collins' assistant still hovering in the periphery. "Is dat yo momma?" She asked a little too loudly.

"Regan!" Margo barked, mortified by her cashier's behavior. The young woman looked up innocently and sauntered over to a rack of dresses. She leaned on it casually, while checking her fingernails for flaws.

Victoria sensed the situation had escalated. She concentrated intently on the contents of her wallet to help Margo save face. She knew she needed to greet Lucy Stewart. It was the right thing to do. Victoria had nothing against the woman, but every time she saw her, Lucy Stewart was rude. Victoria and James Collins were fully aware of the lies Quincy Stewart had spread over the years. Maybe his wife was in on it too. Maybe she believed the hype. Victoria didn't know and purposed to do the right thing, even if it meant she had to speak to that evil acting heifer.

The store remained uncomfortably quiet as Victoria completed her purchase. She wished someone new would come into the boutique or something would happen to change the atmosphere. The radio behind the counter was just loud enough for her to hear, "Your mercy is good and it's kind. Your mercy is brand new every day. Your mercy is everlasting…" She loved the group *Blessed* and smiled to herself.

Will you look at God? He always knows when to send to a little reminder.

No matter how tense it was, she was going to have to show mercy and be kind.

Victoria turned so she could see Lucy who had finally turned around and was fumbling through clothes on a nearby rack. Victoria hated awkward moments. She sincerely hoped Lucy wouldn't give Margo a hard time after she and Tina left the store. Victoria made a mental note to send a gift basket to Margo early next week to make up for today's unpleasant situation.

"Good Morning, First Lady Stewart! How are you?"

Victoria sent Lucy the warmest smile she could muster, but the woman just turned to conceal her face. Victoria knew jealousy was stamped all over it.

Victoria turned to leave, but something about Lucy's face moved her. She could see beyond her affected annoyance. She didn't know First Lady Stewart well, but she knew the face of pain and sorrow when she saw it. She felt the Holy Spirit gently awaken her compassion. God could seem like a jokester, at times, but rather than fight His prompting, she moved toward Lucy.

"Sister Stewart?"

Lucy heard Victoria Collins speak to her, but her eyes stung with tears. She was *not* about to let that woman see her cry. She wasn't going to give her ammunition. Lucy's lips trembled and betrayed her emotional frailty. Lucy tried unsuccessfully to blink back her tears by lowering her head and searching the nearest clothes rack. Victoria placed her purchases across a display and touched Lucy's arm.

"Are you okay, sister?" Victoria whispered.

There was something in Victoria's touch, in her voice. Why was it that when people asked you if you were okay, it often made your tears bolder? Lucy's fat tears rolled down her cheeks and there was no way to stop the flow. Her nose burned and she was embarrassed.

Victoria took Lady Stewart's elbow, shielding her from the earlier spectators. There was no need to uncover her sister-in-Christ even if her spiritual sister didn't treat her very Christ-like. As they moved toward the rear of the store, Lucy's tears betrayed her and she trembled with emotion. She'd held on far too long.

Victoria had never seen an adult this upset. This woman was hurt and she could feel it. James always told her she was too empathetic for her own good, but this was different. Victoria fought back her own tears, guided Lucy into a dressing room. Tina positioned herself directly outside of the door so she could be available to the women inside. Curiosity mounted within the shop.

14

Inside of the dressing room, Victoria Collins' voice was soft and soothing. "First Lady Stewart...Lucy, what is it? Is there something I can do?"

Lucy erupted into deep sobs that racked her body. When Victoria reached to offer a consoling hug, Lucy toppled into her arms. Victoria held her close and let her cry. She had no idea how long they were standing toe-to-toe, in the dressing room. Here they were, two prominent African American first ladies sharing a good cry.

Margo patrolled the space outside of the dressing room. She nearly wore the carpet out with worry. What was going on in there? Was all of this over that suit? *Good grief,* she thought. *If I didn't know better, I'd swear that suit is cursed!*

She'd decided she would order special items for Lucy Stewart too. That would cut out all the nonsense. She couldn't risk losing the Stewart's business and she certainly didn't need that women's crazy husband coming in the shop making a scene.

Margo itched to knock on the door, but was afraid of the woman parked in front of it.

I knew I should have closed for Good Friday! What in the name of God possessed me to open today?

The boutique wasn't busy until these last thirty minutes. Margo made up her mind right then and there that she was going to close the store for the day as soon as the current patrons crossed over the threshold.

With all the drama, Regan didn't care how she behaved. Margo was already mad so she stooped down to see what the two women were doing in the dressing room. Unfortunately, the short lady shifted her body in front of the door to block Regan's view. All Regan was able to see were the two sets of shoes facing each other.

They mighty close up in there, she mused. Regan's immature mind spun with possibilities and she came to her own tabloid conclusions. *Ooh, they must be dykes! This is off the chain! Wait until I call Jennifer and tell her the church ladies were hooking up in the dressing room. She is not going to believe it!*

Victoria released Lucy from her embrace and dug into her Kate Spade bag for a tissue. All she could find was one leftover napkin from Subway. She divided it in half offering the largest piece to Lucy. The two smiled shyly as they patted their faces dry and attempted to help each other repair their make-up.

"I'm not trying to invade your privacy and I realize that we barely know each other, but...you're hurting and I honestly want to help. Is there anything I can do?"

Lucy's eyes filled with tears again, but this time she tried harder to maintain her composure.

"No... I'm okay." Her voice cracked and she lowered her head.

Lucy desperately wanted to unload everything in her heart. She was even willing to tell the woman she'd always considered her nemesis. Lucy knew Quincy would kill her dead if he even suspected that she was nice to Victoria Collins, let alone had confided in her. Yet, there was something peaceful, open and safe about the woman. She was drawn to her. Lucy's heart told her to open up, but her head said shut up and get out of there fast!

Victoria stood and tried to leave well enough alone, but the look on Lucy's face ate at her and she just could not let it go. All of her instincts told her this woman needed serious help and if she didn't help her now, she may never have another opportunity.

"Are you sure you don't want to talk? I know sometimes it is hard for people in our position to confide in others because it often comes back to bite us. But I promise I will not hurt you." She smiled wryly. "Again, I am not trying to pry. I just..." Victoria shrugged in a self-deprecating manner.

The tears began to flow from Lucy's eyes again, but she remained resolute and shook her head no. Her lips trembled as she said, "I want to but... I can't."

Her voice broke in frustration. Victoria reached up gently and took Lucy's hands down from her damp face. On her tip-toes, she leaned forward, pressed the side of her face against the other woman's and began to whisper a prayer softly into her ear.

"Father God, I come before You first asking You to forgive every sin committed by my sister-in-Christ and I. We repent of every word, thought, and deed and ask that you cleanse us of all unrighteousness. Create in us new hearts and renew in us right spirits. Fill us with a new measure of Your Precious Holy Spirit right now. Restore unto us the joy of our salvation and uphold us by Your sweet Spirit. Heal us of every physical, emotional, and spiritual malady and we will testify of Your love and mercy, giving You all of the praise. I ask that You meet my sister at her point of need and hear her heart. You alone know what she needs. I thank You and praise You for what You have done, what You are doing, and what You have yet to do. In Jesus' name, amen." 4

Victoria kissed Lucy softly on her tear-streaked cheek and released her. Before Victoria could move away, Lucy reached out and gripped the woman's hands tightly. She felt peaceful for the first time in years. She experienced an overwhelming sensation of rest when Victoria prayed. She honestly felt like everything was really going to be all right.

"Thank you," Lucy whispered reverently. "Thank you for prayin' for me and...and..." Her eyes filled with fresh tears. "Just...thank you for everything."

"Anytime," Victoria replied. She paused and then she added for emphasis, "Really. Anytime you want to talk just give me a call." She pulled one of her ministry business cards out of her purse and wrote her home number on the back.

Lucy panicked.

"I'm sorry but I can't... I just can't... It ain't nothin' against you. I just can't." Lucy's voice trailed off, but her eyes pleaded.

"What is it then? Your husband wouldn't approve?" Victoria tried to keep her voice even and pleasant, but some of her irritation leaked anyway.

Lucy nodded, bit her bottom lip, and choked back more tears. Victoria wasn't one to encourage women to go against their husband's requests, but this was different. She knew what she felt. This was definitely the hand of God and she wasn't going to ignore it.

"Let's do lunch."

"I just told you…"

"I know, but maybe we could meet somewhere privately—even out of town."

"I don't…"

Inspiration struck and a familiar landmark flashed in Victoria's memory.

"Do you go to Smithfield often?"

Lucy had seen the highway signs for the city and gone to the outlet mall there a few times, but it wasn't an area she frequented.

"I believe I passed through a few times."

"Does your husband spend any time in Smithfield?" Victoria slowly asked as her lips formed a mischievous grin.

Lucy started to smile as well. As many secret rendezvous as Quincy probably had, it was about time for her to have one of her own.

"I don't know, but I doubt it!" The idea had captured Lucy's attention and excitement began to build inside her.

"Okay then. Why don't we meet for lunch around one today - that is if you're available?" Not waiting for a reply, Victoria looked down at her watch. "It's eleven now. Do you think you could make it if I gave you directions?"

"Yes!" Lucy grinned. "I'll be there."

She couldn't believe she was agreeing to go to lunch with Victoria Collins. The two exchanged mobile numbers and Victoria gave Lucy directions to a little diner she'd passed many times. She had no idea what the food was like, but she doubted they would run into anyone they knew. Plus, the food wasn't what they were really going for anyway.

The women quickly hugged and composed themselves. They behaved like scheming schoolgirls and amused each other by briefly speculating about the confusion on the other side of the door. Margo must have been frantic. They checked each other for telltale signs of their tear-fest and Victoria calmly opened the door.

All eyes were on them. Victoria motioned to Tina to gather the purchases, graciously thanked Margo again, and left. Lucy was on her heels. She called to Margo over her shoulder, "Thank you, Margo. I'll see you later, you hear?" and continued on out the door.

Margo stood in the center aisle with her mouth open. Regan stared out of the glass door as their first two customers of the day pulled out of the driveway in separate cars.

She couldn't wait to call Jennifer!

15

James wandered around his Mediterranean-style home feeling lost. Since Victoria had canceled their standing lunch date and the office was closed, he didn't have anything to do. But instead of relieved, he felt disquieted. As tired as he was at times, he was used to being a pastor. But he often forgot how to be James.

I need to learn how to play by myself, James mused with a chuckle. "Learn to play by yourself" was something they had to tell Caleb when he was small and his siblings were tired of playing with their much younger brother.

He walked into his home office and stopped to look at his family photos on the wall. It displayed not only their growth, but the church's as well.

***

The diner was a small, cramped, hole-in-the-wall that smelled like old bacon grease, fried eggs and sweat. The two well-dressed ladies seemed out of place in the truck stop environment and the waitresses stared at them with a marked curiosity. There were a few patrons scattered throughout, but none of them looked familiar. Tina perched on a round, red Formica stool at the short, silver-trimmed, red-speckled counter—just within arm's reach of her boss. With well over twenty-five thousand members and innumerable television viewers, it was impossible to know every face that could be familiar. But somehow, Victoria knew they were covered. God had set this up.

Although she was the one to initiate the plans with Lucy, Victoria was hesitant to break her standing lunch date with her husband. The

Collins' ate together just about every day they were both in town. It was their "private time" and reminiscent of their pre-marital dating days. Lunch was the one meal during the day when they were without any children or church talk and they could simply enjoy each other's company. However, Victoria was curious about whatever plagued the woman who sat across from her. Lucy was noticeably uncomfortable and had difficulty maintaining any eye contact.

She's probably having second thoughts too, Victoria mused. *God knows I've had them myself.*

What if this lunch was some sort of a set up? What if she came out here in the middle of nowhere and something happened? Yes, Tina would be with her, but still. What if Lucy didn't show up? What if someone saw them together and began to associate the ministry she and James worked so hard to establish with the sordid reputation of Quincy Stewart? Stranger things had happened.

The Collins' didn't engage in or endorse the pastoral gossip that went on between churches, but it was almost impossible to avoid Quincy Stewart's messiness. There had been whispers for years about what went on at Abundant Holiness Christian Metropolitan Missionary Fellowship Baptist Church and although some of it was never substantiated, their reputation wasn't the best.

The more she thought about Quincy Stewart, the more Victoria worried. What if James found out about this lunchtime meeting before she had a chance to tell him about her day? Exactly how angry would he be with her? She winced. James and Victoria rarely had words, but when they did, it broke her heart. She couldn't stand for him to be mad at her. Disappointing him made her disappointed in herself.

Then there was the matter of Tina. Tina Wilson was incredibly faithful and dedicated. Victoria didn't know what she would do without her. She'd become a good friend and confidant. From the time Victoria emerged from the fitting room with Lucy Stewart earlier that day, Tina was the epitome of discretion. She hadn't asked any questions or shown any reaction.

Bishop James Collins met Tina during a church conference in California eight years prior. At that time, another large ministry employed her, but James was so impressed with her, he decided she was the one he wanted to protect his wife. Until that time, male security personnel had always flanked Victoria. She didn't like having security around her all of the time, but it was necessary. Not everyone was happy about the work James did in the community or the truth he taught. There were also women who thought James should be *their* husband and hated Victoria just for that. It was amazing what came creeping out of the darkness. When Tina finally agreed to come work for them, Victoria still wasn't sure about her husband's choice for her protection detail. She didn't know *this* woman. The thought of a woman protecting her turned her off.

In fact, the first time Victoria laid eyes on Tina, she was sure her husband had lost his mind! Tina showed up dressed more like a preteen going to Sunday school than anyone's bodyguard. At only five-foot-three inches, she was a hair shorter than Victoria and although Tina had an impressive physique, she didn't read like she could protect herself let alone anyone else. Sensing his wife's reluctance, James had Tina show her stuff at Total Life Center, a gym and conference center on the main campus of their church. They pulled the mats out and Tina took on one of the larger male security guards in hand-to-hand combat. Even Devion Clarke, their security chief, had a smirk on his face at what appeared to be a grossly uneven matchup.

But Devion's jaw dropped when Tina repeatedly whipped Edwards, the guard she'd been paired with. Her moves were precise and looked more like ballet than combat. Every time Edwards hit the mat, his co-workers groaned and looked away. They tried to stifle their snickers for fear they would be called down to the mat next.

Devion wanted to call it a wrap after they left the Total Life Center, but James was on a roll. They drove to Davi's Gun Shop and Range and there, Victoria watched as Tina hit every target square, every time. What impressed Victoria most was when Tina was able to hit the picture of an attacker holding a hostage close to him while the frame was moving quickly in a random zigzag pattern. Despite the difficulty, Tina shot him right between the eyes!

Devion scratched his head dumbfounded. Sure, he had read Tina's resume and knew she had an impressive skillset, but seeing her in action was a different story. Devion was glad Bishop Collins had taken the initiative. Abiding Grace Christian Church desperately needed someone like her in the security department. They prided themselves on hiring the best and she proved to be even better.

That day sealed the deal for Victoria and over time, she and Tina had become close. Initially, Victoria was hesitant about truly getting to know the woman young enough to be her daughter. Victoria couldn't help but be guarded. Tina had left her former employer to come to work for them and that was a little off-putting. What would make her leave? It wasn't until a year later when Tina revealed how she prayed about accepting the position and sought counsel from her former employer that Victoria relaxed. Tina must've had a good rapport with them to be so thoughtful. Victoria wanted to get to know her and she never regretted it. On the ride to Smithfield, Tina didn't say a word and the silence allowed Victoria to gather her thoughts. Tina always seemed to accurately sense Victoria's mood and do the right thing. She was grateful for that.

***

Victoria studied Lucy's face as the woman studied the menu. Everything they sold at this greasy spoon was fried in some way or another and Lucy appeared to struggle with her food choice. Victoria could relate. She'd settled on a couple of slices of wheat toast. As she watched Lucy, Victoria decided that her lunch companion was actually a very beautiful woman. It was obvious that stress had prematurely aged a face that was probably once very striking. Maybe once she was able to get whatever was on her chest out, Lucy would perk up. As much as she tried not to stare, Victoria couldn't help noticing a fresh scar on Lucy's top lip. Although Lucy made a valiant effort to mask the flaw with makeup, anyone with eyes could tell she'd had stitches recently. Horrified, Victoria wondered, *Does that man beat her?* She tried unsuccessfully to avert her eyes, but once she noticed the flaw, it was hard to pretend otherwise. Lucy met Victoria's gaze. She smiled briefly, and looked away.

The two women had been in the diner thirty minutes and had only discussed the weather, local news, and the limited choices on the menu. Victoria was eager to discuss the real reason they were there. She needed to get home and prepare herself for the children's program at her church that night. Her youngest son, Caleb, was in it. He refused to tell her anything about his role, claiming he didn't want to spoil the surprise. At fifteen years old, Caleb was the comedian of the family and the one child Victoria knew was destined for the stage. She could only imagine what manner of craziness he cooked up for the program.

"Don't you have a son in high school?" Victoria asked hoping to direct the conversation toward something Lucy could relate to.

"Yes!" Lucy's eyes lit up. "He'll be graduatin' in June and going to North Carolina A&T to study engineering." She appeared very proud of him.

"What's his name?"

"Michael," Lucy said softly and smiled. "He's my heart." She then proceeded to share an inflated list of her son's accomplishments as only a mother could.

Victoria smiled as she admired the picture Lucy showed her. She knew exactly what the woman felt. One sure way for two mothers to bond was to talk about their children. After hearing all about Michael, Victoria told Lucy about her three precious jewels: Jamie, her newly married college graduate who at twenty-three had already followed in his father's footsteps; Christian, her twenty-one year old daughter who would graduate from UNC-Chapel Hill in May; and Caleb, her spunky sophomore and the family clown. Victoria noticed Lucy's demeanor shift slightly and wondered if she said something wrong. Was she bragging too much? She quickly ended that portion of their conversation, which left them once again in silence.

It was getting late and the two women had been sitting in the diner for nearly an hour. Victoria hated to rush her lunch guest, but they really needed to get the ball rolling. After a few uncomfortable minutes, she took a deep breath and went for it. "So what's going on?"

Lucy looked down and began to play with her place setting.

Victoria tried another tactic. "You were obviously upset this morning and I doubt it had anything to do with a silly little suit, right? Do you want to talk about it?"

Lucy shrugged and moments later, tears filled her swollen cat-gold eyes again. Victoria reached out and touched Lucy's hand. Sensing comfort, she shared her life story with Victoria. Lucy had intended to only tell the Cliff Notes version, emphasizing more recent events, but when she began talking, candid excerpts from the better part of twenty-four years of pain and frustration poured out.

"Wow, Lucy. I am so sorry. That must have been hard. From what you tell me, you were essentially a single mother raising Michael when he was young!"

Lucy nodded.

"I don't know a whole lot like I should. I didn't take to my books when I was coming up. But one thing I do know is Quincy don't have time for nobody but Quincy. He treats me and Michael like women treat jewelry. He put us on to look good, but take us off when ain't nobody around."

Victoria's eyebrows shot up at the powerful analogy. Both women sat silent for a few moments. Then Lucy continued.

"I really wanted me more babies... especially a girl," Lucy smiled. "But God knows what my family is like and I guess He wasn't gonna let another child live with what my Michael lives with."

She glanced up at Victoria and leaned forward slightly as if pleading her case.

"Michael really is a good boy. His daddy just don't take no time with him. Well...that's not true. He just don't take the right kinda time with him. When my baby was small, Quincy walked around the church just a showin' him off and eatin' up compliments. Then when he got home, he'd hand the boy to me and tell me to keep him quiet. He didn't want no cryin' and no noise from him. The only time he seem to like his own son is when someone else is sayin' somethin' nice about our boy. Then he gets all proud and want to act like he done it all hisself. Quincy would never come support Michael when he tried runnin' track. Michael only did it one year and I believe his daddy is why he give it up. But soon as them fast, little girls started callin' and sniffin' around my boy, here come Quincy. Now he wanna be a daddy. I don't know what all he said to our boy, but I do know he gave him a mess of condoms and I don't agree with that!"

Lucy slapped the table for emphasis. She was mad and Victoria didn't blame her.

"You think he encouraged your son to have sex?"

Lucy balled her hands into fists. "I wasn't there when they talked, but that's how he act and since Michael not tryin' to hide what he do, I believe Quincy told him it was okay. I guess Quincy don't know fornication is sinnin' but the way that nasty buzzard act he don't know adultery is sinnin' too!"

Victoria was blown away by the unsettling information she heard but fought to maintain her composure. She thought she'd heard every possible terrible thing about Quincy Stewart but it was worse than she ever imagined. She couldn't allow herself to react negatively though. One wrong expression could do more harm than good. This woman needed an impartial ear and she had to be that person.

Two more hours, one stack of napkins, and several coffee refills later, Lucy finally approached the end of her story. Emptying herself of years of secrets made her feel free. Victoria, on the other hand, was burdened. *Wow,* she thought, *this woman has been living in pure Hell!* Victoria felt a fresh appreciation for her peaceful, relatively uneventful life, and the incredible man God had given her. She also understood how painful it must have been for Lucy to sit there and hear her brag about her three wonderful children after the horrible miscarriages Lucy suffered. By the grace of God, she could have easily been Lucy sitting on the other side of the table.

"So how have things been for you since your car accident?"

Lucy sighed. "It's different in a way. Quincy keeps all my pills now. I gotta ask for everything, aspirin, vitamins…he keeps it all. He only gives me what he want me to have. I guess he gonna make sure I don't make any more mistakes."

Lucy looked down, clearly ashamed. Victoria reached out and took the broken woman's hand in her own.

"I am so sorry."

Lucy smiled. "It's okay. I wasn't going to do that no more no how." Then she brightened.

"You should have seen his face when my Lexus came to the house though. He about had a heart attack. I had to go in my bathroom and run the shower water so I could have a good laugh!"

Victoria smiled.

"He mad though. He forgot I got credit too and them people know us so I did the whole thing on the phone. But now every time he think I'm on the phone, he pick it up and listen in. When he hear all he wanna hear, he just drop the phone down hard. He don't care who I be talkin' too. Usually it's Michael, but sometimes our Assistant Pastor, Daniel, calls. He don't even say excuse me or nothing. Just bangs the phone down."

Lucy shook her head mournfully.

To make matters worse, the story behind Lucy's car accident had spread throughout the church quicker than a gasoline fire. In the past, Abundant was divided between the original members and the newcomers with the old heads having the advantage. Lucy was accustomed to the silent struggle. The original members treated her well, but the other set was a different story. The youngsters didn't openly say or overtly do anything to disrespect her. They just treated her like she wasn't there—as if she was irrelevant. However, that same group treated the church secretary, Stacy, as if she'd just descended from heaven. Lucy could only surmise that Quincy's indiscretions weren't as undercover as he might have thought.

"Them people act like I don't belong there no more."

"Who?"

"Everybody!"

Lucy waved her hands around for emphasis. Seeing Victoria's puzzled look, she explained.

"I went to church for the first time last Sunday. I didn't wanna go, but Quincy made me so I went. I gets there and the mothers who usually greet me, see about me, you know, that kind of thing? Well they wouldn't hardly look at me, let alone speak to me. I have never been so embarrassed in all my days."

Victoria shook her head slowly even as her ire rose.

"So Quincy makes me sit up in the pulpit behind him. We got special chairs up there for us and there is a chair up there for the assistant pastor too. So I go and take my seat like I always do. Once I sit, I always look at everybody and smile and wave, you know."

Victoria didn't do all of that, but she nodded anyway.

"Well I look up and folk starin' at me like I'm a monster. I see some hunchin' each other with their elbows and whisperin'. Some of them young women were smirkin'. I wanted to go home so bad. If my Daniel hadn't been up there, I don't know what I would've done. He smiled at me and I could tell he was wishin' me well. I felt like he had my back, you know? That's what the kids say right? You got my back?"

Victoria laughed aloud. She started to tell Lucy that she *did* have her back but felt an ounce of caution was required. Lucy had shared a lot but Victoria had no way of knowing the accuracy of the information. How would Lucy feel about what she'd shared tomorrow or next week? She pressed on.

"Are you sure they knew? Please don't think I doubt you. I just wonder how something like that could have been circulated throughout the church. Do you think someone at the hospital let it slip? That's a lawsuit if they did!"

Lucy shook her head.

"It wasn't nobody but that Stacy. I know it was her. But I bet you she didn't tell them she was laid up with their Bishop!" Lucy slapped the table again.

Victoria thought it best to leave the whole Stacy/Quincy thing alone for the moment. She had already heard more about those two than she ever wanted to hear.

"So tell me about this Daniel person. He seems to be very supportive of you."

"Oh he is!" Lucy gushed. "That is one sweet boy. He interned at our church when he was in seminary and Quincy hired him right out.

He is so respectful and he knows the Word and is a really good preacher!"

"I sense a but coming."

"No, nothin' wrong with him, except he too good for our church." Lucy blushed from embarrassment. "I know that ain't somethin' I'm supposed to say, but it's true. Quincy knows it too and he does everything he can to keep that boy down. Quincy make him do all the things he don't wanna do. Any suggestions Danny makes, Quincy see somethin' wrong with it. Danny teaches our bible study on Wednesday nights and he does a right good job. We don't usually have but a handful of people, but when he started teachin' everybody startin' comin! Next thing I know, Quincy started givin' Danny things to do on Wednesday night to keep him from Bible Study. And I'll tell you something else, I believe that's why Quincy won't ever let Danny preach on Sundays. He *knows* Danny preach better than him."

Lucy started to sip her coffee then quickly sat her cup back down.

"Oh!"

Victoria jumped, unsure of what happened. Lucy looked bright-eyed and mischievous.

"Let me tell you, my Danny is a real good-looking, young man. But he is so sweet and good-natured. He don't go for women throwin' themselves at him, but honey, when he first showed up at the church, them young girls started smellin' themselves. They started comin' up to the altar every chance they got and just fallin' out and carryin' on like Quincy had the power of God on him." She shook her head. "They just wanted Daniel to look at 'em."

Lucy sighed, more wistful than maybe she intended.

"But Quincy was eatin' it up because he was lookin' like a big man with folk gettin' slain in the spirit all over the place. I ain't never seen so much titties and tail just laid out for everybody to see!"

Lucy flung herself across the booth dramatizing the young girl's shenanigans. Victoria laughed and Lucy righted herself with a twinkle in her eye.

"I fixed them sure enough though. I got me some altar cloths made as big as twin bed sheets. I told them altar ministers as soon as one of them girls fall out, cover them up head to toe. I don't wanna see no part of 'em!"

Victoria laughed.

"I sure did and you know what? Time they started gettin' covered up, suddenly they didn't feel the need to come to the altar no more!"

Victoria laughed even harder. Lucy smiled, happy that she made Victoria chuckle. She missed having girl conversations like this. It had been nearly twenty-five years since she'd had one.

"But I worry about Danny. I done told him to go somewhere else where he can make a difference, but he say to me, 'Mother Stewart, this is where God sent me and this is where I am going to stay until He move me. There is work to be done and I'm going to do it.' Isn't that something?'"

Victoria nodded and mentally added Daniel to her prayer list.

As Lucy continued talking, Victoria sat quietly. She tried not to interrupt Lucy unless she had a question. Occasionally, Victoria would squeeze Lucy's hand, pass her a napkin to wipe her eyes, or nod in understanding. It never occurred to Lucy just how ignored she had been.

Since he'd become older, Michael begrudgingly listened to his mother. Daniel listened, which was a relief, but the moment Quincy noticed, he would call Daniel away and give him something silly to do. Lucy was just supposed to sit in the pulpit behind Quincy with her mouth shut looking pretty. But today, someone actually hung onto her every word and Lucy loved it.

When Lucy finally emptied the closet of her heart, Victoria wiped away tears. Lucy felt bad and immediately second-guessed herself. Maybe her life was just as bad and Lucy reminded her of that fact. Looks can be deceiving. Lucy didn't realize the full impact of her situation until she heard it come out of her mouth. Lucy felt both selfish and stupid because she never considered Victoria's feelings at all. Maybe she was holding Victoria up from something more important.

Lucy started to apologize when Victoria grabbed her hands. She stared Lucy directly in the eyes. It was hard to tell if she was angry or not. Lucy sat worried about how she appeared to Victoria. Her wrinkled brow displayed her anxiety, but she relaxed as Victoria spoke with a fervor that seemed to echo in Lucy's ears.

"You are *so* beautiful, my sister. And I thank God for you. I thank God that you're still here..." Victoria's voice began to break and she quickly composed herself in order to share her heart.

"You're God's most precious asset. You're a survivor and that is a *tremendous* blessing. Do you realize how many people give up every day? How many people out here that can't take even a *fourth* of what you have been through?"

Victoria paused and looked at Lucy with wonderment. "Do you even realize how valuable you are? Do you know that God's so madly in love with you that He rejoices over you with singing daily? The creator of heaven and earth is madly and wildly consumed with love for you. He thinks you're the best thing going!"[5]

Lucy didn't know how to place what she said, so she remained quiet. She hadn't heard anyone call her anything close to valuable since she was back home in Lil' Washington. Lucy released tears of pain and appreciation from her eyes freely.

"The most costly diamond cannot compare to your worth. You are beautifully and wonderfully made. You are a unique designer original created by the Father's own hand. Do you realize that even your toenail clippings are worth more than all the money in the world? You are *priceless*. God exquisitely built you cell by cell for a purpose and no two-legged flawed human being has the right to tell you that you're anything less than what God says you are!"[6]

Victoria was angry and her nostrils flared. She wanted to plant her foot straight into Quincy Stewart's behind so badly that she could just scream!

"Be who God created you to be. Be wonderful. Be creative. Be happy. The joy of the Lord is your strength[7]. Draw from Him and His word daily. You're going to have to meditate on it in your spirit every minute of every day so that you'll be strong. No matter what you choose to live with, God can give you peace. Remember what Paul said? He could be content in whatever state he was in[8]. That level of contentment can only come from the Father. The psalmist David said that even if he made his bed in hell, God would be there.[9] That strength and peace in knowing you are covered regardless of natural circumstances—protected twenty-four seven, three hundred and sixty-five days a year—can only come from knowing the Father and being built up in His word!"[10]

Victoria didn't mean to preach, but she couldn't help herself. She wasn't sure if the other woman caught it but she intentionally said that Lucy chose to live the way she was living. No one can *make* you obey them and take their crap. You *choose* to do it! One of the reasons Victoria and James enjoyed such a wonderful relationship was because they shared a mutual respect and admiration for one another from day one. If he *ever* came home and tried to act-a-fool, he would meet a Victoria Westerfield Collins that he had *never* seen before! But Lucy's Godly esteem *and* self-esteem were so low that she was willing to take *anything*. Victoria refused to see her sister-in-Christ go out like that."

Lucy could feel the passion and conviction in Victoria's words. She felt inspired. Rejuvenated. She wanted to take on the world! Even Quincy didn't scare Lucy at that moment. Her old dreams and desires began to stir inside and it felt good. All Lucy could do was smile a big comfortable smile. Victoria recognized the ray of hope filling Lucy's eyes and she knew she'd said the right thing. She'd carried out her divine assignment for that day.

Victoria graciously explained to Lucy that she would have loved to stay longer, but had an engagement at church that. Deep down they each hated for their luncheon to end because each sensed a special friendship beginning. Before they left, they joined hands and prayed. When it was her turn, Lucy bravely ignored her self-doubt and prayed for Victoria anyway; after all, it wasn't a test or a competition. If God loved her the way Victoria said He did, He wouldn't turn up His nose at her words. When Lucy opened her eyes she realized she must have said all of the right things because Victoria seemed moved. They hugged and agreed to meet again soon.

All the way home, Lucy sang loudly. There was a time when she sang at various church occasions early in their church's history. Of course Quincy and their then minister-of-music coached her endlessly beforehand to make sure her diction, pronunciation, and song interpretation met their standards. Tonight, however, Lucy sang Amazing Grace the way she had before she ever knew her husband. She loved the sound of her own voice. It was a strong, soulful, mezzo-soprano. Her Lexus provided a nice sounding board as she added riffs and squalls to the tune. As Lucy belted out the familiar hymn she couldn't help thinking that it was too bad that some big time record executive-type person wasn't anywhere around. She knew she would have gotten signed to a recording contract for sure and that would have taken her far away from Quincy and all her problems.

Lucy stopped in the town of Garner to get gas and then went straight home. It was almost five o'clock when she reached an empty house. *Good!* She could enjoy her secret for a while longer before the Stewart men came home. Lucy bounced up the stairs and sailed into her room. She was incredibly happy. Remembering how much she liked to sing in the tub as a child, Lucy decided to take a long hot bubble bath where she sang every song she knew to prolong her mood.

When the bath got too cold, she got out and dried off. She sat naked in front of her mirror and let her hair down. She combed it repeatedly and stared at her reflection. She *was* beautiful. It took a minute but slowly she began to see Cretia in the image that stared back at her. Cretia had died one Sunday morning right before Quincy's first sermon. That day had changed their lives.

Funny. He became somebody the day I became a nobody.

Well Cretia was back and Lucy grinned, smiling at herself like she was seeing an old friend after a long hiatus. It wasn't the fake church smile she'd been taught to perform. It was an honest toothy grin she knew Quincy would have hated.

Lucy had no idea where Quincy or Michael were and she didn't care. This was *her* time! She dug through a few drawers in her large white dressing table until she found one of her silky nightgowns. She modeled it in front of her floor-length mirror. The gown was terribly wrinkled after sitting folded in the drawer so long, but Lucy didn't care. At seven o'clock, she snuggled under the covers and for the first time in years, fell asleep without taking any of her pills.

16

James and Victoria Collins held hands in the plush, confetti-patterned theater seats on the front row of the Abiding Grace sanctuary wondering what the church's children had been hiding from them for months. Although the Collins' had been married for twenty-six years they still held hands as if they were dating. Their daughter Christian, oldest son Lee, and his wife Alecia, joined them minutes after they arrived.

Lee was barely seated two minutes before he hopped up and moved over to his father's side. Squatting down he said, "Good evening, Bishop."

James sighed inwardly, choosing to let the matter go this time. Still, his one-word reply said it all anyway.

"Lee."

"I was wondering if you had a chance to look at the proposal I gave to you last week. I believe that…"

"Son, do we have to do this now?"

James shot a glance toward the stage to emphasize his meaning. Lee followed his father's eyes, but because the Dupioni silk curtain was still down, he saw no need to put the conversation off. His father had told him that if he planned to take over the ministry one day, he needed to be more assertive. So Lee pressed on.

"I just need a minute of your time, Dad. They haven't started yet."

Victoria glanced over at the two men feeling sorry for them. James was right, but her baby was trying. There was no winning this round between the two of them and she was not going to get in it.

"Lee…" James' tone brokered no argument, "This is neither the time nor the place. I told you I would get back to you and I will. I know it's a time sensitive issue. Be patient and enjoy the show, okay?"

"But…"

James felt his patience drift and he abruptly interrupted his oldest son.

"Let's let Caleb and the youth have their night. They've been working hard on this a long time."

Lee tightened his jaw. *So have I.* He nodded and went back to his seat. Victoria followed her firstborn with her eyes hoping he would look at her so she could give him a reassuring smile. He never looked up.

Victoria had rushed home after lunch to prepare for the night and to her dismay, James was waiting for her. She could tell he was curious about what had taken her away from him all day, but she wasn't ready for that conversation. He had an annoying way of following her around and just standing there until she answered his silent question, but she refused to give in to the game. If she'd told him where she had been, who she was with, and all that occurred, it would have spurred an all-night discussion. Victoria wanted to see Caleb in his play and didn't want to risk being late. She danced around her husband feigning ignorance, freshened up, and slipped into a simple yet chic, beige Vera Wang pantsuit with a pair of clear mules. They left for the church with James still stealing glances at her out of the corner of his eye. His curiosity tore him up, but she knew he would be OK.

The teens of Abiding Grace Christian Church had written a play and managed to keep all the parents in the dark, including the Bishop and First Lady. Early in the planning stages, the youth ministers assured the pastors that the content would be fine and so they trusted them. Tonight was the moment of truth.

The play, titled *The Master's Plan*, was brilliant! The youth of Abiding Grace went all out in a contemporary parody of Jesus Christ's ministry.

Caleb played a particularly comical Peter. He stole the show. Caleb's Peter tried to cut everybody at Gethsemane.[11] He had the soldiers, the apostles, and even Jesus ducking, dodging, and on the run. Victoria wasn't sure how much of the scene was rehearsed or if the actors really were trying to protect themselves from her wild son. "Peter" also decided to literally cut the people who accused him of knowing Jesus once the Savior had been taken into custody.[12] That part wasn't in the bible but Caleb's interpretation left everyone howling with laughter.

James shook his head with pride. He didn't know where Caleb came up with some of the things he did, but he was proud of him nonetheless. Afterward, the Collins family joined the cast of the play, their families, and attendees in the church's multipurpose room for refreshments. Bishop beamed with pride at each compliment directed toward Caleb. It was a wonderful evening and just about everyone left smiling, talking about the talented youth of AGCC, and trying to guess which ones would eventually end up on the big screen. Of course Caleb's name kept coming up in that discussion.

During a lull, Lee seized the opportunity to approach his father again.

"So Bishop, I was thinking…"

James turned giving his oldest son such a sharp look that it temporarily stole the words out of the younger man's mouth.

"Why don't we save this until Tuesday when the office reopens, okay Son? Relax and enjoy the evening with us."

James then turned to receive more congratulations and well wishes for Caleb. Stymied, a flustered Lee found his wife and went home.

Back at home, Victoria stretched her tired petite frame atop their California king size bed while James showered. She thought about her day and smiled. She rested her forehead on folded arms and wondered how Lucy Stewart was doing. Twenty-four hours ago, she wouldn't have cared about the woman, but just that quickly, Lucy consumed her thoughts. Victoria said a brief prayer for Lucy just as James came out of the bathroom and playfully smacked her on the behind with his towel. He was always so silly but had nerve enough to wonder where Caleb got it. She said "amen" out loud and then looked up at him with one eyebrow raised.

"I was praying."

"No you weren't, you were asleep!" He teased.

She pretended to be offended and got up from the bed tossing her hair as she began to disrobe so she could shower. James started whistling and cat calling as she got undressed. Encouraged, she lost her faux attitude and decided to make the most of the moment. Victoria gave her husband a seductive burlesque show as she slowly took off her suit inch by inch. When she was fully undressed and James reached for her, she bolted to the bathroom and locked the door behind her. James ran behind her and tried the doorknob to no avail.

"Awwwww maaaaaaaaan!" she heard him exclaim.

Victoria laughed hard. James would get his treats when she came out. She would just let him stew for a minute while she enjoyed her shower in peace.

***

Lucy slowly opened her eyes. She had no idea what time it was but the room was dark except for a tiny moonbeam that ran along the wall. She'd had some of the best sleep in years and she was ready to indulge in a bit more, but something woke her up. She knew something wasn't right. The first thing that came to mind was Stacy.

Let them knock themselves out! I hope they catch somethin'!

As she slowly rolled onto her side, a towering figure stood near her bed and she gasped, too shocked to scream.

"Did I wake you up?"

Quincy's voice dripped with sarcasm. Lucy didn't reply and she didn't move. He never came into her bedroom when she slept—at least not since they began sleeping in separate rooms. The thought of him watching her sleep made her blood run cold. She stared at him and for a moment, the room was silent except for his loud, nasal breathing.

After several uncomfortable moments, he spoke again but his voice was so chillingly strange that it made her want to run. She didn't move though, lest she set him off.

"I just came to give you your medicine."

"I'm okay." Lucy whispered.

"You sure? You ain't had your pills today."

How did he know I didn't take what he brought me this morning?

Was he somehow watching her in her room now? Lucy's eyes itched to scan the room for a sign, but knew better than to take her eyes off of Quincy. Instead she said, "I'm fine. I don't need any. Thank you."

"Mmmm," Quincy hummed in a tone that terrified her.

Lucy jumped slightly as Quincy shifted his body weight into another menacing position. Lucy was nervous.

Why doesn't he just leave? What does he want? What did I do wrong now?

Lucy subconsciously pulled the sheets around her a little closer.

"Where'd you go today?" Quincy asked. His voice, although lower than normal, seemed like he was trying to affect a conversational tone. He failed. Lucy was so confused by his manner and the question. All she could reply with was, "Huh?"

"You heard me, fool! If you can 'huh' you can hear! Where'd you go?"

"You told me to go by Margo's…"

"I mean after that," Quincy barked.

"I…" Lucy was at a loss for words. She tried to remember exactly what she *had* done with her day—aside from her meeting, of course.

"Let me see what you got." Quincy demanded.

"I ain't get nothing!"

"What do you mean you ain't get nothin'?"

Quincy's voice boomed and Lucy's heart raced as he took a step closer to the bed. Through the darkness, she could see his eyes bulging.

"She… she didn't have nothing I could wear!"

"You stupid, fat--" Quincy glared at his wife and his anger got the best of him. "--RRRAAAAAAAAH!" Spit flew from his lips as he roared.

"Maybe if you stopped eatin' everything you could get some clothes that fit. I bet you Victoria Collins was able to find her somethin' new to wear for Easter Sunday without a problem! You're not gonna embarrass me this Sunday! You hear me?"

His tone was sharp and accusatory. Lucy thought of Victoria's suit and could have kicked herself for not picking up anything. She walked out of the store with her mind on her upcoming lunch and completely forgot why she'd gone to Margo's Closet in the first place.

Lucy laid still and tried to be brave. She didn't have anything to say to excuse coming home empty-handed, so she lay there silently hoping he would leave.

"So what you gone do about Sunday?" He growled.

Lucy didn't move, hoping he'd get the hint and leave her room. *Where's Michael?*

She tried to steal a look at her digital clock, but her husband's bulky form blocked the way. Whenever his father got this loud, Michael usually came running.

"You hear me talkin' to you? You surely dumb, but you 'posed to be deaf now, too?"

The venom in his voice forced her to answer him. "I'll try and find somethin' tomorrow."

"Uh huh."

He didn't believe her, but she couldn't think up a better response with him lording over her.

"From where?"

"I dunno! Somewhere."

"In Garner?"

Lucy was instantly confused and her face reflected it. She couldn't think of any places in Garner where Quincy would approve of her shopping. Lucy remained silent as she tried to figure out what her husband was talking about.

"That's where you was today, ain't it?"

Lucy's heart raced so fast she thought it would explode in her chest. She couldn't think straight. What was Quincy talking about?

"I…"

Quincy waved something at her in the darkness. She rose up on an elbow to see what it was. It was the narrow white receipt from the gas station where she'd stopped earlier. Suddenly, it all made sense.

Oh my God!

Quincy had been rambling through her purse! Fear gripped her. Victoria's card! Just as quickly she remembered that she had taken the card out of her purse when she got home and hid it among her precious jewelry in her personal safe. *Whew!*

"What was you doin' out there in Garner?" He demanded.

"I…I just ended up there needin' gas."

Lucy was not a good liar. Although she *had* ended up in Garner and she *had* needed gas, the guilt she felt about the lunch showed through. If he pressed her, she wouldn't be able to come up with a solid story even if her life depended on it.

"Uh huh. So you left outta here after ten this mornin' to get some clothes and just ended up on the other side of town at four twenty-two in the afternoon with nothin' to wear?"

Quincy was angry. There was pure hate in his tone. Lucy laid down silently, bracing herself for the first blow and hoping it would all be over soon.

"Who you got in Garner?" Quincy took a step toward the bed. His knee bumped her mattress causing her to yelp from the impact.

"N-n-nobody! I just…went there," Lucy stammered.

In one swoop, Quincy snatched the covers off of her. Lucy instinctively balled up into the fetal position.

"You mean to tell me you just rode around wastin' my money on gas for six hours? WHO was you with?"

Lucy couldn't answer that. She *wouldn't* answer that. If she tried to make up something, she knew she would make it worse, so she simply remained silent.

"WHO WAS YOU WITH?" Quincy roared.

Lucy tried to block Quincy's voice out and silently pray but even in her mind, she couldn't get her words together. Her body filled with fear. But what she experienced that day with Victoria was perfect. She would *not* let the devil in Quincy ruin it.

"Danny, wasn't it? You was with Danny? You old ho! You think I don't see how you be watchin' him and how you always tryin' to get him off alone? I ain't stupid, woman! You think I'm stupid? Huh? Answer me!"

"What?! Oh my God!" Out of all the outrageous things Quincy accused her of, this was the worst. And he had some nerve, since he crept around with women in her own home! Accusing her of being with Daniel was too much. Quincy might as well have said Michael! He was ridiculous! Lucy wanted to protest, but her throat was so tight with fear she couldn't say anything anyway.

"I asked you a question! You think I'm stupid? Look at you! Who you wearin' that thing for?"

Quincy snatched the hem of her gown so hard that the straps cut into her shoulders even as she heard the seams pop in protest. Lucy went into self-preservation mode and tried to scurry sideways up to the head of the bed. Quincy continued his barrage of insults, his voice louder than thunder.

"What happened to your other nightgowns? I warned you about tryin' to embarrass me, didn't I? Didn't I? Was you wearing this for him?"

Quincy grabbed her arm as she made a futile attempt to curl her body back into a ball. He tried to turn her over but she pressed her side firmly into the bed, eyes shut. Inside, she pleaded for mercy. The situation had escalated to a terrifying level and Lucy didn't know what to do. By now, he would have hit her. What was he waiting for and where in God's name was Michael?

Quincy's hand shot out and grabbed one of Lucy's breasts squeezing so hard she thought it would rupture in his grasp. Her piercing scream filled the house and Quincy laughed.

"You think that boy Daniel really wants you? He just feels sorry for you, you ol' wrinkled up nasty retard! With your big self. You as big as a cow now! He don't want you no more than I do. Everybody know you ain't got no milk, don't they? If you did, you wouldn't have left my son all hungry and about to starve when he was a baby?"

Lucy felt a rush of tears press through her eyelids and run down her flushed face onto the mattress.

Why doesn't he stop? Why doesn't he just go away and just leave me alone?

"You want a man, Lucretia? You want someone to make you feel good?"

He slapped her roughly on her butt. The stinging pain made her yelp and throw out her hands to protect herself. Not one to be challenged, he ripped at her gown. Lucy cowered while trying to hold on to the bodice before the lace cut straight through her skin. In a move of desperation, she kicked at him as she heard the hiss and snap of the fabric. Lucy was sure she was going to die before the night was over.

Quincy landed a few solid blows to her side. She stopped moving as she fought to catch her breath. Quincy was sure that whomever she was with, whatever she'd been out doing, someone must have seen her, and he was *not* going to let her embarrass him. She needed to be taught a lesson and Quincy Stewart's rage was going to do the teaching. No man was going to have his wife, even if he didn't want her for himself. She was gone from the house all day and he was no fool. On top of that, she didn't even get what he sent her to buy. Instead she came on home, put on some old nightie, and went to bed. She was just dumb and she must've thought he was too.

That night, Quincy did the unthinkable. Bishop Quincy Stewart beat, raped and sodomized his wife.

When he was satisfied, he left her sobbing, trembling body on the bed. He retreated to his side of the house, slamming her bedroom door behind him.

Removing his gold Mansilk pajama pants, Quincy noticed Lucy's blood sprinkled on them and was disgusted. The pants cost him eighty-something dollars! They were ruined and all because that woman had tried to make a fool out of him. Well he showed her good that night! She wouldn't try that again! He went into the shower to wash her stench off him. He didn't know what he ever saw in her. The only reason he kept her around was to maintain his image and avoid the expense of a divorce. Maybe if he'd met someone like Stacy twenty-something years ago, things would be different now. He wouldn't be forced to go outside the house for attention. He would have everything he needed right at home.

Quincy began to daydream in the shower. He and Stacy would've had lots of children, a legacy he could've been proud of. Maybe even a son loyal to him; one who'd follow in his footsteps. Women like Lucy made you have to keep other women on the side. They made you have to get rough. That was the only way they understood anything. It was like training a dog. Sometimes you had to smack them on the nose and rub it in their mess so they could learn.

Lucy's screams rang in Quincy's ears. She begged him to stop and called on Jesus—as if *He* would ever listen to her. Jesus knew she was stupid and that's why Quincy was convinced God had led him to her purse. God *wanted* him to know his wife was cheating on him. On *him*? Was she crazy? Well sure she was, but he'd finally knocked her sane.

Lucy lay trembling uncontrollably on her bed. She hurt so badly that she could barely stand. He hadn't touched her intimately in over fifteen years and she hadn't been with any other man in all that time. To have Quincy—*her husband*—take her so violently, broke her down deep.

Why?

She thought about what Victoria had said about making your bed in hell. Why did she let him do it? Lucy thought she'd tried to fight him, but did she really?

A guttural sound boiled up from deep within her and spilled out of her lips. Only the labor preceding Michael's birth came close to the degree of pain coursing through her body. Her skin still stung and her insides randomly contracted from his blows. "Oh God," was all Lucy could say over and over again. She slowly slid off her bed and fell into a heap onto the carpeted floor. She tried to crawl to the bathroom, but it seemed so far away she simply lay there helpless. Her body took on a mind of its own and she wet herself; the burning was unbearable.

Her heart cried out to God.

Why wouldn't He just let her die? Why did He keep making her suffer? What had she done so wrong to make Him hate her like this?

She thought He was supposed to be all in love with her. She thought He'd finally heard her prayers and given her a friend. But she now questioned everything. She looked into the darkness with bleary eyes and remembered Victoria's words. "You're a survivor."

Dazed and coming apart fast, she chanted Victoria's words repeatedly as she drifted off to sleep "I am a surviv…I am a survivo…I am a surviv…"

***

Michael Stewart shut off the lights on his Baby Benz as he turned into the driveway. It was just before three in the morning and he didn't want to wake anyone up. Not that they would say anything if he did. He just didn't want to have to make stupid conversation about his night. He'd gone to an Easter jam downtown and hooked up with a honey afterward. He grinned as he thought of his recent conquest.

"Pimpin' ain't easy, is it Playa?" He asked himself as he winked at his reflection in his rearview mirror.

Parking just outside of the garage limited any unnecessary noise. He crept slowly into the quiet house. His parents knew better than to wait up for him anymore. He stole past his mother's slightly open, bedroom door. He hoped she wouldn't call him into her room to get her some water or something crazy like that. He carefully slipped up the steps and into his room. He was glad he'd avoided dealing with his folks until later that morning.

PART THREE

EASTER WEEKEND

17

Saturday

Jason pulled up to the church and was astounded. If he hadn't read the signage first, he would have thought he was looking at a stadium or some building other than a church. Since when did churches get this big? The picture of the church's façade on the web site hadn't done the place justice. He'd read that the actual sanctuary held seating for several thousand, but the sheer size of it didn't sink in until he was up close and personal.

The cream-colored stone building was an imposing and impressive structure surrounded by what was easily thousands of parking spaces. The parking lot was so large it had to be sectioned off with alphanumeric signs so that people could find their cars. He spotted a sign for guest parking that pointed toward the main entrance and another sign pointing toward where the church offices and bookstore were located. He flipped a mental coin and went in the direction of the latter. Jason looked for any sign of the pastor's assigned parking space as he strategized where he would park and what side of the building he would sit on.

Jason circled the church a few times taking it all in. *Could all this be mine?* he pondered meditatively. There were so many possibilities. So many things he could do. He spent a few minutes toying with what demands, if any, he planned to issue to his dear old dad. The man had to be worth a few dollars and when he saw the church for himself, new ideas were sparked.

If his father's church looked like this, Jason wondered what his home looked like. He knew some preachers lived meager existences, but this man didn't strike him as one. From the quality of his suits to his propensity to preach the dollar-sign gospel, there was no doubt old dude had bank. He wasn't broke, yet. If Jason had his way, he'd steamroll 'ol dude and it would serve him right. His mother's dignity lay somewhere in those bricks and she'd sacrificed it along with his siblings, to the benefit of this sorry excuse of a man.

Jason always prided himself in being a brilliant strategist. Thinking on his feet was never a problem. If something ever went wrong, it was so miniscule and infrequent that it was tolerable. Jason was good and he knew he was good. This wasn't a chance meeting. He'd collected more than a month's worth of data—memorizing even the most trivial. After casing the church, he was ready to put his plan into motion.

***

Lucy woke with a start on the floor. She lay there for a few minutes, too scared and in too much pain to move. Once she got her bearings, she slowly crawled to her bed and used the linens to pull herself up. As she came up the side of her mattress she saw droplets of blood—her blood.

Dear God!

She froze in horror for several seconds before continuing her efforts. She knew she was badly injured, but seeing the blood made it even more real for her.

Rolling onto her side to sit, a bolt of pain zipped through her body almost causing her to slide off of the bed.

Oh God! What did Quincy do to me?

She stiffened her wobbly legs and slid into an awkward standing position. Her head spun and her legs felt unsteady. She stared vacantly at the mess on the light-colored carpet. It didn't seem real. Even with the stabbing pain moving across her body, Lucy tried to convince herself it was all an awful dream. It didn't happen. Not in her house. Not by her husband.

As she looked up, she caught her reflection in the mirror near the bathroom door. Her gown was reduced to a few jagged pieces of fabric attached to a barely discernable lace bodice. Quincy was an animal! There were too many bruises, scratches, and bite marks on her chest, upper arms, stomach and thighs to count. Only animals did things like this. If anyone saw her, they probably would think she had been attacked by a bear—not her own husband!

Her husband. Lucy didn't even know what the word meant anymore. It had lost its meaning long ago. The dream the word once held had quickly become a nightmare.

Lucy winced when she gingerly pulled the cream nightgown over her head. She staggered through the pain, and dragged herself to the shower. The water was hot, but she didn't care. A quick scalding would wash away the evil on her. She kept the water running long after it became icy. She leaned against the shower stall, tears singeing each wound on her body.

At some point, Lucy stepped out of the shower. She was fully aware that she needed medical attention, but did not want to risk another trip to the hospital. Another trip this soon would only raise questions. Quincy probably wouldn't let her out the house if she tried anyway. He wouldn't be able to lie and smile his way out of this one. If anything, he might really try to kill her for even thinking about getting help.

Lucy picked up her telephone and called her son's private line.

Michael answered the phone with a sleepy, "What's up."

Lucy had no idea what time he made it home the previous night. She was both worried and embarrassed that he might have heard what his father had done to her. She could never really read him. Sometimes he would be her "Lil' Bookie Boo" again and then other days he had the same devil in him as his sorry father.

"I need you to go fetch me some of that Neosporin from Walgreens. Come to my door and I'll give you the money for it."

"Neosporin?" Michael asked incredulously before continuing, "You just need some ointment or that specific one?"

"I need to heal a cut," Lucy said in an effort to simplify the magnitude of her injuries and hide the truth from her son.

"Oh I already got something for that. I'll bring it to you."

Michael left some Bacitracin he had remaining from his last tattoo session outside her door. Although she was glad he had what she needed, Lucy hated the fact her son felt the need to continually mark up his body like he did. He never paid much attention to her fussing with him about his tattoos and his father acted like it was okay with him. It was what all the kids his age were doing, according to Quincy.

She heard the tube bounce against her door and was glad he didn't try to come in. Once she was sure he was gone, she cracked her door, kicked the tube inside of her ransacked room and carefully got down onto the floor to get it. If what Victoria said was true, Lucy was a survivor. This is what survivors did. They endured.

Lucy glanced up on her dresser to find a small, clear saucer containing two of her pills resting in the center. One pill for each of her prescribed medications. Right away, she knew Quincy must have come back in her room after he'd…

Lucy shuddered at the thought of him standing over her again. How could anyone be that mean? Didn't he have a conscious? Lucy vowed to keep her door locked—anything to keep Quincy away from her.

She sat watching the pills for a long time, but never picked them up. That was what he wanted her to do. No, she needed to be clearheaded. That devil was up to something and she would be ready for him whenever he got the mind to try it.

Lucy donned a more modest gown along with her robe, and stretched out on the rose colored chaise in the sitting area of her room. Shortly thereafter, there was a knock at the door. Lucy swallowed heavily. With a thick voice she said, "Come in…" She surprised herself. She had no idea her voice could get that low.

A familiar face poked around the door. She relaxed and actually managed a smile. It was only Marcelita, their latest housekeeper. Just as quickly Lucy's heart fell as she realized the date. This was more of that devil's doing! He knew they had given their household help the weekend off so they could go to their holiday church services and spend some time with their families and out of town guests. Marcelita asked for the time off over a month ago and they agreed that it wouldn't be a problem, but here she was the Saturday before Easter anyway. Quincy must have called her in to work without caring anything about their agreement.

Old heartless dog!

She doubted he would pay Marcelita a bonus for the inconvenience either. She liked Marcelita and hoped that Quincy wouldn't run her off like he ran off all the others. Lucy wouldn't blame the woman if she quit.

"Good Morning, Ms. Lucy. Happy Easter!"

Lucy had a lump filled with shame and regret lodged in her throat, but managed a weak smile and lifted a hand in greeting.

Marcelita immediately attacked her work with a singleness of purpose. She stripped the bed with almost no effort. Marcelita gathered the soiled linens along with Lucy's destroyed lingerie and headed out of the room to the laundry. Lucy was embarrassed to the point of tears.

Why didn't I just throw that gown away? I could have hidden it under the other stuff in the garbage so she wouldn't have seen it.

The gown wasn't worth washing. It was nothing but rags.

She wondered what her housekeeper really thought of her. Of them. She must have gone home every night with all sorts of interesting tales about the Stewart household. This particular housekeeper did not live with them like some of the others had and after what happened the night before, Lucy was glad. How were you supposed to look someone in the eye after a night like that?

Lucy must have dozed off because the sound of Marcelita's soft voice awakened her.

"Ms. Lucy? Ms. Lucy?"

When she opened her eyes, Marcelita stood next to her with a steaming cup of herbal tea. It was a wonderful treat and never failed to make Lucy relax more than all of her prescription medication combined. Marcelita made it with fresh herbs she grew in her garden at home. Lucy reached out and gripped Marcelita's forearm and thanked her profusely.

"Oh thank you, Marcelita! This is just what I needed. Bless you! You are too good to me and always so thoughtful." She held on to the housekeepers arm a moment longer than necessary before letting go. Without ever saying the words, somehow she knew Marcelita understood all of it. Her astuteness both shamed and relieved Lucy.

Lucy consumed the savory blend of tea as she quietly watched her housekeeper make the bed with clean linens, scrub the stains out of the carpet, and clean the bathroom. Lucy felt obligated to say something more. To make up a plausible cover story. But what could she say? She wished Marcelita had let her sleep through her cleaning so she wouldn't have to see the effort it took to bring the room back to normal. So much destruction in such a short time and for what?

Lucy cautiously studied Marcelita's face for any reaction, but her housekeeper displayed no emotion other than a sense of joy in her work. How could she hum and act so happy on her hands and knees scrubbing someone's nasty piss out of the carpet? Especially when Marcelita knew she wasn't even supposed to be there. If Lucy was in Marcelita's shoes, she would have an attitude! The thought caused Lucy to reexamine the contents of her cup, but she relaxed. Marcelita wasn't like that.

Lucy remained in that comfortable spot on her chaise all day partly because it hurt too badly to move and partly because it felt so good to be off the floor. She remembered that she'd promised Quincy she would find something to wear for Sunday, but she just wasn't able to bring herself to do it. Quincy must have realized she was in no condition to run errands because later in the day, Marcelita knocked on her door with a garment bag and hat box from Margo's Closet.

"Señor Stewart said I must bring you these things for tomorrow."

Lucy did not touch the bag and it remained on the back of her door until Marcelita retrieved it before she left for the day in order to steam the garments for her. When Marcelita returned with it, Lucy told her housekeeper to leave it on the back of her door.

"Are you ready for your pills, Ma'am?"

Lucy was embarrassed beyond words and looked away unable to face Marcelita. There was no way of telling what Quincy had said about her or if he'd even made up a story implicating her mental state as the source of the mess Marcelita had had to clean.

Lucy shook her head

Marcelita immediately looked uncomfortable.

"Señor Stewart said you must take them before I go."

She looked apologetic, which only made Lucy madder at her husband. She grudgingly nodded and Marcelita left to get the medication. Lucy didn't want to put her housekeeper in a bad position and cost the woman her job. It pissed Lucy off that Quincy was using Marcelita as a go between. He was such a coward! He was Mr. Big-n-Bad the night before so why couldn't he face her now? She knew he didn't have anything close to a conscience.

But as mad as she was, Lucy knew better than to get too worked up. Instead, she decided to make a fool of Quincy. She got up slowly and placed the pills that were left on her dresser the night before, into her bathrobe pocket so he would think she took them. When Marcelita returned Lucy graciously accepted the new medication along with the glass of water and sent her housekeeper on an errand elsewhere in the house. Lucy drank the water but flushed both sets of pills down the toilet. She didn't know all of what that devil was up to, but she knew one thing, he was not going to keep her drugged up no matter how hard he tried!

***

Stacy gripped her phone fuming. Time was wasting and this man was playing games.

"The store is about to close and I need three hundred dollars if I am going to get that outfit!"

She sat parked outside Margo's Closet boutique intermittently stealing glances into the store and at the shoppers coming and going at nearby businesses.

"Now Baby…" Quincy intoned, "I done told you what to wear. Wear that yellow suit I like on you. You look some kinda good in that!"

"But I don't want to wear that *again*. Everyone else is going to have something new and I want something too! Your wife is going to be wearing something new!"

"That's different. You know--"

"How?" Stacy demanded. "How is that any different? She has a closet full of clothes, some with the tags still on them. I saw them when I helped you after she tried to kill herself, *remember?* Why can't *she* wear something she already has? I haven't had anything new in forever and I don't have anything in my closet I haven't worn at least a dozen times already! How is her getting something new supposed to be different when she gets *everything* new all the time?"

Stacy's chest rose and fell with a building rage. *I can't believe this man is trying to make me beg for some clothes! This is the least he should be willing to do!*

Quincy had called her and told her to go to the store and pick up his wife's Easter outfit earlier in the day. When she asked him if she could get something for herself, he didn't say "yes" but he also didn't say "no." So while in the boutique, she'd looked around and found the perfect outfit. It was obvious the Stewarts had some type of credit account with the store if the owner was willing to have an outfit boxed up and ready to go for them. Why couldn't she get something on credit too? Just to be sure, Stacy asked the owner to hold the ensemble for her until later. When she delivered the suit to the Stewart's house, she asked Quincy to buy her a new outfit as well but he told her to call him in a couple of hours and they would talk about it. Now she was calling and he was acting dumb.

"Stacy! Come on, Baby. You know she has to sit up in the pulpit for everybody to see. She needs help looking the best she can. You don't need no help. You could wear a garbage sack and still be fine! Come on now, baby!"

"I want that outfit! Call the store and tell them to give it to me!"

Quincy sighed, which only made Stacy angrier.

"When have I ever asked you to do something for me? Anything you want, I give it to you. Hell, I even give you what you don't even know you need, but you can't do this? I do everything for you! Okay. I see how this is now. I guess I thought we had something, but that's okay. You don't have to worry about me. I don't want anything from you that you don't want me to have. Just remember this when you want something from me. OK, BISHOP?"

"Now hold on there, Stacy. You know how we is, girl. Listen. Calm down and listen to me a minute." Quincy paused feeling backed into a corner and not knowing what to do next. He relented. "Go 'head on and get whatever you want. I'll call over there and tell them we doing you a favor or somethin' so don't go in there talkin' about nothing. I don't want that lady all in our business!"

Stacy was only partially mollified. She should not have had to lose her temper to get her way. If things were changing, she needed to stay one step ahead of Quincy Stewart.

"I'll be as discreet as a church mouse," Stacy purred with a smirk and ended the call with fire in her eyes.

18

Sunday

With the early morning sun climbing slowly into the spring sky, Easter Sunday announced itself and Jason lay in his hotel bed staring up at the ceiling. He'd been awake since before dawn imagining every conceivable scenario that could possibly occur within the next few hours: the way he would approach his so-called father; what the man would say to him, what he would say in return, etc. One thing ate at him, though.

What if the man is sorry and actually wants to make things right?

Jason didn't know what to do with that scenario. Could anything ever be done to make all of this right? Maybe he could have the father he always wanted. Maybe he would have the benefit of the relationship for the remainder of his life. Didn't his Aunt Theresa say that God planned it like this?

Jason groaned. He was *not* going to start thinking like his aunt. His eyes slid over to the thin digital clock on the espresso nightstand. It was almost seven o'clock. He could get up and make the church's eight o'clock service, but he didn't want to. He intentionally planned to go to the eleven o' clock service. He wanted to be sure that dear old dad would have plenty of time to hear him out. He had come too far and had waited too long to be dismissed.

His phone vibrated and he checked it reluctantly. It was Denise. Again. He didn't have time to be distracted by her or anyone else today. He had to focus. He would probably only have one shot at the old dude and he couldn't blow it.

***

Victoria slipped into her Easter suit and checked her reflection in the oval, floor-length mirror. The simple suit had been the beginning of an unusual day that turned out to be something special. Her mind drifted to Lucy. She really wanted to check on her but had no way of reaching out. Lucy hadn't given her a telephone number or e-mail address and Victoria knew that calling the Stewart house was completely out of the question. She couldn't get Lucy out of her mind. All weekend Victoria had the feeling that her sister-in-Christ was in trouble. She couldn't stop praying for Lucy. She even woke from sleep several times concerned about Lucy. All she wanted was to hear Lucy's voice and know with certainty she was okay.

Lord, please let all this be a product of my overactive imagination. Please keep Lucy safe. Protect her from that man. Please, Lord Jesus!

James came out of his prayer room and went into the bedroom. He paused briefly to admire her.

"Baby, you look incredible! Is that new?"

Victoria smiled and nodded.

"I like it. I like it a lot. Someone else may have to preach this morning because..."

Victoria swatted his arm with a smile and he leaned down to kiss her nose. He didn't want to ruin her lipstick. He put on his suit jacket and left for church with Devion. Victoria often joked that Devion really didn't work for James—the inseparable two just hung out together all day and called it business.

It was unfortunate for a pastor and his family to have to live a life surrounded by security personnel, but the world had changed. There was once a time when ministers of the Gospel were respected, but that was no more. Their inflated insurance policies attested to the shift. There had been too many "almosts" for the Collins' to not to use precautions. It wasn't a matter of faith; it was a matter of common sense. James ceased being afraid for himself, but was more concerned for his family. However, he also knew that he couldn't help save a dying world if he were dead himself!

Per usual, James had prepared for his sermon all week. Today's message was titled, "It Is Finished: Jesus' Last Will and Testament." He went over it thoroughly Saturday, and had spent his customary time in prayer and meditation that morning. James and Devion rode to the church in their usual silence before James had to preach. It helped the senior pastor stay focused. If he and Devion began running their mouths, he would likely get so sidetracked there would be no telling what he'd say. James insisted on getting to church almost an hour before service started. He needed it.

This particular morning, James really felt on edge. It was Easter Sunday, but there was something unsettling stirring in his spirit. He'd meditated on it in prayer prior to arriving at church, but still felt as if the other shoe had yet to drop. Maybe it was Victoria. She had been a little preoccupied the last couple of days. Normally she processed her stuff out loud, but not this time. He'd been waiting for her to verbalize what she'd been thinking about, but apparently she wasn't ready. James planned to give her another few days before he would call her on it. He didn't like seeing her so wound up.

James took a deep breath, cleared his mind, and began to meditate on Hebrews 9. He had to focus. He wanted to be a clear vessel for God's message and would chat with his wife later.

***

Lucy stared at the colorful suit hanging on the back of her bedroom door. It was the very same suit Margo had tried to force on her on Good Friday. She didn't like it then and definitely didn't like it now. It looked like a box of crayons had exploded all over it and she was sure what was inside of the hat box on her dressing table wasn't much better. She couldn't get her body to move. She had not taken any of her pills since Thursday night and almost three days later, she struggled with that decision. Lucy knew that she had to get dressed or face Quincy's wrath, but she just couldn't motivate herself to move.

She sat in her room a while longer and contemplated her life. For whatever reason, God saw fit to let her live another day. She should have been celebrating Christ's resurrection, but her spirit seemed stagnant. Her bones ached and she felt completely drained. To add insult to injury, thanks to Quincy, Lucy thought she might have a nasty vaginal infection and while it caused quite a bit of discomfort, she could not go to the store to buy anything for it.

The events of Friday still loomed fresh in her mind. What happened drained of whatever life remained after the car accident. She desperately wanted to call Victoria, but she just couldn't bring herself to do it. She was terrified Quincy would catch her, come back into her room and repeat the horror he had perpetrated. Since it was Easter morning, Victoria was also likely too busy with her family to fool with her. It didn't matter, though. Lucy was too ashamed to even pick up the telephone. She felt like she'd let her new friend down somehow.

She remembered how emotional Victoria got just hearing her story. She was sure that Victoria probably wouldn't be able to handle hearing what had happened since then. Deep down Lucy wondered if this was God's way of punishing her for the few times she'd wished she had met someone like Daniel when she was younger. Sure, Daniel was very nice looking, but she didn't want him.

All Lucy wanted was someone nice. Someone not at all like Quincy. If she talked to Victoria, Lucy was afraid she would let that bit of information slip just like she'd let a lot of other things slip. What would Victoria think of her then? There was no need dragging Victoria any further into her life. She probably had better things to do.

Lucy looked across the room at her distant reflection in the dressing table mirror. She searched for any familiar sign of Cretia but she was gone. In her place, were eyes cast in deep purple bags and thick lines on her forehead, just like her mother. Where had they come from all of a sudden? Lucy noted the time and knew if she didn't dress quickly, she would have to deal with Quincy.

With a deep sigh, Lucy slowly eased off and away from the safety of her chaise and began to prepare for a church service she didn't want to attend.

How in the name of God am I going to sit up there with a straight face and support that sorry son of a--?

She immediately repented for the profanity that came across her mind, but dreaded the next few hours just the same.

Ironically, Lucy wished Quincy had given her another black eye or some other noticeable disfigurement so she could stay home. But he must have learned his lesson about that. With her coloring, she bruised easily and the scarring showed for a long time. So he made sure to hurt her where no one would be able to see it. Lucy could never understand what kind of sick thrill it gave him to continually humiliate her—first in private and then in public. He forced her to sit behind him, to silently endorse him, to act like everything was perfect. At least some men hit their wives and then apologized. Quincy never apologized. He did what he did and he meant every bit of it.

19

As Jason approached the main road to the church, he was surprised at the number of people already there. There were cars lined up as far as he could see. Jason left his hotel an hour early to give him plenty of time to get there and park in the space he mapped out the day before. But he still had to wait. He was more than a little concerned. His whole plan was contingent upon him being able to sit near the front of the church. This way, he'd have direct access to the man at the conclusion of the service. He wanted to look him straight in the eye. Somehow he had to maneuver ahead of the endless stream of cars that wound around the church like a giant centipede.

Men in matching bright yellow jackets lined the roadway every few feet directing traffic. As soon as he got close enough to one, Jason let down his window and turned on his best negotiating smile.

"Hey my man… is there another way into the visitor's lot?"

"I'm sorry. It's full. You'll need to stay in this lane if you want to get into the main sanctuary," the burly, middle-aged man replied politely while taking a step closer to Jason's rental car.

"Come on, man! I flew all the way in for this. Can't you open another gate or something?" Jason said, nodding in the direction of a sealed off entrance.

"No, I'm sorry. This is it. If you can bear with us a few minutes, we'll get you in as soon as we can." Jason wasn't so easily deterred.

"You sure, bruh?" Jason asked as he smiled knowingly and held up a hundred-dollar bill he'd surreptitiously retrieved from his wallet.

"Naw, man. Save that for the offering. There's nothing I can do."

With that, the man backed up and began motioning to the departing cars to take another route. Jason nodded his head and rolled up his window. He was getting very angry. This was not how he planned it. This was not how it was supposed to happen.

Jason's long slender fingers drummed nervously on the steering wheel as the car inched closer and closer to its destination. He was never one for patience and this situation was eating him alive. He glanced at the clock again—it was ten forty-eight. He had been sitting in traffic for over thirty minutes. He took a few deep exasperated breaths and turned on the air conditioner to keep from exploding. More traffic controllers smiled as he slowly passed, but he wasn't in the mood.

Jason wondered if there would be any seats left in the front when he finally got in. Surely, there had to be one. Every car he could see had at least two people in it. Assuming people who rode together sat together there had to be one odd seat somewhere close to the front. One was all he needed.

Jason rolled down his window again and addressed the nearest traffic controller. This one was younger and Jason figured there was a chance he could persuade him.

"Hey bruh! Do they usually start on time?"

"Like clockwork!" The parking lot attendant beamed as if that somehow made him proud.

"Look man, I'm running late. Can you do a brother a solid?" Jason asked while exposing the same hundred-dollar bill folded between his fingers, but the attendant put up his hands in alarm.

"Sorry, bruh! Everyone's in the same predicament you are!"

"Come on, man! You know you can open up another lane or something." Jason gave the attendant his most convincing hook-a-brotha-up facial expression, all while wagging the folded up bill between his fingers.

"I wish I could man. Sorry!" The man replied as he waved Jason forward.

I'm sure you are, you damn polyester, yellow-jacket wearing...

Jason raised his window without another word. Everyone was *not* in the same predicament and Jason purposed to do whatever it took to get past the people in front of him. He had to get inside.

***

Theresa White Bonner was busy in her kitchen preparing a large Easter brunch for her family. The aroma of bacon, eggs, pancakes, potatoes, and other breakfast staples in various stages of preparation permeated the house. But neither her heart nor her mind were into what she was doing. The huge, traditional Easter meal was something her mother always did when Theresa and her sister Bridget were small. Theresa wanted to keep at least one memory alive in the family, but this year it was hard. Bridget was with Jesus, Jason was missing, and no one knew anything about where he'd gone.

Anyone who knew Jason well was used to him taking a day or two to sulk when he was mad, but it had been over a month since their last conversation and Theresa didn't blame anyone but herself. She fasted and prayed but just couldn't seem to shake the intense sense of dread that clouded her heart since he walked out of her house that fateful day when she shared their family secrets with him. Jason had yet to respond to a single text, voicemail, email or message left with his secretary. That alone told Theresa this was more than his usual anger-induced, self-imposed isolation. It wasn't like Jason to ignore her or his sisters to this degree and Theresa was worried sick. Donna went as far as to drive to his condo, but she did not see his car and no one answered the intercom. Tyrone denied knowing where Jason was but Theresa knew they were thick as thieves and he could have been covering for Jason. Tyrone had declined his standing invitation for Easter Brunch and that was odd. Tyrone never turned down a free meal at her home. All Theresa wanted was an opportunity to talk to Jason. She'd allow him to yell at her if that would help.

Theresa, her husband, Thomas, and their niece, Donna, went to the traditional Easter sunrise service early that morning at the family church she'd attended since childhood. She gave an extra offering while believing God for the corresponding return of togetherness and normalcy for her family. She wanted to be still and let God be God, but it was hard especially when it seemed like she was being completely left in the dark.

She received the videos she had given to Jason via mail the day before. She would not have minded if he had kept them. In fact, she intended them to be a gift. Donna came into the kitchen just in time to see the worry dance across her aunt's face.

"It's okay, Aunt Terri. He'll be all right. You know how Jason is. He's probably hold up somewhere with a girl!"

Theresa gave her niece a weak smile and hugged her tightly.

"From your mouth to God's ear—wait, then again no. I don't think God wants to hear about Jason laying up with anyone."

Her quip made both of them laugh. Theresa wanted to believe Donna's theory, but something deep inside of Theresa told her otherwise. She did not think she needed to call the morgue, but she knew something was going on. Only God knew what it was and she was going to have to trust Him to keep her sister's baby boy safe. Just then, the phone rang and she grabbed it before it could ring a second time."

"Praise the Lord! He is Risen!"

There was a pause. Theresa hoped the next voice she heard would be Jason's but it wasn't.

"Hi, Mrs. Bonner. It's Denise. Denise Edwards. Jason's girlfriend," the voice said, almost questioning itself.

This was a surprise, but Theresa was happy to hear from her. She really liked this young lady and had been praying as well as dropping hints for Jason to hurry up and marry her.

"Well hello! It is so good to hear from you and you know you can call me Aunt Terri!" Her heart skipped a beat with hope. "Am I going to see you and Jason for brunch? I am almost through cooking and we have our usual spread!"

There was a pause and a knowing disappointment dropped on Theresa's heart like an anvil.

"I'm really not sure, Aunt Terri. Have you talked to Jason lately?"

"Well no, Honey. What's wrong? Please tell me you two are still together!"

"I think so. I just haven't been able to reach him. I went over to his place, but he wasn't there. I know we always get together with you for Easter so…"

"Listen Baby, you are always welcome in my home. Come right on over!"

"I don't know if that's a good idea. I mean, I haven't had a chance to talk to Jason and I am not sure what's going on with us. I don't want to create an awkward situation…"

"Denise, baby, my nephew is going through some things. He has shut all of us out. It is nothing personal. You should know how he can be by now."

Denise laughed feeling some of her concern drain away as Theresa continued.

"He has a lot on his heart and he's trying to work through it. He isn't even talking to us. If you want to come, please come. Our door is always open for you, okay? We'll be eating in about thirty to forty-five minutes so come on."

They said their goodbyes and ended the call. Theresa turned to look at her niece who was standing by with her eyes wide.

"Did you just tell Denise to come over? What if Jason shows up with another girl?"

"He won't. He knows better that to bring just anyone into my home."

Donna grinned. "I told you he was laid up with someone. He's probably cheating on Nieci. That's why she doesn't know where he is."

"He better not!" Theresa replied waving her spatula, "Or else he is going to get reacquainted with this on his behind!"

20

James sat at his massive, handcrafted mahogany desk. His fourth floor office was surrounded by floor to ceiling windows on two sides and provided a near panoramic view of Northwest Raleigh. Devion sat in a club chair within a grouping of neutral toned herringbone furniture in a sunken seating area. Beyond sat a sixteen-seat boardroom with shelves filled with awards, memorabilia, and an eclectic array of gifts the bishop had received over the years.

James silently watched from a private monitor as praise and worship went on in the sanctuary. It was 8AM and the first service was right on schedule. The praise was extra lively and he wanted to get out there to be a part of it. Devion rose and helped James put on his tailored suit coat. He called the Bishop's son, Lee, into the room to collect his father's laptop and Bible.

"Do you need anything else, Bishop?" Lee asked.

James shook his head and clapped his son on the back as they headed for the door. The three exited the office and immediately the additional security personnel who waited outside of the pastor's office surrounded them. Standing in the wings, James took in the congregation, many in the throws of active worship. It never failed to amaze him the number of people who showed up week after week. He knew it wasn't him. For whatever crazy reason, God decided to use him and the people responded in droves.

The first service at Abiding Grace usually had about sixty-five hundred people attend, while the eleven o'clock averaged about ten thousand. That was a far cry from their humble beginnings. He could remember when it was only him, Victoria, and an idea. It had been an incredible ride and he was still amazed by it. James silently watched as many of the people came up and placed their tithes or offerings on the altar. It almost moved him to tears. He knew that each envelope represented hopes, dreams, needs, gratitude, and obedience. He knew his congregants believed in and were loyal to their ministry. Sometimes it was all that he could do not to swoop down onto the altar and attempt to place his hands on each envelope in an effort to connect with the spirits and lives behind them. He often felt incredibly unworthy of their support and feared one day he would let them down somehow. Still he did his best to look out for their welfare.

His eyes scanned the balcony area. Two weeks before, a distraught rejected boyfriend barged in during the eleven o'clock service and tried to take a dive from the balcony. Fortunately, two ushers and a security officer caught him before he could hurt himself or anyone else. It was a momentary blip in the service and was handled so discreetly most people never noticed. Still, it should have never been allowed to get that far. Satisfied at the number of royal blue blazers James counted floating around up there, he returned his attention to praise and worship. He quietly took his place on the platform to join in with those in attendance. He may not have been able to see each one eyeball to eyeball, but in worship, they were all connected. He worshipped with abandon and allowed God to direct the order of the service. James had long since gotten over the whole two fast songs/two slow songs formula some churches still followed. He knew God could do more through people as they worshipped, than in any sermon he could bring forth—no matter how anointed people claimed he was. As far as he was concerned, the jury was still out on that claim.

Praise and worship at Abiding Grace was designed to be personal time with God that released His power in the place. Once the announcement and offering portions were taken care of, James approached the podium and preached the heart of God revealed in Hebrews 9. After completing his divine assignment and covering his flock in prayer, he left the platform with Devion and Lee close on his heels. The other ministers handled the altar calls because Bishop Collins needed to regroup before the eleven o'clock service.

Just as James prepared to turn a corner in the hallway, he heard the quick clicking of running heels. Security went into high alert and surrounded him pushing him toward the elevator. Then he heard a familiar voice calling him.

"Bishop! Hold on one moment, please."

He pushed through security puzzled. Not only had he just left Victoria seated in the pulpit area, but she never disturbed him between services. As she approached him with Tina, in tow, the serious look on her face let him know something was up. She handed him a folded piece of paper.

"You may want to take a look at this."

She hopped up on her toes to kiss her husband's cheek, gave her son, Lee, a big smile and a pat on the arm, then headed back toward the sanctuary at a slower pace. Curious, James opened the note. It was from Elder Carlton, one of the ministry's original members. He was an ardent intercessor and a man whom Bishop Collins respected tremendously. The note simply stated that he needed to speak with the bishop ASAP. James went into his office and because it was rare for Elder Carlton to request an appointment with him, he sent for him immediately.

***

Quincy practically burst with pride at the overflowing crowd filling Abundant Holiness Christian Metropolitan Missionary Fellowship Baptist Church for Easter service. When their driver approached the church, Quincy, cushioned in a luxe ivory leather seat, could not contain himself and had slapped his leg laughing and repeating, "Looka there, Lucy!" She didn't respond, but it didn't matter to Quincy. There was a long line of cars slowly snaking their way up the busy street to the church and each meant dollars for him. An attendant spotted their gleaming black May Bach and opened a side gate to let them in.

As he sat back watching the music and arts team perform, he felt like a king. The people enjoyed the dancers who twirled, leapt, and pranced in the aisles. The praise team was on point and Quincy made a mental note to mention their recently released CD during his opening. It was a good way to get people into the bookstore to shop.

Quincy's eyes traveled down to the front row where Stacy sat in a melon-colored suit that had a short waist jacket and chunky gold chain embellishments. A large organza bucket hat with matching shoes, gloves, and clutch completed her ensemble.

See there, now that's what a first lady is supposed to look like!

He could tell Stacy had spent more than the requested three hundred dollars, but he didn't mind. As good as she looked, she was worth every penny.

Quincy caught movement out of the corner of his eye. He looked over in time to see Lucy fold her hands primly on her lap as she stared at Stacy as well. Quincy quickly averted his eyes in case a visitor noticed where his attention had been and resumed watching the pageantry of their praise and worship.

21

Elder Carlton sat across from James gathering his thoughts. He wanted to relay every detail of the strange vision he experienced three times over the previous week. He knew Bishop Collins had to preach again soon and didn't want to keep him away from any preparation time or rest. James sat patiently across from Elder Carlton. He could tell the man wanted to choose his words wisely, so he remained silent. When he cleared his throat, Elder Carlton began:

"I had a vision of a big dinner. You, your family, and all the leadership of AGCC were there. We sat at this huge banquet table that stretched on forever. There must have been a couple of hundred people there—some I didn't recognize, but most of them I did. There was a ton of food and everyone was eating from plates piled high with food, talkin', fellowshipping and whatnot. In fact, come to think of it, I think you were the only one not eating."

Elder Carlton began to laugh, but James remained stoic. The elder cleared his throat, regained his composure, and continued in a more serious manner.

"All of a sudden here comes this big, wild-lookin' dog, looking like it had been rollin' around in the dirt, you know? It was covered with fleas, ticks, mud—everything. It ran in and jumped up on the table. It started runnin' up and down the table almost like if it was possessed or somethin'! It was a mess. Plates and glasses were knocked over onto the floor and all over everybody. Some people were knocked clean out of their chairs and others just got up and ran away from the table. Then the dog turned around and ran straight towards where you were sitting. I thought it was going to bite you, but instead, it stole a chicken breast off of your plate and ran around with it in its mouth. Clarke and the other security guys tried to catch it but it seemed to stay one step ahead of them no matter how hard they tried. When it stopped running, a pack of dogs came out of nowhere and them dogs fought over that one chicken breast. As crazy as it may sound, the more they pulled at it, the bigger it got! They were rippin' it apart until they each left with a piece of it. You got up and walked straight up to the lead dog like you weren't afraid of it. It finally cowered, lay down at your feet, and then spit out the leftover piece of chicken breast."

Elder Carlton stopped talking and looked at Bishop Collins, who had a perplexed look on his face.

"Well, that's it. I had the same vision three times in three days, Sir. It never changed. There was never any more or any less. It's just that...it seemed so real and it left such unrest in my spirit, I knew I had to share it with you. I know it sounds crazy but that's exactly what I saw."

James sat behind his desk nodding his head slowly. He didn't quite understand what it could mean, but he didn't dismiss the vision either.

"What did you eat before you had this...uh, vision?" James asked with a weak smile. Before the elder could answer, he waved his hand to let him know he was only kidding. He knew Elder Carlton took spiritual matters seriously and wouldn't waste his time on some tuna fish or pizza-inspired dream. Hearing the vision, in fact, had stirred something in James' recent memory.

"Elder this may seem beside the point, but let me ask a crazy question. The dog in your vision, was it a long-haired mutt? Patches of black and brown almost like what you would see on a calico cat with a white underbelly and paws?"

"Yes!" Elder Carlton nearly jumped out of his seat from both surprise and excitement. He didn't know how Bishop Collins knew exactly what the dog looked like. It relieved Elder Carlton of any self-doubt, but also left questions he was too polite to ask.

James sat back in his chair with his fingers intertwined. Decades earlier, when he was in the seventh grade, a stray dog wandered into their yard. Young James tried to keep it as a pet. His father told him to let it go, but James fell in love with the mangy creature. The dog was part of a pack of wild dogs and once James began feeding it, he also had to feed the others too. The pack of mutts ended up trampling part of James' mother's flower garden and dug holes in his father's prized yard. No one was happy with him or the dog. One day, when James came home from school, the dog was gone. His parents insisted it had just wandered off with the others, but James was pretty certain they had something to do with the disappearance of his mangy friend. James had not thought of the mutt in years but a month before, he'd experienced a peculiar dream about the dog.

In *his* dream, Spanky had appeared outside of James' current home and howled non-stop for him to open the gate. Once James obliged, the dog jumped up to lick James and ransacked the property looking for food. James originally thought the isolated dream was the result of an ice cream binge, but now he wasn't so sure.

There were clear parallels to what Elder Carlton saw in his vision. James knew that when it came to dream interpretation, dogs often represented evil, but familiar dogs represented something cherished. Was something he cherished about to destroy him? His family? His ministry? The only thing James cherished outside of his relationship with God *was* his family. He knew the God he served wouldn't destroy what He had built! He tried to reason it out. Food meant sustenance and in both cases the dog had both stolen and eaten what belonged to James. But what did he own that could be consumed? James' mind went a mile a minute, but he knew he couldn't afford to invest too much time on the matter then. He needed to clear his mind in order to preach again. This was going to require some serious thought and prayer later on.

Elder Carlton sat across the desk and watched his pastor process the information. He didn't know whether to get up and leave or to continue sitting there. James had been sitting silent, eyes closed, for about ten minutes. Had he gone to sleep? As the elder weighed his options and readied himself to get up, suddenly James opened his eyes and stared intensely at Elder Carlton. For a split second, the elder thought he saw worry dance across the pastor's face. Then Bishop Collins broke into a smile, quickly stood up and extended his hand.

"I appreciate you sharing that with me. Thank you."

Elder Carlton didn't know what everything meant but he accepted the handshake followed by a hug then quickly left the room.

James slowly walked back around his desk, sat down in his chair, and looked up at the ceiling.

"OK. So talk to me..."

22

Jason craned his neck toward the platform. His eyes darted between the stage and the large screens at each corner of the church.

Man, this place is huge!

Jason struggled to take it all in. It was 11:15 and service had already begun. He'd tried to maneuver his way through the crowd pretending he was looking for someone already seated. It didn't work. The ushers had already filled the first three-fourths of the lower portions of the church and informed him there were no seats left—not even one. Jason was stuck in the rear.

Jason observed a steady stream of people wander up to the stage, so he slipped out of his seat to follow them. Maybe he would be able to find a seat that was overlooked or steal an empty one. As he got closer to the front, he noticed that people in the freewill procession were leaving money and envelopes on the steps that led up to the stage. He fought to control the snarl forming on his lips. These robots were giving dear old dad all of their money like fools. The thought brought back memories of his mother sending in her last dollar to every preacher on television.

Jason felt the familiar hatred and anger build in him again. His temples throbbed and, for a moment, he forgot his immediate purpose. Spinning around, he returned to the seat he had been sitting in without ever reaching the altar. Fortunately, he was still able to clearly see the people on the stage, including the Praise and Worship Team. The music really pumped and was actually kind of nice, but he couldn't get with the dancing. People acted like they were in a flash mob or some sort of musical. He wasn't used to that. Then again, he wasn't used to

180

church period. Jason glanced at a few of the men near him who clapped, sung, swayed, and danced. They were soft. They looked ridiculous and their dance steps would not get them far in the club.

The few times Jason ever ventured into a church, what he saw there was a lot of old people singing slow, dry songs that sounded painful. Every one of the songs had all of the makings of a blues tune or a country western ballad. They sang about struggling up a mountain, trouble being in their way, and begging God to show them a way out of it. The preacher would scream for an hour to keep you from falling asleep, the choir would sing another sad song, and that was it.

But this place was different.

Jason scrutinized the people around him. They were really into this.

I guess that's what happens when you don't have any other outlets.

Jason reluctantly acknowledged the energy in the room, but to him it was all hype and no substance. People just hollered and carried on for carrying on's sake. The energy exploded to another level when a large troop of dancers came out and performed a routine in the aisles. Some had streamers and others had tambourines. They moved in unison and although Jason was impressed with their skill, he felt the vaudeville act was a bit much.

The singers have back up dancers? What's next?

If a disco ball dropped out of the cathedral ceiling, he would not have been surprised. The only thing missing was a magician. Then again, that was what the pastor, his dear old dad, was there for. Smoke and mirrors.

Jason watched the female dancers stretch, leap, and pirouette. He amused himself by wondering about what they had going on under their brightly colored costumes. There wasn't an ugly one in the bunch. He made a few mental notes regarding which ones he would definitely handle some business with if given the opportunity. He'd already had his share of church girls so a few more wouldn't hurt. Church chickenheads were an unusual breed and easy targets. They were all into serving a brother and making sure all his needs were met. He knew his way around them and had game specifically designed for them. While

181

looking into their pastor, he read one of his books on relationships and was really surprised. The man gave his readers the entire 411 on game so he may have to work a little harder to break these females down. But that was the fun part. The challenge. Conquering new territory. The harder, the better.

One song ended and another began, led by a soulful alto who sounded similar to the late Phyllis Hyman, one of Jason's favorite artists. He turned his attention back to the screen where the camera focused on a gorgeous woman belting out the smoky notes. She read a little young, but looked at least a step beyond jailbait. Young and dumb was a good combination for him to work with. His mind went to Tyrone. They did do most of their dirt together. Tyrone would lose his mind in this church if he were with him. Although he would never admit it to Tyrone, he thought about his friend a lot over the past few weeks. There was no denying he missed him, but there was no need to remain friends with someone who didn't care about the things that really mattered to you. A true friend would have understood and encouraged him, especially after knowing all he'd been through. Life was too short to be surrounded by haters.

Jason allowed his focus to shift back to his surroundings. His eyes danced over the sea of people. He remembered reading that it was a multicultural church and that was evident everywhere he looked. He had never been in a mixed church before. Growing up, the only time white people went to his mother's church was during election season. Here, it looked like an everyday occurrence and everyone seemed comfortable.

Jason decided to relax and enjoy the show. With all the beautiful women his eyes took in that morning, he could have an international smorgasbord right here if he wanted to. He wondered if the pastor sampled their goods. If his father's past was any indication, it was likely. Jason had read plenty of expose' articles detailing exactly what these preachers did now-a-days. But who was he to judge? No matter what went down with dear old dad this morning, Jason was definitely coming back to visit this place again. If he knew North Carolina grew females like this, he would have come down south a long time ago!

Suddenly the mood and the music changed again. Much of the crowd kneeled. Some cried, while others had their arms stretched up to the sky. Jason observed this in the videos, but to be surrounded by it was another story. He felt really out of place. These people were emotional junkies and the group up there singing was milking them for all they were worth. He didn't know what to do with himself so he stood quietly, looked down with his hands folded, and waited for it to be over.

The singing eventually stopped but the musicians continued to play a soft ethereal melody that reminded Jason of something out of a dramatic chick flick movie score. He hoped they were finished, so he could sit down. He had been standing for almost forty-five minutes and his shoes felt like they were shrinking by the minute.

Jason's head snapped up and he looked startled as the people began chanting in a language he didn't recognize. It reminded him of French with possibly a Chinese/Japanese flair. He'd heard people talk about speaking in tongues, but he had never actually heard it for himself. It was…different. He watched their mouths. How did they run on and on like that? Did they know what they were saying? As abruptly as it began, the murmurs died down and the people around him fell into a heavy silence. His neighbors looked as if they could hear something, and not one to be left out, Jason started listening too. All he heard, though, was the soft music and an occasional sniffle or cough.

The sudden silence after such a cacophony of noise unsettled Jason. He shuffled his feet. The quiet was so disturbing, he almost considered leaving. Without warning, a woman in front of him collapsed onto the floor. Alarmed he immediately grabbed the chair to move it but it was bolted to the floor. It seemed no one else noticed or even tried to help her. The woman next to her casually glanced down and waved her hand over the woman in a manner reminiscent of Cinderella's fairy godmother. After a second or two, the woman turned back to face the front as if her neighbor wasn't sprawled out on the floor next to her. Nothing else happened. The rise and fall of her chest let him know she was not dead, but to be sure, Jason gently kicked the chair in front of him. She did not move and no one else did either. He continued to watch her to see what she was going to do next. If her head started spinning around or she started spewing green vomit, he was definitely out of there with a quickness!

As Jason continued watching the woman, he heard a woman give what he assumed were the church's announcements. They had a lot going on and he shifted his feet waiting for her to shut up. Why didn't everybody just sit down? As bad as he wanted to, he knew that monitors or not, he wouldn't be able to see everything he wanted to see through the people standing in front of him if he sat. Then a familiar voice drew his attention back to the screen.

There.

As big as life.

Bishop James Elliott Collins.

His so-called father's face flooded the screen.

Jason was so distracted by the drama around him, he didn't even notice when the man walked out on the stage. He looked around and everyone else watched the stage as if in a trance.

As he stared at the Bishop, it finally really sunk in. He was here, in the same room, with the man who got his mother pregnant and then abandoned her. Seeing him in person was a far cry from the videos. Jason could now appreciate the Bishop's height. His presence took over the entire stage. Between his complexion and height, this fool had to be his father. Jason's mother's family was all short. His own mother had been barely 5'4." And at 6'2", Jason and his Aunt Theresa's husband, Thomas, were the giants in the family. But in that church, Jason was in the same room with the giant of a man who had broken his mother's heart. His emotions were getting the best of him. Jason wanted to rush the stage and bash the bastard's head in. Instead, he sat gripping the sides of his seat and biding time. The woman in the row in front of him picked herself up from the floor and a few people helped her fix her clothes. He didn't understand it all, but staring at her and her lopsided wig helped curb Jason's rising fury.

Jason sat with his eyes fixed on the enormous screen flashing the image of his father. He then noticed men with subtle earpieces sitting on the ends of some of the rows. Were they security? Jason's affinity for logistics kicked in. If he were going to rush the stage, he had to estimate how long it would take him to get there, how many alternate routes he could take, and how many of those men he could take on if he had to. As Jason watched the nearest security guard a little too closely, the giant returned Jason's gaze causing him to avert his eyes.

Bishop Collins took off his suit coat, tossed it to a lackey, and jumped onto the main floor to an excited crowd. *Athletic,* Jason noted and wondered how he would fair in a hand-to-hand fight. The pastor talked passionately about something, but Jason could not process the words. He had grown deaf. He was purely focused on his goal.

Bishop Collins started up an aisle. Jason's aisle. How far would he come? The preacher stopped midway and hopped onto a chair while the people, most standing, cheered him on. Jason relaxed in his seat. His time would come soon enough. Yes, there was security all over the place and they all wore blue blazers, but he wasn't worried. Jason knew there was a way around everything and everyone. He would figure it out.

Suddenly Bishop Collins beckoned people to the altar. Jason didn't know what they were going to get, but he went along. He needed to get closer. Whatever they went there for, the folks in line were not trying to let him cut. The crowd was worse than the free butter and cheese lines in the 'hood back in the day.

The group loosely assembled around the stage was roughly ten rows deep. Jason found himself trapped in the last few. There had to be at least three or four hundred people around him and he couldn't seem to press in any closer. Jason noticed that Bishop Collins was back on the stage. He stood stock still staring at the man. He was so close. The crowd jostled him a bit, but he still could not move beyond where he stood.

The preacher began pointing at various people while he spoke to each of them. At one point, Jason could have his old man had looked right at him.

Did he see me?

Jason wondered if God had told dear old dad anything about his long lost son.

People all around Jason had their arms and hands lifted up and a few shouted different things to and about God. At the height of the intensity, Bishop Collins spun on his heels and left the stage through a side exit and several men scurried behind him. People dressed like priests wandered through the crowd assembled at the altar and prayed for each one. Jason turned, pushed through the remaining rows, and left. He neither needed nor wanted their prayers. He wanted James Collins and if he couldn't get to him, there was no need for him to stay there wasting his time.

Although Jason could feel the stares from people he passed, he kept walking. He breezed past his seat and walked out the double doors into the lobby. Once there, he finally felt like he could breathe again. There had to be another way to get to that man. He had come too far.

23

"Are you looking for the bookstore?"

Jason turned to see a beautiful woman behind him. *Does the Bishop have a factory where he manufactures these honeys?*

Her tan skin glowed in harmony with her big, bright eyes and disarming smile. She was like a perfect angel come to earth.

"Uh… yeah…" He lied.

"Follow me," she said, tossing her long, light brown curls over her shoulder. Denise wore her hair like that for him sometimes. He shook the old image from his mind and concentrated on this new picture of perfection walking in front of him.

The bookstore was larger than any of the bookstores he went to in Philadelphia. It was almost as big as a Barnes & Noble! His luscious and ever helpful guide asked him what he hoped to find. He had no idea what to ask for so he simply told her he was interested in videos. That was safe and partially true. Watching the bishop's videos was easier than reading the books.

"Men's ministry? Singles?" She asked as she gave a sly glance at his left hand out of the corner of her eye.

She knew the deal.

"Both," he replied and she began selecting several videos for him, giving her personal commentary on each. Jason tried to pay attention to what she said rather than how she looked, but it was hard. Her pretty brown eyes drew him in.

"I'm sorry. I didn't even ask you your name," she said shyly, breaking him out of his trance.

"Jason... Jason White."

"Do you live in Raleigh?"

"No, I'm here visiting my uh... family. I live in Philly."

Jason could've kicked himself. He had to focus. Philadelphia was a big city. His slip up wouldn't cause any real damage. Nevertheless, he had to get back on point before he made any more mistakes.

"Oh okay. Yeah, I can tell by your accent," she said. "I'm Chanel."

"Chanel?" He inquired.

"Ellis. Chanel Ellis."

"It's a pleasure to meet you, Chanel Ellis. Thanks for showing me how to get in here. So, how long have you been coming to this church?"

"A little more than two years."

"Do you like it?"

"Yes! I really didn't go to church that much before coming here, but since I started, I've learned so much. Lots of good things have happened for me!"

She smiled. He smiled. After an awkward few seconds, she reached out to remove some of the videos she'd piled in his arms.

"No, I am getting these!"

"All of them?" Her eyes stretched wide in surprise. He had at least ten or twelve videos stuffed in his muscular arms.

"Yeah." Jason smiled and revealed his perfectly straight teeth. He knew she was impressed.

"Are you sure? I really didn't mean for you to get every one of them! I was just showing you..."

"I'm sure. I want all of these. I watched Bishop Collins all the time at home and meant to order some of these, but never got around to it."

Jason lied, but she didn't know it. Her southern accent was so cute when she talked about the various videos, how could he put them back? At least one of the videos had to have something he could use on them. Then his eyes spotted Bishop James Collins' mug grinning all over a DVD case and he leaned forward to read the cover: *In Search of Our Fathers.*

Unbelievable.

Jason blinked a few times and would have reached for it but his hands and arms were full. Seeing his dilemma, Chanel snagged it for him and added it to his stack.

"Oooh that was a good one. I think it was his Father's Day message two or three years ago, but it is really popular."

Jason watched her lips move, but his mind raced. What could the man possibly say on the subject? Chanel touched his arm lightly with a puzzled look on her face realizing he had zoned out on her.

"Um...did you need anything else?"

Jason glanced around the bookstore. He had more than enough to keep him busy for a while.

"No, I think this is it."

Chanel moved toward the register, then paused.

"Did you bring your bible in here?"

His bible? He didn't even own one! Jason had to think fast. "No, I left it at home by accident. I didn't realize it until I got here."

"Well you know we have our own bible, right? Bishop Collins has created a Parallel Bible that most of us use, but since you already have your own, you probably don't need it." She flashed him a bright, beautiful smile.

"It has the King James Version and two more contemporary versions in it along with notes by Bishop Collins."

"I'll take it."

She was pleased and led him to the Bibles rattling off tidbits of information. Jason barely paid her any attention. His eyes were focused on two royal blue jacketed men hovering nearby.

He tuned back in when Chanel asked, "Which would you like, the paperback, the leather-bound, or the signature series?"

When in doubt, always go for the best.

"The signature series."

Chanel carefully took the one hundred and twenty-five-dollar bible from its shelf and cradled it in her arms.

As she led him to the checkout line, Jason continued to quiz her.

"This church definitely has a lot of ushers." He nodded his head toward the blue jackets.

"Oh, they aren't ushers, they are security." She smiled. "Everyone who shows up here isn't saved so…"

Jason nodded.

"They are some big guys. I doubt anyone in their right mind would give them any trouble."

Chanel nodded then gave him a once over.

"You're not exactly little. You could fit right in with them. If you decide to move to Raleigh and make this your church home, maybe you could join our security team!"

"You think so?"

Jason tried to appear surprised and flattered. Inside, his mind was whirling. His tour guide had just given him the best idea yet.

"How would I go about doing that?"

"Each ministry has a brochure and application at the Information Desk. You fill the application out and return it there. But you have to be a member first, of course."

They made a little more small talk during his transaction and then Jason gathered his bags and stepped away from the register. He thanked Chanel and made a beeline out of the store. Back in the lobby, Jason collected every bulletin, flyer, pamphlet, and brochure offered. He needed more information. He hadn't planned well and that was a big no-no. Now, he was back on course.

He poured on the charm and made polite small talk with some of the people stationed in the kiosks by the exit doors. It paid off well as he was able to learn that Bishop Collins never stayed in the pulpit through the end of the service. He wanted parishioners to come to the altar for Jesus, not him.

"So you mean to tell me he never interacts with his members?" Jason asked the volunteer who gave him that tidbit of information. He couldn't help thinking of all those suckers throwing their money at the preacher-man's feet and the man couldn't even be bothered to stop and pray for them?

"Oh sure he does. Sometimes he talks to people when they bring their offerings to the altar, but he's a busy man and this is a big church. He comes to as many of the departmental functions and celebrations as possible. He meets every new member that joins and..."

Bingo, Jason thought.

Time for Plan B.

***

Easter Sunday proved to be a grueling day for Victoria. She was used to spending an inordinate amount of time at church on Sundays, but this Sunday felt endless with all of the special elements added in during each service. She was worn out. Back at home, Victoria relaxed in a hot, lavender bubble bath in their Jacuzzi tub to cast away her long day. After the second service, James told her about Elder Carlton's vision and it troubled her. A dog, a chicken breast, and a banquet table. It sounded like the start of a very bad joke and Victoria could not make sense of any of it.

She had consulted her trusty dream interpretation book earlier in the evening, but what she found was more disturbing. Dogs represented fear, cowardice, strife, contention, offense, and unclean spirits. When James recounted the Elder's vision, the first thing that dropped in her spirit were the words "rabid dog" even before he said the words. Reading the book's interpretation of rabid dogs made her very uneasy. Was something evil headed their way?

Deep down Victoria knew what really bothered her. She thought about Lucy. Was Lucy the dog? Victoria had been able to pinpoint some of her issues in their brief time together, but she didn't have the full story. She needed more. Then again, she had all she needed to know about Quincy Stewart, Lucy's husband. God knows he acted like a dog.

Victoria had yet to share her luncheon story with James and the longer she waited, the harder it was to do it. She had consoled a sister-in-Christ and had lunch with her, was that a crime?

Oh who was she fooling? Although James didn't hold any malice toward Quincy Stewart, Victoria knew he wouldn't approve.

James stuck his head in the bathroom.

"Hey baby," she greeted him with a relaxed smile.

"Hey."

"Did you need me?"

"No. Can't a man watch his wife take a bath?"

James tried to force a laugh, but it lacked sincerity. He hadn't been completely "right" since Elder Carlton left his office earlier that day.

"Baby?"

"Yeah?" James replied with his brow raised.

"There's something I need to talk to you about."

James stepped into the bathroom and sat on the edge of the sink and struck his listening pose. Victoria took a deep breath, played with the bubbles in front of her, and spoke without looking at him.

"Remember when I had to cancel our lunch Friday?"

PART FOUR

REVELATION

24

Jason breezed back into Philly like he'd never left. His voicemail was crammed with pleas from his family to call them. Various friends had left early birthday greetings and suggestions for rowdy entertainment, but he deleted the messages without a second thought. He had a plan now and needed to put it in motion. The trip to North Carolina was not what he thought it would be, but it wasn't useless either.

Before unpacking a single item, he went to his desk, retrieved a business card and dialed the number.

"Hello?" A familiar husky voice filled his ear. He was convinced she did it on purpose.

"Amia? Hey baby, this is Jason."

"Well, well, well, Mr. White. What do I owe the uh… pleasure?"

Jason chuckled to himself. She always poured it on thick. "How have you been?"

"Let's cut the crap. What do you *need*?"

"You baby, you know I need you!"

"Umm hmmm…" She purred like Eartha Kitt. "So are you on your way over?"

"No, Sweetness. I'm in the middle of something, but I do need your help."

"Well I can't do very much for you if you're not here, now can I?"

"C'mon, girl. I'm serious. I need a favor."

"Sure, sugar, I'll do *anything*."

"I want to put my condo on the market."

Without missing a beat, Amia went from bedroom to business.

"Oh! Are you ready for something larger? I've got some nice…"

"I am moving out of town," Jason interjected and cut her sales pitch.

"Moving? Why?"

Oh here we go, he thought. Why did women ask a million questions?

"I got a new job making more money. You know me, gotta roll out. Can you handle that for me?"

"Awww, sure baby! You know I'll get you sold, but make sure you come by and see me before you leave town, OK?"

"You know it, Ma! I've got some stuff to handle tonight but you got me, right?"

"I said I would!"

"Alright, but listen, keep my leaving on the low, a'ight?"

"You got it!"

Amia was the realtor who helped him purchase his condo. She proved useful in a lot of ways. Although she wasn't officially part of his regular rotation, he kept the cougar around. She'd recently opened her own office handling sellers as well as buyers. He was glad to throw some business her way.

It's not like I lied to her, Jason reasoned. He *was* looking for a job and he *was* planning to move to North Carolina. He just didn't have all the details worked out yet. Suddenly, Jason stopped cold. Since when he did care if he lied to her or anyone else for that matter? For a second, he wondered if all the reading and video watching he'd been doing was getting to him. He didn't buy into all that religious bullshit. He was just trying to get to know Bishop Collins. This whole thing with his father had him acting out of character and he made a mental note to take some time to catch hold of himself and get centered.

After he hung up, Jason pulled out the Sunday Raleigh News and Observer newspaper he'd brought home with him and searched the classifieds again. There definitely seemed to be a need for people working in Electrical Engineering Management in the Raleigh-Durham area and he was more than qualified. He also planned to skim the web sites of a few professional organizations where he maintained a membership. They usually had the best leads anyway.

Getting a job was not a problem. He knew he was in high demand. Jason didn't see anything new, so he sat down at his computer and crafted cover letters to accompany his impressive resume. Normally, he would have had one of his ladies do it for him, but he didn't want to let anyone else know he was leaving.

The decision to move to Raleigh was a quick and easy one. When Jason left Abiding Grace Christian Church after the Easter Sunday service, he'd driven around the Raleigh/Durham Triangle area for hours thinking. It was a nice. It wasn't anything like the concrete jungle where he grew up. He enjoyed looking at the trees, lawns, and talking to the people. Raleigh didn't have everything he was used to in Philly, but he could make do. He could easily hop a flight anytime he got the urge for a good, soft, street pretzel or a cheesesteak hoagie.

Once he got the idea to leave Philly, it just felt right. He would move to Raleigh and work his situation with James Collins up close and personal. Back at his hotel, Jason had picked up a few real estate magazines and checked out the housing market. The houses were extremely inexpensive compared to what was available in Philadelphia. Raleigh began to look better by the hour.

Anyway, Philadelphia didn't challenge him anymore. Everywhere he went, he ran into at least one chick he'd rolled around in the sheets with. He had done the club thing and knew all the people worth knowing. He had fallen into a rut and North Carolina seemed like a promising new start. Jason was relieved he didn't have to worry about Donna anymore since she was living with their Aunt Theresa. He didn't believe he could do much more for his sister Faye, so moving to Raleigh really wouldn't make that much of a difference. On the one hand, every dime he gave to Faye, she wasted instead of using it for its intended purpose. If he bought whatever she claimed to need, she would sell whatever it was for more money to waste on foolishness. His nephews, Tyreese, Jamel, and Marquis, though, deserved so much better. If he didn't continue to help Faye, wouldn't he be just as guilty as his Aunt Theresa when she failed to help his mother?

The subsequent months were full of activity for Jason. Out of the four choice positions that Jason initially inquired about, three were chomping at the bit to get him. He had a few phone interviews and flew into Raleigh on several occasions to meet with prospective employers.

Each time he went to Raleigh, he made a conscious effort to schedule his interviews at a time when he could also attend a service at Abiding Grace Christian Church. With each visit, he became more and more acclimated with some of the faces there. One week, Bishop Collins was out of town and Jason had the opportunity to compare how things were done when the man was there and when he wasn't. All the information formed a database of miscellaneous facts in Jason's mind.

In mid-June, Jason accepted a position with Instatek Engineering Consortium, a Fortune 500 company located in the Research Triangle Park. They were willing to pay him thirty-five percent more than his current salary. With the cost of living difference, he made out like a bandit. His condo sold quickly and he only had to live in a hotel for a few days before he moved south. The hardest part came when he had to fill people in on his plans.

Finally, after tearful goodbyes at his aunt's house, he prepared to leave. No one received the news well, least of all his nephews. But they weren't the ones who had to live a lie all these years. They couldn't understand. He was ready to embrace his new life and finally get some answers about the past. Hoping to avoid further argument or inquiry, Jason left Philadelphia under the cover of darkness two days earlier than planned.

Thirty-six hours later after tearful goodbyes at his aunt's house, seeing his nephews and arguing
with Tyrone, Jason was finished. He had said goodbye to everyone he planned to say it to. He was
irritated at the way his news had been received, ready to embrace his new life and to get everything he felt
he was deserving of starting with some answers. So, under the cover of darkness, Jason checked out of his
hotel room two days early and left Philadelphia.

Thirty-six hours later after tearful goodbyes at his aunt's house, seeing his nephews and arguing
with Tyrone, Jason was finished. He had said goodbye to everyone he planned to say it to. He was
irritated at the way his news had been received, ready to embrace his new life and to get everything he felt
he was deserving of starting with some answers. So, under the cover of darkness, Jason checked out of his
hotel room two days early and left Philadelphia.

***

Lucy stared out of her bedroom window as her son, Michael, backed down the drive in his BMW. She rarely saw him anymore and it broke her heart. However, his frequent absences were preparing her for his departure for college in a few months. Going away to school would get him out of harm's way. After the incident at his high school graduation ceremony, Lucy wanted him as far away from that Stacy woman as possible. The memory never failed to boil Lucy's blood.

As Michael's graduation ceremony began, the Stewarts were seated on the Raleigh Civic Center floor facing the commencement stage. Just as the principal gave his opening remarks, a commotion stole Lucy's attention. She watched in horror as Stacy climbed over several seated families to get closer to the stage. She pressed on, in spite of the glares she received, until she made it to the row just below the Stewarts. Quincy saw her and had the nerve to smile. Lucy could have shot fire out of her eyes.

Who invited her?

Lucy cut her eyes at Quincy. She was livid. Each student was allotted a small number of invitations because of space. She had requested only two invitations, one for her and one for Quincy; other graduates had larger families. How did this heifer get an invitation, let alone three extra?

"Hi! Sorry we're late! These are my girlfriends Lisa, Quanda, and Jerica. Girls, this is Bishop Quincy Stewart."

Stacy made her introduction with a flourish. Her friends smiled and said hello even as people seated behind and beside the Stewarts shushed them.

"That's his wife, First Lady Lucy." Stacy added dismissively without even looking her way. Lucy didn't bother to react or respond to the lame introduction. She turned her head and stared at her husband who stared back unmoved. When Lucy would not break her gaze, his eyes went cold. The still fresh memory of Good Friday made her acquiesce. She tried hard to ignore the four women dressed in bright neon colors. Together, she thought they looked like a bag of Skittles.

Lucy managed to maintain composure even when Stacy took it upon herself to shout out to Michael, who then noticed them from the stage.

She has got some nerve!

Again, Lucy glanced at Quincy.

Have you no shame?

If it wouldn't have made an even bigger scene or led to a fight later on, Lucy would have walked out. But it was Michael's day and she was his mother.

After the ceremony, Stacy and company stayed close as if they were part of the Stewart party. Lucy glared at her. Stacy gave Lucy a prolonged frosty perusal as if to challenge the first lady. Just as she was about to put the church secretary in her place, Michael walked up with his black gown billowing about him.

"Class of 2002 in the Hiz-ouse!"

"Congratulations, Son. I'm proud of you!" Quincy beamed while patting Michael awkwardly on the back.

Michael hugged Lucy in a long embrace. Michael was flush with joy and a little embarrassment.

"We're fixin' to go eat. Where you want to..." Lucy began.

"My little Michael! Look at you! All grown up! You're a man now! Come meet my friends!"

Stacy swooped in and corralled Michael away from Lucy so fast, the first lady's mouth dropped open midsentence. Stacy had a proprietary arm wrapped around the young graduate as she introduced and gushed all over him. Lucy stared at Quincy, who finally seemed a bit uncomfortable but made a valiant effort to keep smiling.

"Sooo, I got you a little something. I know how much you like the water and Quanda has a condo at Myrtle Beach. She said you can use it for an entire week. How would you like me to take you to the beach before you go away to school?"

That was it. Lucy spun Michael around to face her.

"I don't think so!" She fumed. "If you want to go to the beach, we'll take you. You not goin' anywhere with her!"

"Bishop…" Stacy said wistfully, but Lucy barked an emphatic, "No!"

Lucy fired a look at Stacy that would melt steel. Full of the fury of seven hells, Lucy declared, "Let's go!" She marched out of the civic center and into the parking deck never once letting go of her son who was humiliated.

She was sure every bit of that incident would make its way into the church's grapevine before they made it home that night, but she didn't care. Stacy could have her husband and the sometimey people at church, but she was not getting Michael. Not her baby. She would kill over that boy.

It didn't matter to her what those people over Abundant Holiness thought anymore anyway. She had finally stopped going to the church. Quincy didn't ask her why or demand she show up and it was just as well. None of the older mothers who had been her prayer partners on Wednesday nights bothered to call and check on her. She could have been dying, but they didn't seem to care. To Lucy, it felt as if she no longer existed to anyone outside of the house.

On her last visit to Abundant Holiness, she had been ogled like a space alien. They whispered without even disguising their rudeness. Tired of the foolishness, she decided not to sit in the pulpit. She was certain Quincy would notice and call her up there, but he behaved as if he hadn't noticed her absence. With her back to the majority of the congregation, Lucy sat on the far end of the first row—far away from Stacy who sat directly in front of Quincy on the other end in her short skirts crossing and uncrossing her thick shapely legs and hanging onto his every word. Maybe she was sitting there to coach him.

Lucy refused to look Stacy's way. Instead she stared at the choir members' red robes. The gold stitching of the church acronym, AHCMMFBC, ran from their shoulders to their thighs. It had to be the longest set of letters a church ever had. She looked at anything except the man in the pulpit and the harlot in front of him. After the service, no one came to see about her needs or walk her back to Quincy's office.

If she wanna be the first lady so bad, she can have it. These folk are gonna turn on her just like they turned on me.

She hadn't been back since.

After the graduation ceremony, Lucy climbed the steps to her bedroom. She looked through the white banister rails and saw Quincy standing below glaring at her. His focus on her was unnerving. Her heart skipped a beat, as her gait stuttered as well.

Quincy's eyes traveled to her behind and he sneered as he watched it move from left to right as she climbed the stairs.

Jesus, no!

Unwanted memories flooded her mind as her wounded body seemed to throb in sync with them. She moved faster up the long flight of curved steps.

"Lucy!" He barked.

She broke into a run and stumbled up the last few steps into her bedroom. She locked it with shaking hands, even as Quincy's loud tread thundered up the steps. He pounded on the door.

"You hear me talkin' to you, woman? Open up the damn door!"

Lucy backed away from the vibrating door and looked for refuge. Her eyes spied a pair of her highest heeled shoes in her open closet. She hadn't worn them in years. She grabbed one intending to use its slender heel as a weapon.

"I said open this damn door and let me in. Don't make me say it again!"

The doorknob jiggled and a loud bang signaled Quincy had kicked the door. Lucy locked herself in her bathroom. She realized she should have grabbed her phone, but she didn't dare leave the safety of her en suite. Her eyes spied the disposable razor she used to shave her underarms on a shelf in the shower. With more strength than she knew she possessed, she broke it apart freeing the blades. Quincy could come in there if he wanted, but he was going to regret it.

After several very intense minutes, Quincy finally left her alone. She sat in the bathroom for several hours afraid to leave. If she hadn't already planned never to return to their church again, this was enough to seal the deal. How was she supposed to sit in that church knowing that within hours of preaching, he could rip her open again? At night, she kept her bedroom door locked and even pushed her chaise against it for extra security. Her razorblades were also hidden nearby, just in case.

Lucy pulled her robe around her body. She wanted to talk, but the available candidates were slim. She didn't feel like calling home. All her mother would talk about was the latest news in Lil' Washington and it was minor compared to what Lucy lived with every single day.

If Lucy called her sister Juanita, she'd eventually ask for money. Lucy wasn't going to be the bank for her anymore. The role got old several years and many defaulted "loans" ago. Lucy had talked to Daniel so much in the past that she'd run out of excuses to call him. Plus, if Quincy ever caught her speaking to Daniel on the phone, he would fly off the handle again. Lucy didn't want that. She prayed for Daniel to leave Abundant Holiness and get on with his life. Maybe he'd meet a nice girl, get married, have a few kids, and get his own church to pastor.

Lucy had often thought of Victoria Collins, but she never tried to contact her. After all, who was she fooling? They barely knew each other. Victoria simply caught her on a bad day and was nice to her. That was all. The woman probably hadn't given her a second thought. She doubted Victoria even remembered what they talked about.

A familiar knock at her door startled Lucy and she rose to unlock it. Marcelita was there and Lucy welcomed the company. It was all she could do not to hug the woman every time she saw her.

"Hola, Ms. Lucy! How are you today?"

"Fine! How are you?" Lucy grinned.

"I have great news! Guess what?"

Marcelita beamed at Lucy, clapping her hands together and rocking on her heels.

Lucy shook her head, her eyes reflecting the woman's excitement.

"Well…" Marcelita began, unable to keep the joy out of her voice. "A certain little boy has kept himself dry all night for a whole week!"

"What?!" Lucy squealed and high-fived her housekeeper.

"Aye, Ms. Lucy! Thank you so much. I did what you tell me and it worked! I hated having to keep getting up all the time all night, but he no pee the bed so I am glad!"

"I am so happy Marcelita! No more diapers and Pullups for you! He's your last one, right?"

"Yes. He is the baby, but he is almost five years old! I am tired of buying the big boy diapers, so I not sad for that. I am sad my baby is growing up."

The two women laughed. Little did Marcelita know but Lucy lived vicariously through her. Her stories made Lucy feel like she had a happier life. Lucy would shoulder Marcelita's burdens when she had a dilemma and got excited about her victories. If she'd had her way, Lucy would have had Marcelita move in with them so she could have a friend. But that would never happen. Quincy would not approve of it, especially because Marcelita was married with four children. The last thing he wanted was "a house full of Mexicans." He said he only hired them for cheap labor and tolerated them only as long as they did their jobs.

It was partly because of her husband's prejudices that Lucy constantly made an effort to treat their household help exceptionally well. She frequently slipped them monetary bonuses from her allowance. So far, Marcelita was her favorite and she was willing to do all she could to make sure she wouldn't quit like their other housekeepers. Lucy didn't blame any of them for leaving; she'd only wished she could too.

The ladies chatted, while Marcelita cleaned. All too soon it was time for Marcelita to leave and Lucy hated to see her go. She was a prisoner in her own house. Quincy's irrational behavior forced her to keep her bedroom door locked all day just so she could relax. She didn't trust that devil for one second.

With Marcelita gone, Michael out for the evening, and Quincy MIA, Lucy was bored and lonely. Sitting close to the TV, she tuned it to a popular Christian cable network, hoping to catch the Abiding Grace Broadcast. She never knew when Quincy would come home so she kept the volume low and sat close to the television. It had become her daily spiritual boost and gave her temporary peace of mind. It was hard to worry or be afraid with the way some of those preachers went at it. She listened to the sermons with an unprecedented hunger and even called into some of their prayer lines using a fictitious name. She was desperate to recapture the feeling she had when she prayed with Victoria Collins. Lucy felt God in that little diner and craved it now that she knew beyond a shadow of a doubt that it was possible.

Out of all of the ministries she viewed, the Abiding Grace broadcast was her favorite. The sermons were richly woven with good ol' life truths that made her see the Bible differently than she had before. More than anything, Lucy looked for a glimpse of the woman who had selflessly ministered to her on that afternoon months prior. In those brief moments, when the camera fell on the other First Lady, Lucy could keep in touch. Victoria appeared so happy, peaceful, content, and beautiful—everything that Lucy coveted. Victoria and James were often seen standing in their pulpit holding hands and smiling. Their connection was what Lucy had wanted once upon a time. It was what she thought she was getting when she married Quincy.

Some of Lucy's old jealousies resurfaced and her tortured heart manufactured bitterness. Victoria had everything, while Lucy had nothing. Lucy found herself lost in a cyclical paradox of envying the very woman she also admired. No matter how hard she tried, Lucy could not let go. Why didn't God love her like He loved everybody else? What was so wrong with her that everyone treated her so badly all of the time? She couldn't seem to shake the thick cloud of depression that surrounded her. She hadn't taken her pills in almost three months, but each time Marcelita brought them to her, the temptation to indulge became greater and greater.

25

Victoria sat at her desk with a small, pink piece of stationary clasped between her delicate hands. She thought of Lucy Stewart daily and waited patiently to hear from her, but it never happened. They were supposed to keep in touch and reunite for lunch again, but that hadn't happened either. She was concerned about her sister-in-Christ and she longed to hear from her.

Victoria woke from some very disturbing dreams about Lucy over the last few months and always prayed earnestly for her afterwards. James told her to leave the Stewarts' situation alone, but she couldn't. She couldn't help feeling like she and Lucy had bonded spiritually and was sure Lucy needed a friend.

When Victoria shared the details of her afternoon with her husband, James listened intently without uttering a sound. She wanted him to show some emotion or say something but he didn't. When he finally responded, his voice was heavy. She regretted not coming clean sooner.

James Collins trusted his wife but her confession thrust him between rock and a hard place. Victoria possessed uncanny discernment. He never doubted that she felt led by the Holy Spirit to help Lucy Stewart, but after hearing Elder Carlton out, he shared her concerns.

If the Stewarts represented the wild dog, then it very well may have been a warning for her to leave them and their business alone. She could always pray for them from a distance. The Holy Spirit would easily bridge the gap. James preached that message time and time again.

At the same time, though, he didn't want to tie his wife's hands if God was leading her in a different direction.

"Vick, I can't tell you what to do on this. I'm not getting the mind of God on this one way or another. I need to really pray about it. As your husband, though, I really think that you need to leave well enough alone. Don't disregard the Holy Spirit to comply with my wishes, but...be careful."

Victoria nodded through teary eyes. The situation weighed heavily on her and she couldn't help getting weepy. James patted her arm lovingly and walked out of the bathroom. The bath water had turned lukewarm, but she sat a while longer. She'd hoped to get clearer direction, but all she heard in her heart was: *pursue.*

***

As the bright June sun forced its way between the slats in the blinds, James left Victoria alone in their bedroom and busy at her desk. He went through his office, and into his prayer room. It was formerly a walk-in closet for the bedroom turned office, but he had transformed it into a place where he could commune with God undisturbed. He sat down with his back against the wall and his long legs extended. He stared at the closed door in front of him. A favorite worship song filled his head. He hummed a familiar tune and James rocked from side to side slowly, as his heart recited the lyrics.

Speak to my heart, Holy Spirit. Give me the words that will bring new life. Words on the wings of a morning, the dark nights will fade away, if you speak to my heart.

Lately, it seemed harder and harder to clear his head. He desired a direct, unpolluted channel into the presence of God. What used to take him a couple of minutes, now took ten times as long. This was an unfamiliar spiritual space and his soul was disquieted. The past few months left him weary. There seemed to be a gray cloud hanging over everything and it even dampened Christian's college graduation.

Normally every Collins family member was celebrated with fanfare, but his daughter's big day was strangely low key. Because it was also Mother's Day, Victoria and Christian were joint guests of honor at an unusually sedate family dinner. Everyone appeared to be caught up in his or her own thoughts. Everyone except Caleb, of course. James' youngest son complained about the overall mood he sensed and declared them all a bunch of boring old people as he rushed into the basement to play videogames. James loved his youngest son's spirit. He wished he could be as unburdened.

James didn't mention it to Victoria or even Elder Carlton, but he'd dreamt about his childhood dog, Spanky, again. The dreams began shortly after talking to Elder Carlton on Easter Sunday and had increased over the past few months. Many times the dreams started innocuous. But then they would shift and Spanky would appear out of the blue. Sometimes the dog would simply stroll through a room and other times the mutt would seemingly run or play in the background of an unrelated dream sequence. He was a tiny blip at first, and would magnify until he was the star. And just as soon as he appeared, he was gone.

Initially, James excused the dreams as a by-product of hearing Elder Carlton's vision. But the dreams were hard to dismiss. Through them, James had recalled people he hadn't seen or thought about in over twenty-five years. Friends. Women. Experiences. The only thing that linked them was Spanky's presence.

He prayed about the disturbing trend, but couldn't soothe his troubled mind. Maybe he was too emotionally invested to hear from God properly. The only thing that James got from his prayer time was an increasing sense of dread. It seemed red flags were everywhere, but James couldn't figure out what they meant. James sat in his prayer closet and sought the Lord yet again. God was strangely silent. He'd given the requisite thanks and repented feverishly to no avail. He'd have to be patient and wait, a lesson he could preach but not easily implement himself.

***

Victoria stared thoughtfully at the envelope for a moment before rising to leave. She needed to contact Lucy and believed she had devised a sure-fire method to accomplish that goal. She had tried everything else. She'd visited Margo's Closet and hung around making frivolous conversation waiting to see if Lucy would show up. She even casually asked Margo about First Lady Stewart. It was if Lucy had fallen off of the face of the earth. After running out of options, Victoria decided to go back to Margo's one more time with a definitive plan of action.

26

Margo unpacked the new deliveries and marveled at the garments inside. She'd discovered a new designer at the buyer's mart earlier in the year and this was her first shipment. They were classy, sassy, elegant, and fiercely unique. There seemed to be a little something in her shipment for all of her frequent customers.

The package could not have come at a better time. Business wasn't bad, but it certainly could have been better. People weren't coming in the shop the way they used to, but when they shopped, they made large purchases. Lucy Stewart, most noticeably, hadn't been in the shop for months. In fact, Margo didn't think she'd seen her since the suit incident on Good Friday. Everything appeared to end peacefully that day, but First Lady Stewart hadn't returned as promised. Her husband had come in a few times, but Margo did not wait on him. Something about that man gave her the creeps. She always felt like he leered at her. He never failed to pick out the same bright heavily ornate style of suits for his wife but Margo didn't feel they were a flattering cut for her. Nevertheless, she didn't think Bishop Stewart would appreciate her honest opinion the way his wife did.

Margo hung up the new pieces and called Regan to steam. Margo had called her best clients to let them know about the new shipment. Maybe her personal touch would create the shopping traffic she was accustomed to. She didn't like standing around the store twiddling her thumbs. Margo reached several clients, but when she got Victoria Collins' voicemail, she was disappointed. She had counted on connecting with her. It was a guaranteed sale if not an absolute buyout with First Lady Collins. Margo decided to put a few pieces aside for her until she could reach her. After all, not only was she Margo's best customer, she was a walking billboard for the shop.

When Margo got to the S's, she hesitated over Lucy Stewart's card wondering if she should she call her. What if her recent absence was due to her being offended over First Lady Collins' Easter suit?

Well there's only one way to find out.

After a few rings, a bright, melodious voice answered the phone.

"Good afternoon, Bishop Stewart's residence."

"Good afternoon. May I please speak with Mrs. Stewart?"

"May I ask who is calling, please?"

"This is Margo from the boutique."

"One moment."

Margo couldn't help smiling. The person on the other line was so jovial that it was contagious. She heard another line pick up and a familiar voice said, "Thank you, Marcelita."

There was the subtle click of a receiver resting in its cradle when her client proceeded. "This is Mrs. Stewart."

"Lady Stewart this is Margo from Margo's Closet, how are you?"

There was a painful pause and Margo didn't know if she should continue speaking or wait for a response.

"Yes, Margo. What can I do for you?"

Margo could not interpret Lucy's tone. Her voice sounded decidedly older, heavier, and more tired than she remembered.

"I just wanted to check on you. I hadn't seen you in a while…"

Margo let her statement hang in the air, as she silently debated if she should bring up the fact that Victoria Collins had asked about her as well. She decided against it. No need to get into something that was none of her business.

"My husband been doin' my shoppin' lately."

"Yes, I have seen him in here. I hope you're well?"

The uncomfortable silence returned and Margo didn't know where to go from there.

"I received some new things in today and thought you may want to see them for yourself. Are you familiar with Estelle Claire?"

Lucy knew the name and her ears perked up slightly. "Yes!"

"Well I handpicked several pieces...one of a kind. I doubt you will see anyone in this area wearing these. They came in today and I wanted you to be able to have first pick before they're all gone." She lied. In Lucy Stewart's size, she probably *would* have first pick.

"Well thank you, Margo. It was nice of you to call."

Was that a thank you but no thank you?

Lucy Stewart's tone was flat. Margo had done all she was going to do and wasn't trying anymore with this woman.

"Okay, well you take care and I'll see you next time you stop by."

"Thank you for calling."

Margo hesitated, then quickly said goodbye before she heard the click of First Lady Stewart's receiver. She knew Lucy Stewart could be intense but she had never known her to be *that* rude! Margo shrugged it off. In her business, the divas and wannabe divas could have their moods. She was still tempted to snatch that one card out of her file and trash it, but instead, she continued down her list and called her other clients. As she contemplated the move, Regan barged into Margo's office with all of the graciousness of a charging bull.

"That woman wanna see you."

"What woman?" Margo asked with marked agitation. Sometimes the girl had absolutely no grace. Margo honestly didn't know why she kept her around; she was a liability.

"Collins." Regan said, pursing her lips like the name tasted badly.

"Victoria Collins?" Margo jumped to her feet and brushed past Regan muttering a sharp, "Excuse me."

"Yessuh, Massa," she grumbled under her breath. She closely followed behind her boss to get a front row seat to another potential spectacle.

Victoria nervously glanced around the shop. As she ran a silk camisole through her fingers, Margo breezed onto the sales floor gushing.

"First Lady Collins! How are you? I just tried to call you, but got your voicemail. I received some *very* lovely things in today that you have *got* to see!"

Victoria smiled. Margo tried so hard. It was almost too painful to watch at times.

"So I see. I look forward to seeing them, but I actually came here for another reason."

Regan's ears perked up as she heard Victoria Collins' reply. What would she want with Margo other than some clothes? Her recent actions pricked panic in her mind. Regan had told Jennifer about seeing Victoria Collins and Lucy Stewart doing it in the dressing room before Easter. She didn't think her best friend had told anyone, but what if she did? Regan was antsy and moved closer to hear everything. She'd curse Jennifer out later.

Victoria glanced up in time to see Margo's assistant hovering in the shadows. She didn't care for that girl. She got the distinct impression that the child was devious.

"Is there somewhere we can talk?"

Margo was flustered. Had she done something wrong? Was there a problem with a previous purchase? Not knowing what to expect, she stammered out her reply.

"Uh well...uh...we can go in my off--"

"Let's step outside."

Victoria didn't want to be in earshot of the eavesdropper and anywhere indoors would be fair game for the little sneak.

"I'll be right back," Margo shouted over her shoulder to Regan who appeared to ignore her as she positioned herself by the front window so she could at least see the two women talking.

Victoria looked up and made direct eye contact with Regan through the glass. The girl was bold! She neither blinked nor looked away. Victoria turned her back to the little spy, looked her favorite boutique owner squarely in her face, and spoke quickly.

"Margo, I've been shopping with you almost from day one and I think we've developed a trusting relationship, right?"

Margo nodded, but her heart was in her throat.

"You've always been honest with me and graciously hooked me up with things that make me look good. I appreciate that. You've never let me walk out of your establishment with something that would make me look bad even if it cost you a sale, right?"

"Right!" Margo stood a little taller. She prided herself on those things and having Victoria Collins notice and respect those traits made them even more important to her.

"I've always counted on your discretion and integrity. That's one of the reasons why I give you all my business. Now, I need your help with an important personal matter." Victoria paused and surveyed Margo's serious expression before she continued.

"I need you to contact Lucy Stewart for me. It's an emergency."

"Well I don't know what I could do," Margo stammered. "I don't have the same type of relationship with her that I have with you so--"

"This is all I need you to do." Victoria slipped the dainty envelope out of her pants pocket and pressed it into Margo's hand. She glanced at Tina. Her eyes were trained on the store, which undoubtedly meant that the little snoop was still busy.

"I need you and you *only* to give this directly to Mrs. Stewart. Do *not* give it to her husband or anyone else — only to *her*. And please, don't let *anyone* even see you giving it to her. Can you do that for me please?"

Margo's face was solemn as she nodded her head firmly. She would not disappoint her most important client even if it meant calling that evil woman again. Victoria's face warmed with Margo's assurances and she thanked her.

"Now, let me spend some money," Victoria said in a more jovial tone. She motioned to Tina to join them then led a bewildered Margo back into the boutique.

27

Lucy stared at the note in her lap and read its contents again: *Lucy, I need to speak with you. It is urgent. You have been in my spirit constantly and I think it is time we got together again. Please call me even if you choose not to meet with me. I am really concerned about you and how you are doing. Please stay in touch.*

Victoria's phone numbers were listed at the bottom just in case Lucy had misplaced them. Lucy stared into space, unsure of what to do. She had been so sure Victoria Collins wasn't giving her a second thought, but this note proved otherwise. Lucy placed the note back in its envelope and put it in her safe next to Victoria's business card. She was still confused and the last thing she needed was to drag anyone else into that confusion.

***

Rolling over, Victoria opened her eyes and looked at the clock. It was almost midnight and her sleep had been disturbed again. She glanced at James snoring contentedly. She wanted to pout, but being prompted to pray for someone was a privilege. Still, Victoria knew when she got to heaven she planned on asking God what He had against afternoon prayer time.

She laid in bed a few more minutes and prayed silently. When she caught herself nodding off, she got up and went into the bathroom. She tried praying using what Lucy shared, but Victoria was incredibly tired. It had been weeks since she left the note for Lucy at Margo's boutique. Margo confirmed Lucy's receipt of it and that all but let Victoria know that she didn't want to talk to her. Apparently God knew different, so He kept waking her up. Victoria could only hope Lucy was losing sleep too. At least there would be some justice in Victoria's restless nights. She sat on the commode lid and prayed until there were no more words. Then she let the Holy Spirit do the rest

.

28

The praise and worship at Abiding Grace was especially powerful on this particular Sunday. The music and arts ministry had gone over their allotted time, but Bishop Collins insisted the service never run on man's schedule. Only God's. For that reason, the church didn't pass out programs or bulletins. Bishop Collins desired for God to set the tone and agenda every time they met for worship, not some folded up piece of paper. A spirit of unity filled the church and liberated the congregation as their voices joined in sincere praise.

Lucy Stewart sat crouched in the balcony enjoying it all. She'd watched this on television, but the feeling in the sanctuary was something else. She never felt anything of that magnitude before. Lucy waved her arms first timidly and then boldly, her limbs seemed to swim amongst the sea of worshippers. She wanted to dive in and bathe herself in its sweetness.

In a flash of self-consciousness, she adjusted her hat in order to shield her face. She feared someone would recognize her from the huge, tacky billboard Quincy had purchased on the Beltline. Lucy tried to downplay her style of dress for the day, but everything she owned was bright. She stuck out like a sore thumb and it made her nervous.

Glancing over at the woman next to her, Lucy envied her freedom. Marcelita and her family had accompanied her to Abiding Grace and she, in particular, seemed to float carelessly on the wave of worship. All she had to do was let herself go and trust the Spirit to carry her, but fear had her bound, at least initially. When she finally threw caution to the wind, she jumped to her feet, lifted her voice, and began to sing as loudly as she could. She was happy to be in church again. It had been a long time coming. She felt like a tiny leaf caught up in a rushing mighty wind[13] and it was the most edifying thing she'd done for herself in a long time.

***

On the main floor, below Lucy Stewart's seat in the balcony, Jason White closed his eyes and allowed the singing to envelop him. Since he'd officially became a North Carolina resident, he had faithfully attended every single service for the past month and this particular song was a favorite. The singing quieted the voices in his head. It temporarily soothed the burning anger in his heart, and it made him forget the pain that so frequently fueled it. He'd become better acclimated to the flow of service and actually looked forward to going.

Who would have ever thought that he would be in church three times a week, every week? Although he would feign sincerity during other church rituals, his participation during praise and worship was authentic. He allowed himself to clap, rock to the music, and even sing a little bit. He hadn't graduated to the whole hand raising or crying thing though. Something seemed soft about it and he didn't want to be seen that way. He'd developed a fan club, which watched him constantly and he felt more compelled to maintain his cool.

Yet, something was different this Sunday. Somehow he just knew it would be the day he would get the opportunity to look that man in the eye and finally put his plan in motion.

Bishop Collins came out from the back earlier than normal and as the people left their money on the edge of the stage, he hugged them, shook their hands, kissed their babies, smiled, and said a few words. There was a time when Jason would have rushed up to the stage and taken advantage of the moment, but he'd changed his tactics. Now he was more focused, more deliberate. He was patient. If the people wanted to be stupid, let them. They could give their beloved bishop as much money as they wanted, it would all be Jason's anyway.

A smirk formed on Jason's lips. His train of thought was interrupted by the short skirt and big thighs sitting next to him. If she

219

moved any closer, she would end up sitting on his lap. She wasn't his type and as much as he ignored her, she continued to do everything conceivable to make her presence known. Her desperation turned his stomach.

This nonsense started when he visited from Philadelphia, but since he moved to North Carolina, it was out of control. Even though Jason was used to having women chase him, he didn't really expect it at church. Not in the ways that he'd seen it since he'd been coming there. It seemed like every time he pulled into the parking lot at least one woman shoved a business card in his hand, left her number on his car, pressed up against him, or threw herself at him. Discretion was in small supply.

Jason felt stalked and somewhat disappointed. It wasn't like he was Mr. Christian now or anything but he had watched the singles videos he purchased on his first trip. He read the books and heard the sermons. Their pastor gave them great advice on how to conduct themselves as women-of-God. Much of what Bishop Collins said made sense and Jason couldn't argue with it. Either these chicken-heads missed those teachings or didn't care to follow through on their pastor's advice. There was a time not too long ago when he would have seized the opportunity to hump and dump his way through the entire building, but that incident with Nadine at his mother's funeral seemed to have left him more than a little paranoid. Before he hooked up with another female, he had to make sure he did his due diligence. Once he felt comfortable, it would be on. But until then, he would just take matters into his own hands. God help the next woman because he had a backlog of loving to let loose.

He often thought about the beautiful woman who'd shown him around the bookstore on his first visit. She seemed pretty cool and he wouldn't mind running into her again. What puzzled Jason the most was he recognized many of the women, especially those who got on his nerves. They performed with the dance troop, sang in the choir, worked in the bookstore, and did other prominent things at church. He eventually realized that a person didn't have to act saved or know much to participate. Some of the very ones he saw running up to the altar crying and falling out like they were crazy, pushed up on him thirty minutes later in the hallway like they had never been prayed over.

There was nothing Jason hated more than a fake woman. Which was interesting because part of what bothered him was he fact that he really thought what he was experiencing at Abiding Grace was real.

There were even times when Jason was tempted to go down to the altar with everyone else. He just couldn't bring himself to do it. Sometimes Jason thought something really special, almost magical, happened there at the altar. But then, after seeing how these women acted, he knew that nothing could be really happening. It was just another well-orchestrated show.

Regardless of what *their* motives were, Jason purposed to concentrate on the service. More specifically, on the hypocrite who was trying to convince him of how he should live. Every time James Collins said something funny, Miss Desperation sitting next to Jason would nudge him then lean over and laugh. He ignored her. He should have moved earlier, but now that service was just about over, he decided to stick it out. He was on a mission and firmly believed—no, he *knew*—this would be the Sunday he had been waiting for.

Just as Jason shifted his body away from the pest next to him, he thought he heard it. He looked around and saw some people moving out of their seats. He stood up holding his bible.

"Again, if you believe the Lord has called you to be a part of this church family, come forward now, so we may receive you."

He'd been waiting all month to hear the invitation.

Much to his needy neighbor's dismay, Jason quickly moved out of the row and away from her. He was finally going to join the church. Jason had never joined one before. Although he told himself he was doing it just for the opportunity to meet his father face to face, he secretly felt like he'd made his mother's spirit happy.

As the band played a high-spirited tune, Jason made his way to the expansive area in front of the stage with about thirty or forty other people. Standing in front of all of those thousands of smiling faces was intimidating. Seeing the church from this vantage point made it feel even bigger. He wasn't sure what he was supposed to do, so he mimicked everything the guy next to him did. Jason wasn't "saved" but he believed that there was a God and that was good enough for him. He joined a church; he wasn't asking to preach a sermon or anything.

The new members were ushered out of the church sanctuary down a long, brightly lit hall. Along the way, ushers sporadically smiled and greeted them. As they turned a corner, they were led into a large, elaborately decorated meeting room. Jason looked around. The space was nicer than some of the five-star hotels he had been in! It was full of dark woods, bright bursts of the church's blue and gold colors and outfitted with furniture fit for a three-diamond establishment. James Collins spared no expense when it came to aesthetics.

A middle-aged Asian woman stood on a small platform in the front of the room. With a sharp commanding voice, she called the crowd to order, and gave them instructions with all the flair of a drill sergeant.

"Good Afternoon, Brothers and Sisters. I am Elder Li and I am the Minister of Membership Training. I would like to thank you for your interest in joining the Abiding Grace family. We believe each of you has something valuable to contribute to our church and we are excited to have you here. While we thank you for your interest in Abiding Grace, you're not members yet."

She turned her head slowly allowing her eyes to travel over the lot of them. For a brief second, she met each one of their eyes.

"In order to become an actual member of your church you will be required to attend a three-month New Members class. It meets at seven o'clock on Sunday mornings, every Sunday, rain or shine."

A low groan spread across the room and a few of the current members chuckled.

"You are allowed two absences. In the event that you are absent, you are responsible for getting the information and/or materials you missed. Understood?"

No one responded.

"If you miss more than two classes, you will be dropped from the roll and you will need to retake the course once it is offered again."

Elder Li held up four books, one at a time.

"These are your textbooks. You will be required to purchase them from the church bookstore. As a member in training, you receive a discount. If the cost is a challenge, we do offer scholarships to help aid your purchase."

A fellow member yelled out a question.

"Will there be a test?"

It lightened the mood and made everyone laugh until Elder Li replied.

"Yes. You will have one test every month so there will be three in all. Failure to pass a test will result in your having to repeat the course."

A hum went around the room as the shock of what they had gotten themselves into set in. Jason was relieved. He wasn't the only one who thought this was over the top. They were joining a church, not enrolling in grad school. No wonder James Collins had people throwing money at his feet. He probably brainwashed them in the guise of this new members' class! Jason wasn't worried. He was a good student and had developed a strong will.

Elder Li was unmoved by the buzzing crowd. She lifted her tiny hand and silenced the room without uttering a word.

"You must understand that you are joining a powerful army of the Lord and in order for our platoon to be effective, we have to be on one accord. This means we have to be on the same page."

Jason understood the logic, but still. As far as he was concerned, this whole thing was excessive and he was skeptical.

"It may seem like a lot, but thousands of people with various educational, cultural, and environmental backgrounds mastered this class the first time around long before you," she assured them. "Look at the person to the left and right. Get to know them. Make friends. Have study get-togethers. They are on this journey with you," she continued. "Please enjoy the refreshments we have prepared and use this time to ask the existing members any questions you may have."

Puzzled, several of the newbies began to look around for the refreshments. Unsure of where to go, many conversed amongst themselves. Suddenly, a low whirling sound drew their attention to the rear wall, which collapsed and revealed a palatial reception hall.

Waiting for them was a receiving line of smiling faces, and the first was James Collins.

29

Jason swallowed hard. He'd waited for this moment for what seemed like forever and now that it had come, he was deeply moved by the reality of it. His mouth felt dry and his feet weighted. He'd never considered how he'd react when they met. Now that the defining moment had come, Jason fought to maintain his composure.

The crowd of members and newbies filed past him as he stood awestruck. Most of them entered the elegantly decorated hall before he could manage to take a first step. A member of the orientation staff walked up alongside of him.

"Impressive, isn't it? I was surprised the first time I saw it myself."

"Uh… yeah," Jason replied without looking at the person who spoke to him. His eyes were fixed on James Collins. "I, uh, wasn't expecting that."

Realizing his odd behavior, Jason quickly regained his arrogant demeanor and fell in line behind some of the other Abiding Grace neophytes. Each step took him closer and closer to the man who was supposed to be his father.

As the line inched along, Jason kept his eyes on the pastor's every movement. A steel jawed security guard materialized at the Bishop's left elbow assessing each person who approached. Jason could only assume the man was poised to strike should any encounter with the Bishop prove to be less than friendly. He watched James Collins smile broadly at each member trainee, shake hands, have a brief conversation, and then send them on their way. The anticipation surrounding his turn almost made Jason lose it. A few folks took a little too long chatting with the pastor, but Bishop Collins didn't seem to mind at all.

Jason speculated about what he would say once he finally got his turn. What exactly was a person supposed to say the first time he speaks to the man who jacked up the lives of his entire family?

The closer Jason got, the clearer his view became of the petite woman standing next to her husband. She was so small, she looked like a child compared to the large man next to her. Jason had to admit she looked even better than her pictures.

He has good taste.

She was attractive, but she wasn't as beautiful as his mother had been. This woman lacked the earthiness of his mother; a way about her that she'd worn like a badge of honor. The Bishop's wife looked too fragile and Jason couldn't help but feel contempt for her. She was the woman his father married instead of his mother. Jason wondered if she ever worked three jobs to take care of anyone a day in her life. He knew she hadn't and it made him hate her more. She met his gaze and gave him a warm smile. Jason looked away; he didn't have anything for her. She had already taken enough away from him.

After more than twenty minutes of waiting, Jason found himself face to face with his biological father. Jason was disappointed when he realized he fell a couple of inches shorter than him. He wanted to loom over the preacher and not being able to, added to his resurging fury. Jason's previous state of anxiety suddenly turned to full-fledged anger—surprising even him. It was all he could do not to jump on James Collins right there and pummel the hell out of him. For an awkward moment, Jason clenched and unclenched his fists. He felt the sweat form in his palms and figured he better act now and get it over with or scrap the whole thing.

The two men stood eye-to-eye, toe-to-toe for a tense second before Jason wiped his right hand on his trousers leg and slowly reached out to accept the pastor's freely extended one. He then quickly withdrew it again. He didn't want the man touching him. Jason struggled to hide his contempt as he carefully took in every mole and every line on the bishop's face. James Collins spoke to him, but Jason's mind was so full that all he could hear was the fierce beating of his heart. He gave a weak smile. Bishop Collins looked a little confused and gave a lopsided smile. He slowly asked, "Your *name*, son. What is your name?"

Son. That word shot darts into Jason's heart. He'd never felt this much contempt for anyone in his life. Through his peripheral vision, Jason noticed the security guard shift his weight. Jason wasn't deterred.

"Jason White," he replied with an unnatural amount of bass in his voice. He stared Bishop Collins straight in the eyes without blinking.

For a split second, James felt uneasy. He sensed something off about the young man in front of him, but he couldn't put his finger on it. And when he called him son, he could've sworn he saw hatred flash in his eyes. But to James' knowledge there was no reason for the young man to hate him. He'd never seen him before a day in his life. Maybe he took the term of endearment as condescension. Despite his first impression, James greeted the young man warmly.

"Well, welcome Jason White. We're glad you want to be part of our family!"

Jason couldn't hear anything else.

You have got to be kidding me!

Did this man know what he was saying? First the whole "son" thing and now "welcome to the family"? He felt his self-control slip and fought to regain it. He managed it just in time to hear the Bishop ask, "How long have you been visiting with us?"

"About six or seven months. I just relocated to the area."

"Well praise God! It's nice to have you here with us!"

Now it was Jason's turn to nod his head up and down slowly while giving the Bishop a clean head to toe sweep.

The Bishop's wife took her cue and extended her tiny, delicate hand. It was warm and soft. He didn't want to indulge her sweetness and part of him wished she'd disappear.

"Hello, Jason! It is so nice to meet you. I'm Victoria Collins, but you may hear some of the members call me Lady Vicky." She gave a polite laugh. Jason managed another fake, but charming smile.

"Please make yourself at home," She said with a delicate pat to his forearm.

Face to face she was incredible. His plan would be even better if he could turn her out and make her leave dear old dad for him. Then, he'd turn around and dump her as a bit of karma for her trifling ass. Maybe then she would know what his mother had to live with all her life.

Jason nodded at the First Lady and moved past the Collins' so the next newbie in line could say hello. He'd finally met the man, so he quickly made his way down the line shaking hands with people and avoiding any further conversation. Jason was ready to end the whole meet-n-greet session.

Bishop Collins' eyes tracked Jason's movements as he continued to greet the other new members. Jason's name burned in his brain. There was something about that boy that James could not shake and he was determined to find out what it was.

After Jason shook his last hand, he made his way over to the hors d'oeuvres. He'd been too anxious to eat breakfast, but after all the hoopla, his body was ready for sustenance. Just as he began placing fruit on his plate, the beautiful woman he'd lusted after on the praise team breezed into the room from a side door hastily giving apologies for her tardiness to everyone who crossed her path. He took a long look at her and continued placing food on his plate. He kept an eye on her. Today was her lucky day. He had every intention of rolling up on *that*. It had been too long and he needed a release. Maybe he could teach her how to hit some new high notes if she played her cards right.

"Her name is Chris," a vaguely familiar, deep voice said a little too close to Jason's left ear.

Jason turned to see the face of the orientation staff member who'd spoken to him earlier. Jason gave the man an acknowledging head nod and tried to bypass him. Instead of moving off, the man extended his hand. Jason begrudgingly accepted it. He wanted to get rid of the man before his dessert could walk away.

"I'm Darryl Newkirk. How long have you been visiting with us?" he asked.

Is that the standard question? They probably taught that in their new members' indoctrination too.

"About six or seven months," he replied while following Chris with his eyes.

As a reformed predator, Darryl could smell a familiar stench on Jason and he wasn't about to see one of Abiding Grace's young sisters go out like that. Especially not *that* one.

"Actually, her name is Christian Collins," Darryl said. "She's Bishop and Lady Vicky's daughter." Darryl eyed Jason to gauge the new member's reaction. The information had its intended effect and Darryl was satisfied. Jason was disappointed and was likely no longer interested. Darryl couldn't resist teaching this newbie a lesson about how they did things at AGCC.

"Would you like to meet her?" He asked.

"Sure!"

To Darryl's surprise, Jason called his bluff and now he was going to have to deliver. The two men made their way over to her. Seeing them approach, Chris' face lit up with a bright smile. Her entourage stepped forward almost blocking her, but she pressed past them.

"Hey, Darryl!" she said, giving him a quick side squeeze.

"Hey, Chris. This is Jason. He's just joined the new members class."

"Oh, OK! Well nice to meet you Jason!" She grinned.

"Likewise," he said slowly. He could barely look her in the eye.

She's my half-sister? Damn!

"You have an accent. Where are you from?" Chris asked, fixing her eyes on his as he glanced up.

He wasn't sure if she was trying to flirt, but he couldn't touch her now anyway. Not until he figured out if what his aunt told him was true.

"Philadelphia."

"Oh great! I was up there about a year ago or whenever it was the last time daddy went there to preach! So what brought you *here*? School? Job?"

Inside, Jason shuddered at the realization that James Collins had been in Philadelphia and he didn't know anything about it. On the outside, he smiled at the fact that she still called her father daddy.

"Actually, I moved here to be closer to my family and was able to find a job. It all worked out."

"That's wonderful. So does your family come here too?"

Amused, Jason eyed her and couldn't hide his cat-that-swallowed-the-canary smile. She smelled of sweetness, innocence, naïveté, and everything that was bubble-gum good. Her face was a perfect oval and now that he knew the deal, he could see she favored her mother quite a bit. She had an angular nose that had a cute way of wrinkling as she heartily ate from a plate someone handed to her as she talked with him.

Christian wasn't petite like her mother but she was thick in all the right places. Jason tried to keep his eyes focused but it was a challenge. Every man standing near her had the same glazed look on his face, and that included Jason's self-appointed babysitter, Darryl. Immediately, he switched to Plan C. There was no use putting all of those goodies to waste.

"Actually, yes," he responded and wanted to laugh at the irony of it all.

Before she could inquire further, a few other people rudely joined their conversation. Jason quietly slipped away, but not before noticing an intense stare from one of her guards. He returned the look and held his gaze before exiting the group. He wasn't scared of these clowns. What happened to the welcome wagon? Did talking to Lil' Miss Chris cause them to unhitch it?

Across the room, James Collins took in the interaction between the young man and his daughter. Devion Clarke picked up on it as well and went into bulldog security mode. He was about to signal Chris' security detail to interrupt her conversation when James touched his arm to stop him.

"She's OK," he said quietly, keeping his eyes trained on the situation. Nothing inappropriate happened and there was no need to cause an unnecessary scene. In his mind, James ran down the extremely short list of men his daughter had dated. Had Jason White been one of the few that James had run off? He didn't think so but he couldn't shake the sense that he was dealing with a very personal grudge. Even if his intuition was correct, he had no idea what the grudge was about.

James' best guess was that it had to do with something he'd preached, but if that were the case, why join his church?

Devion nodded, agreeing to James' request to stand down, but not agreeing with his pastor's assessment. Devion did not like this new kid. Everything in his spirit told him that this one was trouble. He didn't like the way the punk came off or the way he looked at Christian. Devion was determined to get this Jason's new members' card and do a thorough background check on him before he got any further access to the Bishop, his family, or their church.

James Collins watched Jason leave the crowd surrounding Christian and take up residence in the conference room. Something about the young man both troubled and fascinated James. He decided that maybe he needed to try to spend some one on one time with him like he used to do with so many other members back in the beginning of his ministry. James really missed that one-on-one interaction and jumped at the challenge of personal discipleship.

Without hesitation, James moved across the room in Jason's direction. Devion was on his heels, but halfway across the room, James told Devion to back off. He obeyed, but remained close enough to neutralize the situation, if necessary. When it came to his pastor and friend, Devion trusted a precious few. The boy could be another jilted boyfriend, someone the Bishop pissed off in one of his many ministerial trips, or a hired hand courtesy of one of the many political figures who would love nothing better than to see James Collins disappear.

***

Bishop Collins walked up to Jason smiling, but the young man appeared oblivious to his presence.

"How is everything?" He offered.

Jason looked up from his food to see James Collins standing in front of him.

He gave a slight nod and mumbled, "Good."

"Wonderful! We're blessed to have skilled caterers in-house to provide all of this. Can I get you something else?" James extended a hand toward the food.

"No." Jason replied. He was mildly impressed by the whole can I get you something move" as if the world-famous Bishop would actually fix *his* plate. It was the type of approach Jason would have tried himself. Kill them with kindness. But Jason was one person who couldn't be played so easily.

James Collins studied Jason. He behaved as if he really didn't want to be bothered. In fact, other than a few one-word answers, James realized he was being completely ignored. He wasn't used to that type of response, but he adapted. Why would someone who acted like they didn't care for him, join his church? It didn't make sense, so he pressed in again and tried to initiate further conversation.

"I see you've already met my daughter, Christian."

"Yes."

"I also have two sons around here somewhere," James' eyes panned the room looking for Lee or Caleb, but didn't see either in the crowd.

He frowned. They knew better than to miss the new members reception. Their absence was inexcusable. James had sent Lee back to the office for something, but he should have returned by now. James made a mental note to discuss protocol with his children, but he continued his conversation with Jason as if everything was perfect.

"One of my boys is probably about your age."

Jason looked up sharply in surprise and stared at James for an awkward second. He then dropped his head just as quickly. He forced himself to sample the food on his plate and completely ignore the Bishop's sad attempts at conversation. If James Collins had a son the same age as him…well, Jason didn't even want to think about it. That was probably why he abandoned them. He had already started a family somewhere else! Jason pretended to eat but the food was tasteless and his appetite was shot. Bishop Collins, never at a loss for words, continued talking unaware of the effect those words were having on Jason.

"...he serves as my adjutant here in the ministry. I'm really proud of him. He's only twenty-three, but he's definitely sold out for the Lord. He wants to pastor one day and I know he'll be excellent. One day soon, I'm going to have to turn him loose to..."

Jason's tone was low and gruff as he hastily interrupted the pastor. "Twenty-nine."

"I'm sorry, what was that?" James asked.

"I'm twenty-nine," Jason replied while never taking his eyes off of his food.

"Well you're a little older than Lee, but I would still like for you to meet him." James said as he looked around again. "I'm sure he's around here somewhere."

Jason nodded and kept eating. He was no longer hungry, but it was something to do to keep from overreacting. He needed time alone to process everything.

Starting or maintaining a conversation was never difficult for James, but this young man wouldn't crack. He didn't consider himself a prideful man, but Jason brought something out of James he didn't realize was there. James didn't like not being able to reach and relate to people outside of the pulpit like a regular guy. He was determined to change that. He stood in front of Jason for another ten minutes trying to connect with the young man, but he got nowhere.

The conversation remained very stiff, but James did not stop trying to knock the invisible wall down. One thing he knew for sure was Jason seemed to be an angry young man. Providing mentorship was James' specialty and he was going to make this man his personal project. *If this boy needed a father*, James thought, *then I will be it*. With God's help, James wanted to set this man free from whatever emotions imprisoned him.

There was a reason why the membership of Abiding Grace Church was sixty-percent male. Their men's ministry was like no other. God had used that ministry to change the lives of thousands of men by teaching them what it meant to be Godly. He couldn't wait to see Jason White go through the transformation so many others had gone through before him. After a painful silence, punctuated only by the sounds of Jason chewing and the people around them socializing, Bishop Collins excused himself and fellowshipped with the remainder of the new members' class. Jason never so much as lifted his head to watch him go.

Devion Clarke kept his eyes Jason. He looked for a reason, any reason, to stamp the nagging suspicions he had towards him. He couldn't hear what was said, but a blind man could see that Bishop Collins tried to be friendly and the boy was rude. *He probably has authority issues.* It was as if Devion could see the nefarious wheels turning in the boy's head.

Devion's military instincts were on point. Somehow that boy was a threat and he made a point to have his personnel stick close to Jason. Devion made sure everyone on his staff was aware of him. He called a few of his men over to him and casually pointed Jason out. This boy was not going to get over on Devion Clarke.

30

L ucy Stewart ran up the steps two at a time to her bedroom door. She slammed it behind her and locked it. Panting, she stripped out of her church clothes. She never intended to be gone so long, but traffic out of Marcelita's church had been a bear! Quincy and Michael were due home any minute, and she had to get right. Lucy went to the sink and scrubbed her face but it was no use, she was too "tooted up," as her mother would say, to have been at home in bed all day. Desperate, she spun around, turned on the shower, and jumped in. She didn't want Quincy to smell her cologne or see anything to alert him to what she had done that morning. Still breathless, Lucy got out of the shower and dried herself off. She grabbed her pantyhose, suit, and slip and tossed them into a laundry bag that she then hid in a back corner of her closet like she told Marcelita she would. She settled on her chaise and tried to relax.

She had been thinking about Victoria for weeks, especially after she received her note, but she hadn't been able to do anything about it until a chance conversation with her housekeeper. The week before, Quincy had been out of town and Lucy enjoyed her freedom. One day, while Marcelita made her bed, the Abiding Grace came on the television. Much to her surprise, Marcelita clapped with delight and informed Lucy the church was where she and her family attended. The two discussed the recent televised services and Marcelita told Lucy all about the church. Marcelita's descriptions made Lucy want to go more than she already did and her housekeeper helped her devise a plan to make it happen. And on this particular Sunday, Lucy sat smug and satisfied; she had stolen the cheese without springing the trap.

Lucy must have dozed off for a moment because she was startled awake by the sound of voices coming up the stairs. *They must be home,* she thought as she prepared to get up and greet Michael. A stifled giggle and a rustling outside of her door caught her attention. It wasn't Michael.

Lucy quickly cleared the distance to the door, flipped the lock, and opened it. Crouched outside her doorway was Stacy with a church program in her hand. Lucy eyed her with a burning contempt that she didn't try to mask. The younger woman, taken by surprise, stood erect and looked at Lucy wide-eyed. Lucy's hand itched to slap her, but she was too much of a lady. Stacy would probably run straight back to the church claiming that she was attacked. Instead, Lucy's eyes formed slits that threatened to shoot daggers.

"I...I...I mean, you weren't there so..." Stacy stammered while holding out the program.

Lucy was no fool. She knew Stacy didn't care a thing about her. She must have put something ugly in the program she wanted Lucy to see. Either that or she was giving it to her to somehow garner favor with Quincy. Regardless, the loose heifer was wrong and she *knew* it.

"His bedroom is across the hall," Lucy hissed, snatching the bulletin from her outstretched hand. Stacy stumbled backwards a few steps. Lucy had finally acknowledged what was always a silent understanding.

If only she'd lean over a lil' to the left, fall down them steps, and break that evil neck of hers.

To Lucy's disappointment, that didn't happen. Instead Stacy turned, scampered down the steps, and out of sight.

How dare she come back into my house!

Lucy fumed when she returned to her room. Quincy wasn't probably an hour out of the pulpit and here that slut was in their house. *Her* house! Didn't they fear God at all? Why didn't God just open up the ground and swallow them whole like He did those disobedient Israelites back in the day![14] What happened to His immediate vengeance?

Lucy felt herself getting worked up and that was exactly what the enemy wanted. But she wasn't going to let any of them win this time. Lucy closed her door, ripped the program into fours, and tossed it into the trashcan. Then she went back to her chaise. She couldn't help, but smile. It was a victory. She'd stared down the face of the devil and made her run away. Today was a good day.

***

Victoria laid across the bed as she watched her husband sulk around the room. He had moved about ten things only to place them right back where they were originally. Victoria had learned a thing or two over the years and one of them was to steer clear of James when he was deep in thought like this. He wouldn't see her if she tried to get his attention anyway. Once his mind was locked in, the world could explode around him and he wouldn't know anything about it until he came out of his trance.

Something had happened to him at the new members reception. It was something between him and one of the young men that joined the church. On the way, home she asked James about the young man, but he didn't mention anything new about him. It took some time, but he did tell her that he had never met the young man before. He mumbled off and on about how disrespectful the current generation was, but she didn't indulge his rants. Victoria had also noticed Devion tense when she asked about the new member. He must have picked up on the weirdness as well. He was loyal to James and would do everything in his power to protect him and the Collins family, if he perceived a threat. She was sure of it.

***

Jason stood in front of the bathroom mirror in his relocation suite and stared at his reflection. It had become a ritual he carried out every time he saw James Collins. Jason constantly looked for definitive traces of the Bishop in his own appearance. Sometimes he wanted to see some similarity, while other times he wanted to prove there was no trace of him. Today was a day for the latter. Because of their encounter after church, Jason now saw James Collins as a small, pathetic man and he didn't want that sort of blood running through his veins. That clown had stood there like an overgrown puppy begging for attention. Jason refused to give him an inch. It was disgusting to see a grown man act like that. It was sad. Jason wondered what his mother ever saw in James Collins. Jason was disappointed with how things had gone, but their first meeting wasn't appropriate for his big reveal. That time would come soon enough.

One of the first things on Jason's list was to meet Lee. After the way James bragged about him, Jason wanted to see what made his "chosen one" so special. Actually, he wanted to see both of his half-brothers. He needed to know what they were like. Jason saw dozens of pictures of Victoria Collins and read that the couple had three children, but the children's lives were so under the radar, he'd forgotten there was a possibility he might have additional siblings. Even in his seminal sermon, *In Search of Our Fathers*, James Collins only gave a brief nod to his own fatherhood but seemed to focus on everyone else's. It seemed that outside of their church, the Collins children were some sort of secret and Jason wanted to know why.

Because he had been so focused on the Bishop, Jason never intended for his plan to include the Collins' children. They actually might make things a little easier for him. They were James' weakness and he could tell from how he glared at him during his conversation with Chris, just how far he'd go to protect them. Jason turned off the bathroom light, sat in the lounge area of his suite, and fixed a drink. He had a lot to think about.

31

James Collins lay wide-awake as his wife slept. He felt a little foolish. It wasn't like him to be fixated on a person without a clear reason. In the past, James expressed concern for his members, but such care usually grew because of a mitigating counseling session or something God specifically revealed to him about them. This was different. James knew nothing about Jason, and God hadn't given him any cheat sheet to work from.

James prayed. He needed to know the purpose of all of this, but all he had was a deep sense of dread. He was exhausted and almost feared what would come next. But he knew better. He'd preached against getting paralyzed by such situations. He knew a strategy of the enemy was to wage war within a person's mind and he knew this was the enemy's strategy of choice for him.

James couldn't go on like this. He made a mental note to have his secretary, Vivian, call Jason White and set up a lunch meeting. This wasn't something he did much in recent years, but in the early days of the ministry, he enjoyed getting to know his parishioners this way. Some people needed a more personal touch. He would hate to see such an angry young man get lost in the crowd. He was certain Victoria would understand. Finding some resolution, James rolled over and found the sleep that had eluded him earlier.

In his dreams, a ghost from his past appeared in the form of a girl named BB. It was strange because she didn't fit into the storyline. She was just there kind of like his old dog, Spanky, was in his dreams before. Were the two related? Perturbed, James awoke with a jolt, contemplating the possibilities but not getting any clarity. She was just someone he knew when he was younger. A memory, just like Spanky. They both came into his life for a short period of time and then just as quickly, circumstances caused their interaction to end. He couldn't make sense of any of it and began to wonder if they were some sort of distraction to keep him from seeing a threat coming from somewhere else.

James was stumped. He tried to recall the girl who literally just walked through his dreams. I wondered how she could possibly relate to his former pet. He briefly considered what might have become of her. He would have to call his cousin, Boobie, in Philadelphia and ask him if he knew.

Glancing at the clock, James realized he would be groggy in the morning if he didn't get back to sleep soon. Still, he pondered everything a while longer before allowing his previous slumber to overtake him.

***

James sat calmly in the rear private dining room of 115 Midtowne waiting for his guest. He'd rushed back to Raleigh after preaching in Wyoming just so he could make this appointment. Periodically, he checked his Rolex to verify the time. He had arrived early, but there was still no sign of Jason White.

His secretary, Vivian, made the appointment a week ago and she attempted to confirm the day before but Jason didn't have the decency to even respond. Because James insisted that a non-answer did not necessarily mean there would be a no-show, he sat waiting. The manager, who was also a church member, was kind enough to give them this room. He only hoped his guest would show so all of the staff's efforts would not be wasted. He believed his intuition was right, but only time would tell.

James glanced over to the rear of the room. At a single table almost hidden by the server's wall, Devion sat brooding. When James indicated he had a private lunch with Jason, his security chief did not hesitate in expressing his dissatisfaction.

"That's not happening, James."

"Uh, yes I am. I already made arrangements to meet with him today. I wanna get to know him. Find out what's going on with him and how I can help."

"All of a sudden you're conducting one on one meetings with every person who joins the church? You not only can't keep that up, as soon as someone catches wind of it, you'll be seen as playing favorites. You're setting a bad precedence and it's going to backfire on you."

"Oh really? I did it with you, didn't I?

James' retort shut Devion up for a moment. When they'd first met early in the church's inception, James had taken a similar amount of time with Devion. At the time, he was a very angry, jaded man in a failing marriage. Those lunches, games of basketball, and just hanging out had not only helped heal Devion's spirit, but created a brother-like bond between the two.

"That was different and you know it," Devion protested. "Back then, the church was smaller and different. You didn't have the schedule you do or as many people counting on you for one thing or another. I'm telling you, man, you start singling people out for special attention and it's going to cause a stink."

"I am here to do the work of the Lord and I couldn't give two cents about how it offends anyone. There is something about this young man that calls me. I can't shake it and I feel I'm supposed to do this."

"With all due respect, you don't have the time to take on a pet project. Do you really want to start something that you will not be able to maintain or finish?"

"What part of 'God said...'" the Bishop interrupted.

"But you didn't say 'God said.' You said you were here to do the Lord's work and you felt strongly about the guy," Devion pointed out, feeling confident in his argument.

"Pepsi/Coke, Dee. Don't get into semantics. I am going to meet with the young man and that's it."

Seeing his friend and employee's frustration, James added, "Look, I have no intention of holding his hand and walking him through his Christian journey step by step. I just want to get a feel for him and his needs. Then I will gladly match him up with one of the strong brothers, one who has been where he is, in order to be mentored and discipled. Who knows, I may turn him over to you," James chuckled.

Devion made a derisive noise deep in his throat.

"Bishop, I'm really not trying to be insubordinate, but I cannot allow you to leave this property and go to lunch with this guy alone. It violates all protocols we have in place—protocols you and the board put in place."

James did not look pleased, but Devion continued.

"I haven't had the opportunity to vet this guy. You and I both know he is hostile. That bad attitude came off him in waves. Can you really trust your judgment or feelings enough to step out on a limb and go off alone with him? If the shoe was on the other foot, would you allow me to do that?"

James released an exasperated sigh.

"Look if it makes you feel better, you can come. But hang back, OK? I don't want to push him further away."

Consequently, Devion drove James to the restaurant. He had an additional security person follow them, and he sat partially hidden at a little table for two. He was more impatient than James as he waited.

He probably has his hand on his gun, the Bishop mused as he shook his head. James had no idea where the rest of his security detail was in the restaurant, but he knew with Devion in charge, reinforcements were nearby.

Listening to the low hum of the patrons dining just beyond the French doors separating them, James took another sip of water. He smiled at the waitress who poked her head in the room to see if his guest had arrived. The clock moved at a snail's pace and James fought the urge to drum on the table, accentuating the beat of the piped in jazz.

He wasn't sure how this whole lunch thing would go, but he was determined to get to know this new trainee, if for no other reason than to satisfy his curiosity. He wondered why the young man stayed on his mind so much. It was as annoying as a familiar face that he couldn't place or a song intro he knew, but couldn't recall the title.

James didn't have much in the way of any planned conversation topics and if Jason gave him the silent treatment again, it was going to make for a very quiet lunch. One of the things he did pick up on were the mannerisms of a young gigolo. He noticed how Jason carefully cut his eyes to watch the women at church and how he'd stared at Christian so intently before approaching her. Given his observations, Bishop Collins felt it was only appropriate to give the young man the same speech he'd given many of the similarly focused single men that joined the church. It was his famous "every woman in this congregation is my daughter and I will not allow some knucklehead to infiltrate this house, steal her virtue, destroy her spirit, disrupt the unity here, or harm them in any way, so if that's you, get right or get to steppin'" speech. James had given it more times than he could count and figured that it could account for at least five minutes of the meal.

Just then, his Nokia phone vibrated. He pulled it from his jacket pocket and noticed the church's phone number. He answered it with a concise, "Bishop." He was concerned his secretary, Vivian, was calling to inform him Jason would not attend the lunch after all.

"Hey Dad, it's me." Lee said. "I went by your office hoping to catch you before you went to lunch, but you were already gone."

"I'm about to have a meeting. Is something the matter?"

"Oh!" Lee said in surprise. "Your calendar was blank so I thought…"

"I didn't put it on the main calendar. Is there something you need?"

Lee hesitated, then said, "Well, no. I just wanted to run something by you." He paused again. "Is everything alright with you? You're not at the doctor or anything?"

"No, Son. I'm not." James sighed. "I'm meeting with a young man who is new to the church. I'll be back in the office later and will call you when I get there. OK?"

Once again, Lee paused before replying with a simple, "Sure."

Lee hung up, perplexed as to why his father had an off-the-calendar meeting with someone from church and why he hadn't been invited to join him. He knew Devion was with his father because another staff member told him he had witnessed the two men leave together. Why didn't they include him? It annoyed Lee that he had been shut out of so many of the day-to-day things regarding the church and had not been taken seriously by anyone including his father. He didn't know how was he supposed to lead if he never knew what was going on.

Jason entered 115 Midtowne. When he met the hostess, she briskly walked him to the rear of the small restaurant. Jason entered the private room with his eyes on James Collins, who was seated in the center of at least a half dozen square tables. For a moment, Jason wavered. He wondered what the outcome of this one-on-one would be. *What if Aunt Terri really did have it all wrong?* He doubted it, but now in the face of destiny, it was worth considering. *What if this man somehow already knows who I am? What if he actually has a plausible explanation for everything that happened?* Jason waved off his doubts along with the hostess, and confidently walked up to the table.

James rose to his feet with his trademark broad smile and extended his hand. Jason never took his eyes off of James and he didn't accept the Bishop's outstretched hand. Not one to prolong an insult, James graciously gestured for Jason to sit down.

Devion watched this transpire from his vantage point in the back corner. His hand itched to release the safety on his gun. The preliminary information he received about Jason was a little too clean to be believable. This new guy had been an honor student and stayed out of trouble, but all that meant was that he was smart enough not to get caught if he did wrong. Devion knew in his gut that somewhere there was more about this one. He still had two more sources that had not reported back. Devion needed something concrete to justify his urge to plant a foot firmly in this young buck's behind.

Before James and Jason could engage in any awkward conversation, their waitress appeared to take their drink orders. When she disappeared back through the heavy doors to get their appetizers and beverages, James struck up a safe conversation about the weather, sports, and current events. Jason responded, but his words were careful and targeted. The younger man appeared to be void of any emotion— at least any positive emotion.

A bevy of common mental disorders ran through James' mind as he tried to classify Jason's behavior. Just before the food was served, James launched into his pre-planned "don't mess over my spiritual daughters" speech. Jason simply stared at him without revealing any sense of comprehension, which left James a little perturbed. James wasn't sure what would happen next. He realized he would have to revisit the topic at some point to ensure the message was received. In the meantime, he would try to learn more about this Jason White.

The waitress appeared and placed their appetizers in front of them. James prayed a brief blessing over their starters and they began to eat. Between bites, the two ventured into more personal territory when James commented on Jason's accent. With the same blank stare, Jason replied, "Philadelphia," then turned his attention back to his food. Their meal had begun to get less strained and James didn't want to go back to one-word answers. A toothy, mischievous grin appeared on his face and the Bishop reminisced.

"Philly? Really? I used to visit there every other summer when I was in junior high and high school. I have some family living up there and I used to hang pretty tight with one of my cousins. We raised too much sand for either one of our parents to want us two years in a row!"

He chuckled, as the memories flashed through his mind.

"Wow! You know, I've got to call him! It's been a while. Time can slip up on you when you're busy. I'll tell you, sometimes it's hard to maintain relationships when you let yourself get too busy, you know? Never put your friends and family on the backburner, son. Always keep them in the forefront so you don't have to play catch-up after twenty years."

Jason's thoughts jerked to a halt. He felt warm under his collar.

I swear if this old man calls me son again I am going to have to make an example out of him.

Jason wanted to ask him was if he ever planned to stay in touch with Bridget White and her kids or if that was one of his regrets too. As bad as the moment seemed to call for it, he knew the question would have come too soon. His nostrils flared and he struggled to swallow the mini quesadilla he had in his mouth.

Sensing the mood shift, James decided to turn the conversation to more spiritual things.

"So, how long have you been saved?"

Jason looked at him for a moment. He took a sip from his glass, and picked at his appetizer. James was familiar with this type of avoidance so he pressed further.

"Son, you are saved, aren't you?"

Jason swallowed. He knew he'd better correct him now before he had to beat this fool's ass all over the city.

"Don't call me son," Jason said with a barely contained rage that caused Devion to slide out of his seat and stand flush behind the ficus tree. He couldn't hear every word the two men said, but he was a master at reading body language and this punk was looking a little too aggressive for his liking.

Jason took a moment to compose himself before calmly stating, "Define saved."

James was taken aback. Realizing he offended the young man, he sighed. He hadn't meant to sound condescending. Calling a man "son" was a habit. A term of endearment. It was not an indictment.

"Have you accepted Jesus Christ as your Lord and Savior?"

"I believe there is a God."

"But have you accepted…"

"I've accepted that there is a God who pisses on those He hates and blesses those He loves. Unfortunately, I was born into the first group."

James was about to respond in God's defense, but Jason raised his palm and cut him off before he could form the first word.

"Don't bother quoting me any scripture. I've already had this argument with other people. I believe what I believe and that's all there is to it."

Instinctively, James was ready to take Jason on for deceiving the church by claiming that he was saved and he also wanted to show Jason the error in his thinking, but something quieted him. He suddenly felt like he needed to listen rather than talk.

"What would make you feel like God hated you?"

Jason openly sneered, but James wasn't surprised. He suddenly felt like the mask had come off and he would finally be able to see who he was dealing with. Without moving his lips, he led his heart in prayer.

"Because of the life He gave me. The family He gave me. He just didn't think I should have it any better and this is what I got. But you wouldn't know anything about that now, would you?"

James saw that he was going to have to pull information out of Jason slow and easy. "Okay then, so tell me about it."

Their waitress returned to clear the remnants of their appetizers and serve their entrees before disappearing again. Devion retreated to his seat. He did not want to not miss anything going on at their table. Jason began to speak as if he were reciting a well-rehearsed speech. Only his tone revealed that was trying to remove himself from the very real pain of his tale.

As James listened intently, Jason gave the highlight reel of his life.

"One summer, my mother met this guy. One thing led to another and by the time she found out she was pregnant, he was long gone. She tried everything she knew to get up with him, but he never returned her letters or even called her. My grandparents weren't going to have a pregnant kid at home, so they kicked her out and refused to pay for her college education. My mom had to get help from strangers because her entire family turned on her."

Jason's voice trembled with anger, but James mistook it as the younger man fighting back tears. He looked away, hoping to give the prideful young man his dignity. Jason continued sharing his story.

"So there she is with only a high school diploma and pregnant with twins. She ends up living with one of her friends for a while and gets a job working fast food. By the time she had us, she had government assistance and lived in one of the nastiest projects you can imagine. There were rats this big." Jason held his hands three feet apart.

"They would come into the apartments through the walls like they owned the place."

James shuddered.

"Yeah, it was like that. So one night when we were about eighteen months old, I guess one of them tried to feed on my twin sister. She ended up dying. By then, my grandparents had split up and my grandfather disappeared. My grandmother got sick and my mom took me and moved back home.

James looked relieved, but Jason shook his head.

"No, things didn't really get better. My mom lost it for a while and ran wild. She ended up with two more children. And then my grandmother died. Long story short, we ended up right back where we started, in the same nasty projects. My mom worked like three and four jobs trying to take care of us. My sisters' fathers helped out some with them, but not with me. They always made sure to let me know I was not their responsibility. My mother had to do everything for me on her own. Those niggas didn't even like me. They would beat my ass just for breathing."

James didn't so much as flinch at the profanity. He welcomed the honesty.

"Nothing ever went right for us. Thanks to my mom's sister I got scholarships to cover college, but my family has always been really messed up. I don't know how else to explain it."

Jason took a sip of his sweet tea and James took the opportunity to ask a question.

"Were you raised in church?"

Jason guffawed.

"Ah yes, church. Well my mom found God when I was in the third grade and made us go to church with her. My aunt has always been that way and took us a time or two before my mom went all in with the whole church thing. In fact, she used to watch you on TV. My aunt still does. She has your tapes and everything."

Jason eyed James coldly and nearly broke his fork in two when the Bishop looked pleased at that news.

"Really?"

"Yeah," Jason replied with an icy stare.

"Moms sent you money too. She may not have been able to feed me or buy me what a lot of the other kids had, but she always had money for you."

Suddenly James felt the sting of what seemed to be an accusation. He thought about what Jason said for a moment and asked a clarifying question before offending his lunch companion again.

"You're speaking about your mother in the past tense. Is she no longer living or is she just no longer involved with my ministry?"

If the young man was here to ask for his mother's money back because she no longer liked his television ministry, James wasn't sure what he would do. Stranger things had happened. He could just imagine the endless I-told-you-so's he would have to endure from Devion.

A sad smile crossed Jason's face.

"Both I guess. She died in February."

"Oh I am so sorry to hear that. Had she been ill?"

Jason shook his head still wearing a sad smile.

"No, she died of a brain aneurysm. It came out of the blue. One day she was here and the next…"

He paused to fight back his tears. Then Jason cleared his throat.

"A lady in our building who used to keep us while my moms worked, told her a long time ago that she was going to work herself to death and I think she did. She was always working."

James felt for the young man across the table, but before he could say the words, Jason began to speak again.

"My mother never knew what it was like to go away some place nice on vacation. I tried to take her but she was always worried about missing work or what would happen to my sister while she was away. She never got to retire. She was just forty-five when she died. Forty-five. All she ever did was work and go to church. She never got to know what it was like to relax and enjoy life and now it's too late."

"I am so sorry to hear this. I can only imagine the pain you've experienced and are still experiencing."

"Really?" Jason asked and the sarcasm wasn't lost on James.

"I know that sounds trite, but I mean it. Sadly there are never any perfect words to convey the proper empathy for another person's pain."

James decided to shift gears a little. "So is your mother why you ended up coming to Raleigh and joining our church? You said she watched us so…"

Jason was swallowing his sweet tea and nearly choked from shock and amusement.

"Yeah. She was, actually. Funny you should ask."

James nodded slowly and decided to suspend discussing the young man's mother for a while. He seized the moment and tried to speak life into the hurting young man.

"As hard as it was and as awful as your life may have seemed, it could have been a lot worse. I need you to understand God does love you. He kept you through all of that when so many others living in similar circumstances didn't have the strength to make it. You have to learn how to appreciate where you've come from, forgive everyone and everything that hurt you, and use all of that as stepping stones to propel you forward in life. You said your father rejected your mother and I guess by proxy rejected you, but you know what? The Bible says that even if your father forsakes you, God will adopt you. He is a far better father than any man could ever be. Did it ever occur to you that you might be so special in His sight that God couldn't trust your natural father to raise you? God divinely removed that man so He could fill that void. Instead of looking at it as a bad thing, it may have been the best thing that could've ever happened to you!"

Jason's anger reached a dangerous level as James tried to speak words of comfort and reassurance. His case for a loving God had fallen on deaf ears.

"Whoa. Hold on a minute. I have heard some ridiculous stuff but this?"

James was taken aback at Jason's reaction. The younger man shook his head as the anger rippled through his core.

"You don't get it. If that punk ass nigga had stood up and been a man when my mother told him she was pregnant, none of the things that happened would have happened. My grandparents would have never split up, my grandfather would still be around and my grandmother would probably still be alive!"

Jason's voice rose and Devion moved back into position behind the ficus. They taught their staff to be observant not nosey, but, given the circumstances he had been both. He wasn't sure if Jason was yelling at James or just upset, but Devion was ready.

"Do you know my grandfather left because my grandmother wanted my mom to come back home with me and my sister? He didn't want any of us in his house. I never knew the man and he hated me that much. He blamed me. My grandmother died probably blaming me for her husband leaving her. I never got a chance to say sorry because I never knew all this stuff until my mother died!"

He continued angrily as tears demanded an exit, but he refused to give in.

"Do you know that if my father had been a man, my sister would probably still be alive? Everything wrong in my life began the moment that boy let off in my mother."

"Are you saying you wish you hadn't been born?"

"If it would have changed the outcome of my mother's life, then yes."

James didn't know what to say. Jason's words concerned him.

Jason blinked back the tears and looked at James through squinted eyes.

"Let me ask you something. Why did you invite me to lunch? Why did you have your secretary even call me?"

Relieved at the change, James smiled at him.

"When I met you at the new members reception, something about you struck me. To be honest, I sensed hostility and wondered why you wanted to join the ministry if you didn't seem to like me." He shrugged. "I guess I thought I would take a minute to get to know you. I'm glad I did. I see it wasn't personal. It's all of that unforgiveness bottled up inside you. I really want to help you with that if you will allow me the honor."

"Unforgiveness? Yeah, I think I have earned the right to not forgive my birth father. Were you raised by your birth father or even a stepfather? Did your mother work herself to death because your father wouldn't bother to take care of you?"

James tightened his lips not wanting to give the young man the satisfaction of making the point he could see coming a mile away. It was a version of the grass is greener and he was not going to play that game.

"Yeah, I thought so." Jason intoned, not waiting for a reply. "So it's easy for you to talk about forgiving your father."

Rolling his eyes, Jason turned his head to the left to take in the rest of the room. He noticed a familiar face staring at him, through a tree in a shaded corner. He nearly laughed aloud. The whole super agent thing was ridiculous.

"I see you brought the men in black with you. What did you think I was going to do? Oh that's right, you said I was hostile."

Jason cut into his cold salmon then dropped his fork without ever tasting it.

Devion moved out into the open. He had heard enough to understand at least some of the young man's issues. Part of him wanted to cut the guy some slack, but the other part still didn't like him. He did think James was messing up though. His friend was definitely out of his element and he planned to gently encourage him to leave the counseling to those who were better trained.

James sat staring at Jason. Jason stared back. Before a staring match could get into full swing, their waitress reappeared to ask if they needed anything. Neither of them had made a dent in their meals.

James found himself frustrated. This lunch had not gone according to plan. Granted, he learned a lot about Jason's family history, but no positive change had been achieved. If anything, he was more haunted than ever before. At least he knew how to pray for him, but outside of assessing his spiritual needs, this lunch may have been a waste of time. The boy hadn't even pretended to take any of his advice and James was certain he hadn't reached him. Just as he sensed the urge to end the meeting, Jason spoke suddenly.

"Would you like to see a picture of my mother?"

James beamed thinking maybe he had broken through. It was obvious the boy's mother meant a lot to him. Seeing this picture revealed Jason's vulnerability, so he jumped at the opportunity.

"I would love to," he said full of hope.

Jason carefully pulled a short envelope from out of his jacket. Devion took a few steps closer. His hand slipped to his gun as Jason handed James the first picture.

"We took this last summer at her church. It was about eight or nine months before she died."

James looked over the 5x7 family portrait. He noted Jason's two sisters, and commented on the good-looking family. Jason studied James' face and realized the Bishop hadn't recognized her.

Reaching back into the envelope he said, "Here's another one of my mother when she was younger. It was taken a year or so before she had me. It's one of my favorites."

Jason handed James the worn snapshot of his mother from when she was sixteen years old. James' mouth went dry. He stared at the picture in disbelief. This is unreal. What were the chances that a person he hadn't thought of in almost three decades had been immortalized on the film Jason had placed in his hands? He felt dizzy.

After staring wide-eyed at the picture for a few seconds, he glanced around the room. He shook his head at Devion, but his friend didn't catch the signal to go back to his seat. James felt cornered.

"What's going on here? Just what are you trying to pull?" He asked, slightly perplexed.

James reached for Jason's family picture. He stared at the picture of Jason's mother.

"I asked you a question! What are you trying to pull, boy?" He growled.

Devion moved closer. He was ready to handle the rude youngin'. James waved Devion away, but the security chief was too focused and he missed the signal.

"Dee!"

Finally hearing his boss, James shooed Devion away. He took a few steps backward, but stayed in range.

Sensing James' vulnerability, Jason struck.

"Actually you asked two separate questions. And I'm not trying to pull anything, Dad!"

Jason's words were soft but seemed as if he'd shouted them from a mountaintop. Taken aback, James struggled to compose himself as he tried to assume a more congenial manner. Devion froze. He was certain he'd heard wrong.

"Dad? Listen. I didn't mean to call you boy. That was insulting and I know better. You have issues with your father and that was inconsiderate of me. Forgive me. What I should have said was…"

"But you are my father. Aren't you, Dad?"

James stared in a state disbelief that quickly turned to fury. Devion could not deny what he heard that time. He stared first at James and then at Jason. He blinked. There was a definite resemblance once he looked close enough. He stood and his eyes ping-ponged between the two men. How did James have a son and why did he never tell him about it?

James barked questions at his luncheon guest.

"Who sent you here? Who are you working for? Just what are you after? If you think for one moment that I…"

Jason cut James' diatribe and spoke in a chillingly calm voice. He began to recite verbatim from the first part of James' sermon, *In Search of Our Fathers*,

"…and to you man-children, that's right, you who've upended the integrity of our virtuous sisters-in-Christ with your self-centeredness, aimless living, and shallow integrity, I'm talking to you. That's right…that's right. Your seeds…broken, discouraged, and forever searching, need YOU for their harvest, but YOU were nowhere to be found. Crops untended easily spoil, BUT by the grace…Oh, the mighty grace of GOD...His children are NEVER, do you hear me, NEVER left alone!"

Jason spoke with such fervor, his eyes burned with unshed tears. He would not let James Collins see him cry. James' face was pale and his mouth moved silently in unison with Jason's over key phrases. Devion stood back watching the men and a sickening feeling filled the pit of his stomach.

When Jason paused, James stammered, "How do you get off..."

"Are you kidding me?" Jason raised his voice. "Are you trying to say you never met my mother?"

James shook his head and opened his mouth to speak, but Jason cut him off.

"Don't bother. Are you saying thirty years ago you didn't fu..."

He took a breath and continued.

"Are you trying to say you didn't get with her like that? Huh? Are you trying to say you never knew you got her pregnant? Don't sit here and lie to me, Man-of-God!" Jason emphasized mockingly.

James continued shaking his head. "I knew her. I mean, I admit I wasn't perfect when I was younger, but I didn't... I haven't seen her since... I don't know what you want me to say!"

"Don't bother saying a damn thing," Jason snarled as he jumped to his feet, retrieved one picture from the table, and snatched the other from James' hands.

"Thanks for nothing. Lunch was great. Let's make plans to do it again," Jason said with undisguised sarcasm. He barreled out of the room without ever looking back.

Devion was at James' side in a flash. Numb, James sat staring at the place where Jason had been only moments before.

What just happened? Is there any way Jason could be my son?

There was no way! How in the world did he find out all of that information and get his hands on those pictures? What kind of game is he trying to play?

James counted back thirty years. *Oh God,* he thought. The gnawing in his stomach told him that this was very real. As much as

James wanted it to be a coincidence, everything in him told him it wasn't.

Sitting there, James relived his final summer in Philadelphia. He could smell the city's subway, street vendor foods, trash, the hot sweat of young bodies, and old concrete doused in hydrant water. He remembered all of the great music that marked that summer: The O'Jays' "Backstabber," The Staple Singers' "I'll Take You There," and James Brown's "Get On The Good Foot." He tried and failed to dance like the Godfather of Soul back then. They had so much fun that summer running the streets, playing street hockey, and honing their sexual prowess with whatever young lady they could talk into it. They were invincible.

Fear gripped his heart and he began to feel as if he would lose his lunch.

"Bishop? Bishop? James!"

At the sound of his name, James jerked. His mind fell with an unsettling thud back to the present. Devion stood next to him, concern etched on his face. James ran a hand over his eyes before looking over at his security chief again.

"Let's go."

"What's going on, man? Did I hear that guy just call you Dad?

James replied coolly, "You didn't hear anything."

"The hell I didn't!" Devion replied. "What is going on? Why did he call you dad? I thought I knew all your kids. Why didn't you tell me he was…"

"Dee! Enough already! You heard nothing. Nothing. Understood? Now go take care of the check and let's go."

"Yes, Bishop."

Devion immediately tossed his familiar hat aside for a more professional one. He was hurt and confused, but he did as he was instructed. James instantly regretted blowing up at Dee but he could not talk about this yet. He had to wrap his own mind around what he'd just heard. There were other people he'd have to share this all with. People like his wife. When it came to her family, she was territorial and he was not sure how she would deal with this at all.

In the church's navy, Lincoln town car, Devion watched James through the rearview mirror. He wasn't sure he knew the man anymore. He'd respected his pastor and friend tremendously. He'd argued more than once that he wasn't like Quincy Stewart and a few other shady pastors. But now? Now he wasn't so sure. That hurt him. It was a given that James had mentored him back in the day as a pastor. Devion had bared his soul to that pastor. No one ever said your pastor had to bear his soul to you in return but this was different. He had watched James' back because he believed him to be a man of integrity. But if James had skeletons in his closet like this, there was no telling what else would fall out. And Devion was sure he didn't want to be involved.

"Keep your eyes on the road, please."

James didn't bother looking his friend's way when he said it. He could feel Devion staring at him. He was ashamed and felt blindsided. He couldn't go back to work in this condition.

"Where's your car? At the church?"

"No sir, it's at my house."

The formality of Devion's reply hurt. He deserved it and let it go.

"Swing by your house. You can get your car and I'll take this one home. I'm not going back to the office. Tell Viv to cancel everything for the rest of the day and tomorrow."

Devion's eyes found his friend in the rearview mirror again. James did not cancel appointments willy nilly. He knew he would probably catch grief for asking, but he had to find at least something out.

"Bishop, Sir. May I ask you a question?"

James sighed. "Cut it out, Man. I'm sorry for blowing up at you. Are we good?"

Devion nodded, not feeling at all mollified, but choosing to accept the apology it if meant he could feed his curiosity.

"I have a question."

"I don't know if I can give you an answer right now."

Devion nodded. That was fair enough.

"Did you know you had another son?"

James shook his head.

"Do you think he really is your son? How did he find you?"

"I have no idea. None at all. He talks a good game but I don't have any proof. I mean I do, but I don't." He snorted in disbelief. "His mother watched me on television and I guess she told him about me. Maybe she lied. I don't know."

"But why now?" Devion slammed on the brakes suddenly. He had nearly sent them sailing into the back of a CAT bus stopped at a red light.

"Let's not talk about this now. You're acting about as shook as I feel."

Devion remained silent as they drove the rest of the way. He parked in front of the garage at his townhome and turned in his seat to face James.

"So do you honestly think he's yours?"

"I don't know what to think."

"Do you want him to be?"

James looked at him strangely. "Why would you ask me something like that?"

Devion raised his hands to let James know he meant no harm.

"I just asked because you seemed to be so taken with him and now he ends up claiming you're his father. That's all. I didn't mean anything by it."

33

J ason tried to maintain his composure as he exited 115 Midtowne. His face must have betrayed his true emotions because the few patrons gathered inside the door quickly cleared a path for him as he charged past. As he bolted out the front door, he caught the familiar scent of Clinique Aromatics. It was his mother's favorite cologne and the only one she would wear. He almost turned around to search out its source, but he needed to distance himself from James Collins. He knew his mother wasn't there. She was gone.

He got into his car before the first tear fell. Jason spent the better part of his life never shedding a tear, even when Donna's father used to beat him for the slightest infraction. But now? Over the last seven or eight months, he had cried more than he had in the three decades of his life. Jason hastily wiped the tears away with the back of his hand before anyone in the parking lot could see. He glanced back at the front door of the restaurant. Would James Collins come after him? He knew better. The man was a coward.

Jason backed out of the parking space. His thoughts and emotions collided. He looked in the rearview mirror just in time to see a large man in a dark suit hastily exit the restaurant and stop short to watch him pull off.

"So pops came with reinforcements. Punk ass! He can't even handle his business himself," Jason mumbled.

Using his rearview mirror, Jason prominently displayed his middle finger to the bodyguard and pulled out of the garage, tires squealing.

Jason hadn't had a drink in months and his taste buds craved one. Ironically he hadn't had a drink since sometime after he began his research on James Collins. He still refused to believe all the religious crap he'd exposed himself to had rubbed off on him. He'd just been too busy, too focused, to enjoy himself. But those days were over. He was about to indulge in a big way.

As he drove, the aroma of his mother's cologne tickled his nostrils. He felt like he had been snatched back in time and could just about taste the peanut butter sandwiches he'd survived on as a child while his mother worked. He became somewhat nostalgic and several poignant memories occupied his thoughts. When the walk down memory land was over, his body seethed.

"I'm gonna get him, Ma," he said. "Don't worry, I'm gonna get him."

Inside a local liquor store, Jason stocked up on all of his old friends: Johnnie Walker, Grey Goose, Cruzan, and Courvoisier. He hadn't had a decent bar at his place for a while and this shopping trip was past due. These friends would help ease the throbbing in his head and deaden the pain in his heart. They always had.

***

Lucy Stewart pulled her Lexus into the garage as she pressed the remote. She glanced in the rearview mirror to admire the hairstyle she received that afternoon. It had been a while since she'd had anything done to it. The hair and nail appointments at a new salon relaxed her and lifted her spirits. When the double door lifted, she blinked at the two vehicles in front of her. Quincy's black May Bach was parked in its usual space but beside it, where she usually parked, was a new, pearl gray Toyota Sequoia with 30-day tags. Confused, Lucy exited her car to look in the vehicle's windows but there was nothing on it or in it to identify the owner. Curious, she entered the house, leaving her vehicle idling. She opened the door that led from the mudroom, stepped into the black and white kitchen, and stopped short. Stacy Lewis was in *her* refrigerator, wearing *her* apron and judging from the smell of chicken boiling and the groceries on the counter, using *her* stove.

"Just what do you call yourself doing in my house?"

Stacy, dressed in a neutral linen pantsuit, covered by one of Lucy's frilly red and white plaid aprons, turned to look at Lucy. The older woman gasped, her eyes fixed on Stacy's neck. She could not believe what she saw. Around the church secretary's neck was Lucy's specially designed, handcrafted necklace. She'd found it at a flea market years earlier. The pop-up shop allowed patrons to choose beads, faux jewels, and charms, as well as the type of chain, collar, ribbon or heavy thread they desired. Although the three-strand necklace ended up being less than thirty dollars, it never failed to garner compliments from nearly everyone who saw it. Lucy didn't wear it often so she had no idea it had been missing from her jewelry box.

"Where did you get that?" Lucy asked, pointing at the young woman's neck.

At first, Stacy seemed confused. She put her hand to her neck and just as quickly, her confusion turned into a smirk.

"Oh this little thing? I found it a few months ago when I helped Bishop Stewart pack up a few things to take to the hospital."

The reference was not lost on Lucy. Stacy had been in her bedroom while she had been lying in the hospital recovering from the car accident. *The nerve!* She shook with anger. *How dare Quincy have this floozy in her personal space pawing over her personal belongings!* She could just imagine Stacy touching her things and it made her want to knock the other woman senseless.

"You thief! You triflin' little thief! What's wrong with you? Why you always take what I got? Don't you know how to have somethin' for yourself?"

Lucy advanced on Stacy and reached out to snatch the necklace from her. Stacy batted her hand away as she backed around center island.

"Keep your crazy dyke hands off me!"

"What did you just say to me?"

"You heard me! I don't want your nasty dyke hands on me!"

The women completed a full revolution around the island. Stacy did not appreciate the fact that once again, Quincy's crazy wife had her

261

on the run. She hadn't been able to help herself when she saw it in the jewelry box.

Feeling confident that she could out maneuver the older and heavier Lucy, Stacy began to taunt the other woman, hoping to rattle her into doing something to prove to Quincy once and for all that he was better without his deadweight of a wife. If Stacy played her cards right, she just might get Lucy to try to kill herself again.

"Why don't you just leave, huh? Everybody knows Quincy doesn't want you. If I had known you played for the other team, I would have told him to send you on your way a long time ago. All you're doing is holding him back and making him and your poor son, Michael, miserable. Why don't you go off with your girlfriend somewhere and leave us all alone?!"

Caught off guard, Lucy stopped stalking Stacy for a few moments and stood staring at her. Stacy laughed.

"How dare you talk to me like that?" Lucy shrieked.

"Ha!" She laughed, "You didn't think I knew? Everybody knows Lucy! Everyone!"

"Everyone knows you will say anything to get what's mine and if I find out you've been spreadin' rumors about me, I swear to God…"

"You swear to who? You can't do anything. You can't even kill yourself! Next time do us all a favor and try a little harder, OK?"

Lucy reached for the nearest thing, which was a heavy glass lid for the Dutch oven. She hurled it at Stacy. It caught the woman in the arm then bounced off and onto the floor where it broke.

"Ow!" Stacy yelled. She looked down at her arm and her inattention was all Lucy needed. She was on her in a flash. The two women slammed into the island and smashed against the lower cabinets, wrestling. An 18-piece cutlery block set slid across the granite countertops and hit the floor. Knives skid in every direction. The women toppled to the floor. Stacy grabbed handfuls of Lucy's freshly styled hair and tried to slam her head into the floor. But Lucy clawed at Stacy's face. They shrieked and screamed, as each threw punches, pulled hair, clawed and bit each other. Lucy managed to roll Stacy off of her. She slapped and punched the adulteress. All Stacy could do was scream and flail on the floor.

"Get off her!"

Strong hands yanked Lucy off of Stacy. She got in one more punch and yanked the necklace off the other woman with all of her might. Beads exploded into the air, bounced on the floor, and rolled in every direction.

Quincy spun Lucy around and shook her. "What's wrong with you?"

"She tried to kill me!" Stacy shrieked. "Call the cops. She's crazy. She was going to stab me with those knives!"

Stacy pointed dramatically to the scattered knives although none were close to the site of heir brawl.

"Liar!" Lucy lunged at Stacy, but Quincy's firm grip kept her in place.

Stacy was wide eyed. "I'm bleeding!" She screamed, touching her face. Blood dribbled from one of her nostrils. "Call the cops! She tried to kill me!"

Quincy released Lucy with a rough shove and helped Stacy from the floor. He held her to his chest as he glared at his wife. Lucy stared back in disbelief. He'd boldly chosen Stacy over her. There was no telling what else the girl had helped her greedy hands to. Lucy never felt so empty, betrayed, and alone.

Lucy opened her mouth to speak, but Quincy yelled, "Shut up! You done embarrassed me in front of my company. You need to apologize and see about her. I was feelin' poorly this morning so I come home and what Stacy do? Out of the goodness of her Christian heart, she come over here to fix me some soup only to have you attack her? Was you here to see about me? Where were you when I was sneezin' and carryin' on? You need to apologize right now!"

Lucy stared silently at her husband. There was no way she was going to say she was sorry for anything. She just looked from Quincy to Stacy and back again. There was nothing normal about this situation but they were acting like *she* was the crazy one. Stacy held onto her left side and whimpered, "I think one of my ribs is broken. She flopped her big self on me and broke my rib!"

Quincy looked at his mistress, his face full of concern, then he turned to his wife full of anger.

"Why you do it, huh?" He asked.

Lucy stared back not uttering a word. Her eyes lidded with resignation.

"You can't talk now? Cat got your tongue?"

"Tuh," Stacy sucked her teeth. "Victoria Collins' cat got her tongue. Isn't that right, first lady?" Stacy eyed her with a nasty smirk. "That is what you all do, isn't it?"

Quincy looked over at Stacy with his brow furrowed. "What you talkin' bout?"

Stacy preened with satisfaction.

"Your little friend at that store told me that your wife and Bishop Collins' wife were in one of their dressing rooms making out right before Easter. She said you could hear them doing it all through the store. She said people were in there shopping and heard them. It was embarrassing for everyone there and I guess they couldn't get it like they wanted to because she said they came out of there smiling and left together." She turned a triumphant smile at Lucy. "Ain't that right?" She asked, as she mocked Lucy's strong southern brawl.

Quincy spun to look at his wife. Shock, horror, and anger warred for control. Lucy quickly and repeatedly shook her head. She couldn't believe this was happening.

"That's not true! She lyin'! She just tryin' to make me look wrong 'cause I caught her stealin' my things!"

Quincy snarled, "Come here!"

She knew that look. He wanted to hurt her and she could not let him do it again especially in front of that woman. Lucy's eyes darted around her on the floor but all of the knives were behind Quincy and there was no way she could get past him. She also would have to pass him to get to her bedroom if she wanted to hide with her razorblades. He lunged for her and she spun on her heels, ran out of the house, hopped into her idling car and floored it.

***

James pulled onto the familiar gravel driveway, past the lush manicured lawn and several elaborate flower gardens that decorated the vast front yard. As he stopped in front of the carport, a tall, slim woman with hair the color of storm clouds came out onto the porch wiping her hands on a white 'Kiss the Cook' apron. James sighed. He was home. And his mother stood on the porch waiting for him. All his pain and confusion came to a head and all he wanted, all he needed, was for her to make it all better the way she had when he was five years old.

He stepped out of the Lincoln and inhaled the fresh country air as his mother greeted him.

"Hey Baby, you alone? Where's my Devvy?" His mother referred to Devion who had become like an adopted son.

"He's at the church, working," James replied. His mother frowned.

"Well, come give your mother a kiss."

He took the five steps in two strides and enveloped her in a bear hug. She smelled like Dial soap and the onions and meat she had been frying. She rubbed his back before gently moving back to look at his face.

"What's troubling you? Don't even try to tell me you just came by to see us. I can look at you and tell something isn't right. Come on in the kitchen and talk to me while I finish fixing supper. We're having Salisbury steak, mashed potatoes, and the succotash I made last night. Are you gonna stay and eat?"

James opened the door and they moved down the short hall to the kitchen.

"I'm not really hungry and don't know how long I'll be here."

She briefly glanced back at him as she checked the meat cooking in a large, black, cast iron skillet. Her eyes danced over him critically.

"Get yourself some lemonade out of the refrigerator and come talk to me."

James complied.

"Do you still have those boxes of my high school and college things around here?"

He tried to be casual, but knew immediately the attempt had failed. His mother, a retired educator, not only had the memory of a dozen elephants, but when it came to anything concerning him, she was a pack rat. He was pretty certain she still had the first booger she ever cleaned out of his nose somewhere in a glass cube. She was scrapbooking before it became popular and her only child was her muse.

"Are you looking for something in particular?"

James sat in the small breakfast nook. The oak bistro table, nestled in a bay window that overlooked the back yard, was too small for him now and he had to push his chair away from it in order to stretch his legs. He shrugged nonchalantly.

"I had something come up and I wanted to look over some of the things from my high school graduation up through my freshman year at State."

Beulah Collins put a hand on one of her slim hips while using the back of her other wrist to wipe across her damp brow.

"Things like what?"

Before James could try to form an innocuous answer, the sound of a toilet flushing in the hall bathroom signaled the arrival of his father, retired District Court Judge, Edsel Collins. The tall, broad shouldered man strolled into the kitchen and headed straight for his son with an outstretched hand. James clasped it while giving into the pull to stand and embrace his father. James palmed the top of his father's head and gave it a quick familiar rub as they hugged.

"Alright now, don't mock me. Yours will be gone soon enough."

The two men laughed and stared proudly into eerily similar eyes before finally letting go.

"So what brings you out here to the country to see the little people?"

James rolled his eyes at his father's dig, but before he could answer, his mother piped up.

"He's got some trouble and came home to go through his old things to find the solution, right, James?"

There was no getting anything past her. He blew air out of his nostrils while twisting his lips. To confirm it, would mean an immediate interrogation. To deny it, would be to lie. He opted for a diversion.

"Hey, Daddy what *actually* happened to Spanky?"

"Who?" The elder Collins asked with a frown.

"Wasn't that the old mutt you kept feeding?" His mother asked.

His parents shot each other a look. His mother chuckled and his father looked sheepish.

"That dog and his pack were tearing everything up. They ruined a perfectly good garden and tore up your mother's flowers!"

James gave his father a look that said, "And…"

"Well I'm sorry, son. I wasn't honest with you. I called a buddy of mine at animal control and they came out here lickety-split. Rounded up those dogs in a couple of hours and took them to the pound. I'm really sorry."

James was horrified and his face reflected it. Although it happened decades earlier, it still hurt. He loved that mangy dog.

"So what does that mutt have to do with your graduation things? Don't think I didn't notice you never answered my question," Beulah said as she retrieved a covered Tupperware bowl from the refrigerator and sat it on the counter.

"Are you in some sort of trouble?" Edsel asked.

James pursed his lips and nodded. "I just very well may be."

"What's going on?" His father asked.

"It's really complicated."

"Well simplify it," his mother said.

With a few, quick, flicks of her wrist, Beulah extinguished the fires on the stovetop, covered the pots, and wiped her hands on her apron.

"Let's go sit out on the sun-porch where it's cool. The food can wait."

Edsel looked like he was going to argue that his evening meal could not wait, but his wife chimed in.

"He's going to simplify things, aren't you James? So waiting a few more minutes won't hurt your supper."

As the three sat in rocking chairs, a ceiling fan whirled lazily above them.

"I met with a young man today who believes I'm his father."

"What?" Beulah exclaimed.

"Jesus!" Edsel shouted on cue.

"This isn't anything recent," James quickly added. "He's twenty-nine years old."

"You weren't married yet." Beulah said softly and James could hear the relief in her voice.

"How did this come about? If he's is twenty-nine, then you couldn't have been more than seventeen or eighteen…"

"Jesus, Son! How in the world did this happen? You need to explain. Why didn't you come to your mother and me? You know you could always tell us anything."

"That's exactly right!" His mother chimed in looking both wounded and angry.

James blew out air.

"I'm sorry. I am not trying to excuse my behavior, but how many eighteen year olds walk up to their conservative, Christian parents and announce that not only had they started having sex, but also some random girl in another state said he got her pregnant? She never sent any proof, so why risk getting in trouble?"

His parents said nothing.

"I was completely blindsided today by the whole thing. I can only tell you what little I know. This guy joined our church a couple of weeks ago. He's a tall good-looking fellow, but he has a massive chip on his shoulder. So when we greeted him at the little reception we have, I got a chance to talk to him. He acted like he couldn't stand me. Devion was about ready to kill him on sight. I tried to feel the guy out, but he was locked up tight. After that, I could not get him out of my head. It wasn't so much a pride thing for me. I just wanted to find out what was troubling him and help."

"You can't help everyone!" Beulah sniffed, agitated.

"So I decided to invite him to lunch away from the church, the way I used to do."

His father groaned and James stopped rocking.

"He was in my spirit, dad. I felt this was something God wanted me to do. I was booked up for several days but when I saw an opening, I had Vivian make arrangements. I met with him today. So he gets there and eventually starts telling me his life story. Long story short, according to him, I abandoned his mother and ruined all their lives."

"Wait a minute, son. Back up. Who did you abandon? Do we know her?"

James got up and walked over to a corner of the sunroom. He stared out at the yard his father prided himself on keeping up. He caught sight of the garden peeking at him from the corner of the house. The plants looked healthy and strong. He got his words together then turned to face his parents.

"She was a girl named Bridget. I met her the summer of my high school graduation when I was up in Philly visiting Boobie."

Beulah harrumphed and folded her arms under her small breasts.

"She was just a girl. I was young and dumb, OK? I had just discovered..." James glanced at his mother not wanting to be disrespectful. Her eyes bore into him.

"You just discovered another use for your penis? Is that it?"

He nodded sheepishly.

"That summer, Boobie and I were just having fun hanging out, meeting girls, and doing things. She was really cute, but really clingy. I understand the ties of the soul now, but I just thought she was whipped. She would not leave me alone. I tried to get with other girls, but she would show up and block me at every turn. I ended up being with her the most not because I wanted to, but because she was convenient. She wanted me to go to Temple that fall so we could be together. It was like she already had us married. When I left to come home, I didn't even tell her because by then she had really gotten on my nerves."

Beulah sat rocking and staring into space. Slowly she turned her eyes toward James.

"Was she the one writing you those letters?"

"Yes!" James exclaimed.

Beulah nodded sagely. "And you want to see if we still have them?"

He nodded again. Edsel had stopped rocking and was bent over with his head in his hands.

"Tell the whole story, Son. Put it all out on the table."

"So a few weeks after I got back, I got a letter from Bridget because Aunt Josephine gave her our address. She wrote that she was pregnant and wanted me to come back up there or to send for her to come down here. I didn't believe her so I wrote to Boobie. He called me over Christmas break and told me she was lying. She had been pestering him about me and he thought she was just trying to get me to come back up there to go to school with her. It seemed like every week I got another letter from her!"

"I remember," Beulah murmured. "She had that big loopy handwriting and always used those airmail envelopes you could get from the post office. I haven't seen one of those in a while. Do they still sell them?"

"I have no idea, Ma, but I am glad you remember them."

"How could I forget? You didn't get mail much before then."

"Exactly. Well, after a while I stopped opening the letters because they were a version of the same song and dance. I really thought she was crazy. Then sometime during my first semester at State, I came home and there were no letters waiting for me. I figured she had moved on to the next guy. I even asked Boobie about her later that semester because I wanted to know if she was still bothering him. He said he'd seen her at a party and she didn't look pregnant. She was about this big," James said holding up a pinky finger. "So if she were pregnant, you would be able to tell. After that, I just went on with my life and you know what happened on my end."

"But what happened on hers," his mother asked.

"According to Jason, that's his name," James added, "she was pregnant with twins and got kicked out of her parent's house. They didn't pay for her college education and she ended up working minimum wage jobs and living in the projects. He said she tried to reach out to me, but I never responded. She had a girl and a boy. The girl died and she raised the boy then had a couple more kids. I think her parent's split up over her getting put out of the house. I'm not sure of all the details, but it sounds like she had a really hard life and Jason is bitter. He blames me for everything."

"So what does she want now?" Edsel asked wearily.

"That's just it. According to Jason, she died earlier this year. He's the one who came looking for me, not her. The weird thing is, he said she watched me on TV and even donated to the ministry. That's just…odd. If she wanted to blackmail me, don't you think she could have done it years ago?"

His parent's murmured noncommittally.

"It could be that she told her son about you, but respected the call on your life and didn't want to interfere. It's either that or she, unfortunately, held you blameless. It could even be both, actually."

Beulah said this while eyeing her son. Edsel wasn't convinced.

"How do you know any of what this young man said is true?"

"He had pictures of his family and of his mother when she was teenager. I remembered her. Actually, I had a few dreams about her recently. The dreams weren't really about her, but she was in them and so was Spanky."

"I've been wondering what that dog had to do with all of this," Beulah said wryly as she rocked.

James shared with them the vision Elder Carlton revealed.

"And you think those dreams were the Lord speaking to you about this matter?" His father asked.

"I'm not sure. Recently Vicky sort of befriended Quincy Stewart's wife and…"

"Oh my God! What in the world?!" Beulah threw her hands up. "Why would she want anything to do with that woman? They're bad news, James! Bad news! You don't want to invite that mess in your life."

"I know...I know..." James replied, patting the air to calm his mother. "I thought that the visions were a warning about them until today. Now I'm not so sure."

"Don't allow yourself to be taken for a ride. With technology today, pictures can be manipulated all sorts of ways. You need to find out definitively if this boy is any relation to you. What does Victoria say about all of this?"

James sighed. "I haven't told her yet. I came straight here."

Edsel eyed his son disapprovingly. Beulah shook her head.

"You didn't tell her you were coming to Oxford?"

"I did. I just told her something came up and I would be home later."

"What about the church?"

"Well, Devion was there and he heard some of the conversation but..."

Edsel shook his head frowning. "I mean what about your work at the church. What about the ministry? You're usually in your office until at least six, but today, you're here."

"I took the rest of today and tomorrow off. I needed some time to get my mind wrapped around all of this."

Edsel continued shaking his head.

"You are messing up. The last thing you need to do is neglect the ministry God gave you. You know better. Get concrete facts and take action! Don't sit around here moping and licking your wounds. Are you sure those dreams were from God? Satan is a counterfeiter, you know. He has a doctorate in deception. Don't think you are immune just because you have a big successful ministry and people know your name. You hear me?"

James nodded, ready to put the whole conversation to rest. He was tired. What his father proposed was easier said than done. For years, James had taught his congregation what it was to be a real man. He taught them how to handle their responsibilities, not run from them. He even had to remove an elder from the AGCC leadership team for his repeated failure in those very areas and now here he was being called out on the same offense. How could he possibly look that former elder in the face and continue to keep him from serving when James' own personal life was a mess? After all of his preaching and teaching, there was a distinct possibility that he failed his own children and now one of them was dead. No wonder Jason hated him so much. This was a disaster.

After a prolonged silence, Beulah Collins rose, and adjusted her apron.

"The food should be ready in about thirty minutes. You need to eat something James. The garden is running over with cucumbers, squash, snap beans and zucchini. I'll gather some up for you to take home to Vicky."

***

Margo was working alone and had her back to the door when Lucy Stewart burst in. One look at her customer and all she could say was, "Oh my Lord!"

The woman's hair looked like it had been caught in a ceiling fan. Her mint green sundress was rumpled and there were drops of what appeared to be blood near the neckline. Her face showed signs of fresh bruising and her eyes were wide and crazed.

"First Lady! Are you okay? What happened? Do you need me to call someone?"

Lucy advanced on her looking like Beelzebub himself.

"How could you? All the time I shop in here and give you good money and you gonna lie on me?"

Margo noticed her fists. Glimpses of jagged broken nails were visible each time she unclenched her hands. Margo backed up a few steps. There had been whispers of Lucy Stewart having some emotional problems, but she never thought they were anything but gossip. Now, the woman looked extremely unstable and Margo wasn't near a phone to call for help.

"I just heard that you all been tellin' folk that I'm a homosexual!"

Margo looked horrified.

"What? Where did you hear that? I've done no such thing!"

"My husband's secretary said you all told her that I was with Vicky Collins in that there dressing room having sex before Easter! That's a lie and you know it!" She shrieked. "She told my husband that! She told my husband and he believed her!"

Margo winced, hoping beyond hope that Mrs. Stewart's appearance wasn't the price she paid for her husband hearing that lie. Lucy sobbed as Margo's heart dropped into her stomach. She rushed to the front door, flipped the closed sign, secured the door lock and turned to Lucy.

"First Lady, I promise you that I had nothing to do with that!"

"Lies! Everybody lyin' today! You was here that day and saw us go in there to talk. That's all we did was talk," Lucy screamed as she dropped to the floor with her back against the short wall of the checkout counter and wept.

"I am not lying to you. I would never do that. Can you tell me what she said?"

And Lucy did. Margo shook her head. She should have known Regan would do something so stupid. That girl loved to gossip with her friends. Something like this could potentially close her shop down!

"I am so sorry, first lady. I think I know what happened. My sales associate has assisted your secretary the few times she shopped here. Regan must have said something to her. Teenagers today don't think about consequences. I promise you I will deal with her. You never have to see her again, OK? I can have her write you and your husband a letter of apology. I'll do whatever it takes to fix this mess."

Lucy didn't answer. She cried with her knees drawn up and her face buried in her hands.

"Do you know if First Lady Collins has heard this rumor yet?"

Lucy shook her head then seemingly snapped out of whatever had possessed her moments before.

"Oh my God! Victoria! We gotta call her!"

Oh no we don't, Margo thought.

Lucy clumsily rose from the floor.

"I ain't got her number with me. I know you probably got it cause you call me sometimes. We gotta call her right now! I need to talk to her!"

"Uh… maybe we need to hold off on that. How about we get you to a doctor? You look like you've been through something today."

"Call her!" Lucy insisted.

Margo was not about to do that but Lucy continued to press her until she finally said, "I can't."

"Well give me her number and I'll call her. I really need to talk to her right now!"

"I can't do that."

"Please!" Lucy begged but Margo looked away.

Lucy stared at her. Even Margo was turning her back on her. It looked like today was the day she was going to find out exactly where she stood with people. The hurt was all over Lucy's face and Margo felt terrible but she was in a bad position. Keeping her store alive was paramount. Without another word, Lucy turned and left the store.

***

Inside his apartment, Jason lounged in a club chair with his shirt unbuttoned and his tie askew. He was drunk, but his mind had never been clearer. Although his meeting with James Collins had not gone exactly how he wanted it to, he still managed to say what he wanted to say to the man. There was no doubt he had the man on the ropes and floundering.

Any hope Jason had of James accepting responsibility for his neglect was gone. He still seethed at the arrogant and condescending way the Bishop had spoken to him. He was a grown man but he'd talked to him like he was a three-year-old. Jason was certain he would have been able to maintain his composure a lot longer if James hadn't started talking about how God did all of this to Jason on purpose. That nonsense didn't work in Jason's world. He believed that people should own their mistakes. Now he only wished he had punched James Collins in the throat for saying that shit to him. He had no forgiveness for that man. None.

James Collins needed to be knocked down a peg or two. After today, Jason doubted there was any chance he could join the security team at the church and use that access to mess with the Bishop's head. He still had new members class. Jason wished someone would try to keep him out of it when the class began in a little more than a week. He was not above showing his ass if need be.

As Jason poured himself another shot of Johnnie Walker, he thought hard about revenge. He wanted to hit the man where it hurt. Humble him. His mind circled around to one thing: the Bishop's kids. He went to great pains to keep them out of the spotlight. Jason still had to figure out which one of the flunkies surrounding the Bishop was his son. He had made a few guesses, but wasn't sure. He also had yet to see or meet the youngest kid. But he had met Christian.

"So sweet. So pure. Precious little Christian. Daddy's perfect little songbird," Jason muttered in a dark singsong tone.

He had just the thing for her. James Collins took his sister, JaLisa, and now Jason was going to take his daughter. He was sure the bible said something about an eye for an eye or at least his aunt quoted it like it was scripture. Ol' James should be able to relate to that type of justice then.

Jason swallowed the contents of his glass in one gulp and fished out his mobile phone. He smiled to himself as he hit a familiar number on its speed dial.

"Hey man, it's me."

**

Lucy sat in the Wal-Mart parking lot in Durham watching people go in and out of the store. She had been sitting there over an hour waiting for Michael's call. After leaving Margo's Closet Boutique, she had driven around the 440 Beltline twice before exiting onto Interstate 40 and driving to Durham. She had nowhere to go. Quincy had called her phone several times, but she did not answer his calls.

Realizing she had no cash, no clothing and no place to stay the night, she stopped at the Wal-Mart. It took her nearly thirty minutes to gain the courage to go in the store. She was terrified that someone would recognize her. She knew she looked like something the cat drug in. She hastened to the store's bathroom and fixed herself as best she could. She needed a few items and risked using the credit card Quincy had given her. She was afraid he might have canceled it. She was able to buy underwear and toiletries. She couldn't bring herself to buy the clothes. She just had to make it through the night and then maybe she would be able to get to her things.

Back in the car she called her son, Michael, who answered on the first ring.

"Mom! Where are you? Everyone is looking for you!" He sounded anxious.

"I'm okay. I need you to do something for me. It's a secret, so you can't tell your daddy."

There was silence.

"Michael? You hear me?"

"Is it true?" He asked. The tone of his voice was reminiscent of a much younger version of the young man on the other end of the line.

Her heart fell. She wouldn't put it past that woman to try to fill Michael's ears with vicious lies. He deserved to know the truth so if he asked her about Victoria Collins, she would tell him everything.

"Is what true?" she asked.

"Did you really try to kill Miss Stacy today? She said you tried to stab her."

Lucy's shoulders drooped with relief.

"I lost my temper, but I did not try to stab her. I hit her and slapped her a little, but that's it. I shouldn't have done that much. She just made me so mad I couldn't help myself."

Michael was quiet again, then softly said, "They're talking about putting you in a mental hospital. Daddy's been on the phone all afternoon. He said if you called me I was supposed to tell you to come home. We're supposed to keep you here, then some people are going to come get you and take you away."

Tears slid down Lucy's face.

"Are you going to tell him I called you?"

"No," he replied, but she wasn't convinced.

"I really, really need your help right now. Can you do this one thing for me and I won't ask you to do nothin' else, okay? I don't want to get you in trouble with your daddy."

Michael sighed. "You don't have to beg, Momma. What do you need?"

She gave him explicit instructions. She had him repeat them back to her twice so she was sure he had it right. Now she sat waiting for his return call and feared it would never come. Fortunately, the Wal-Mart was open twenty-four hours though she had no intention of sitting in the parking lot all night.

A while later, her phone rang. Glancing at the caller ID, she answered.

"Hi, Bookie Boo."

Michael groaned, "Don't call me that."

"You get it? Your daddy see you? What they doin' now?"

"Yeah I got it. He's too busy worrying about what you're doing and trying to keep Miss Stacy from calling the police and her friends at church that he's not thinking about me."

Michael slowly recited the numbers to his mother and she slowly repeated them back to him.

"Why are you calling her? I didn't think you knew those people."

"It's a long story and I'll tell you everything as soon as I can, but I need to make this call before it gets too late."

"Momma?" Michael hesitated and it sounded to Lucy like he was trying not to cry.

"Yes?"

There was a choking noise then to her surprise and confusion, Michael burst out laughing. In between guffaws he gasped out, "I can't believe you finally beat down Miss Stacy! Oh my God! I wish I'd seen it. I've been waiting for you to knock her out for years! I keep trying to imagine you punching her in the face and..." He started laughing even harder. "You gave her a black eye and you did something to her nose because it looks really messed up. It's all swollen and everything!"

Lucy laughed too and soon both of them were laughing uncontrollably.

Finally Lucy said, "I gotta go, silly boy. I'll call you later on."

"I love you, Mama."

Lucy's heart swelled. "I love you too, Baby."

She held her phone to her chest basking in the love and laughter they shared. She hadn't lost everything.

Glancing at the digital clock on her dashboard, she carefully dialed the number Michael gave her and listened as the phone rang.

***

James stood in the doorway of their master bedroom watching Victoria read. Even without makeup and her reading glasses perched on the end of her nose, she was still the most beautiful woman in the world to him. He loved her more than he could ever begin to express and the last thing he ever wanted to do would be to disappoint or hurt her. He was certain he was going to do at least one of them now. He had no other choice.

"Like what you see?" She said with a smile as she secured her place with a bookmark and closed her book. She grinned at her husband for a second then pretended to pout in sympathy at his long face.

"Hard day?"

He nodded, stepping into the room. His heart thudded at the inevitable. Victoria got a better look at her husband. Her brow furrowed.

"What's wrong?"

James sighed. Just then Victoria's phone began to play a jaunty conga tune. She reached for it but James put up his hand, signaling for her to stop.

"Can that wait? I need you right now."

Victoria gave James a sly knowing smile before realizing he had a different need in mind. Still she glanced at the phone to make sure it wasn't one of her children calling. She didn't recognize the number, which relieved her.

"What is it? What happened? Are Mom and Dad okay?" She asked referring to his parents in the familiar way she had since they were dating.

"They're doing alright. Mom wants to wring my neck right about now but other than that, they are fine. Oh, she also sent you some things from their garden. I put them in the kitchen."

Victoria nodded but did not lose focus on her husband's countenance.

"So what is it? You're starting to scare me."

James recalled his father's admonition to just "come out with it" when talking to Victoria even if it meant he had to wake her up to do so. His heart continued to thud in his chest as he spoke.

"Remember I told you I was having lunch with that new guy today?"

"Of course, how'd it go?"

The look on his face answered for him.

"Not so good, I take it?" Victoria said.

James shook his head even as he blew air out through his nostrils. "I can't even say."

Victoria patted the bed beside her. "Come here and tell me about it."

ABOUT THE AUTHOR

Sharon D. Moore is a writer, people watcher, and an avid reader. She relies on her vivid imagination, sense of humor and understanding of human nature to craft stories that cause readers to feel deeply and laugh loudly. A former world-traveling, military brat, Sharon now lives in North Carolina with two cats and a host of other wild life that stop by regularly for meals, protection and affection.

Visit Sharon D. Moore at:

www.sharonmoore.net

ACKNOWLEDGEMENTS

God gets all of the credit because not only is He my Creator and Keeper, but I truly believe He gave me the dream that spawned this novel. I want to thank my parents, Doug and June Moore, for everything they have contributed in every way to get me to this point.

I also want to thank my sister, Patsy, for her loving support, encouragement and creative spin on the world.

Over the years. several other people sowed into this effort via encouragement, answering my questions, and even giving me money. Others suffered through reading early drafts of this work. To the latter, I owe a huge apology. These individuals are (in no particular order): Preston and Cheryl Stokes, Festo Kyanda, Chambrea Daniels, Deidre Johnson, Adolfus McGee, Zoe Herndon, Sumit Deshpande, Candace Williams, Luther and Kimball McNeill, T'Sa Looby, Kanika Looby, Najuma Thorpe, Wanda Moore, Brenda Kinyon, and Lorin Coakley.

Finally, I would like to thank Tracey Michae'l Lewis Giggetts for believing in me and helping to mold the writer in me.

END NOTES:

[1] Exodus 32:16
[2] Acts 5
[3] Mark 12:42-43 / Luke 21:2-3
[4] Psalm 51:9-12
[5] Zephaniah 3:17
[6] Ephesians 2:10, Psalm 139:14

[7] Nehemiah 4:10b
[8] Philippians 4:11-12
[9] Psalm 139:8
[10] 2 Chronicles 16:9, Psalm 34:15, Proverbs 15:3

[11] John 18:10
[12] John 18:16-17, 25-27
[13] Acts 2:2
[14] Numbers 16: 30-33

Made in the USA
Lexington, KY
12 September 2016